As Aaron ... **suite, he** ... **member** ...

Bonnie sat on the floor, her knees pulled up to her chest and her face hidden behind her hands as she cried. Her long sandy-blond hair fell like a curtain, shielding her face from view, as well.

"Hey," he said, taking a seat next to her. "You're going to get mascara all over your pretty pink dress. And I heard that's not easy to get out."

Bonnie lifted her head and wiped her cheeks. "I hope you believe me when I say I have never done anything with Mitch. Nothing is going on between us. I don't know why he thinks he's in love with me when he was about to marry Lauren."

Typical Bonnie. She was the most humble person in all of Blue Springs.

"I believe you. Mitch told me he hadn't said anything to anyone about how he felt until today. Bad timing, huh?" he asked, trying desperately to get her to smile just a bit.

Dear Reader,

Who doesn't love a wedding? I know I am a huge sucker for weddings. It doesn't matter if my best friend is getting married or a distant cousin, I get choked up every time the bride comes down the aisle, her eyes locked on her soon-to-be husband. It's such a magical moment in time. So what in the world made me write about weddings that get called off? The drama of it all!

A Bridesmaid to Remember came to be when my former editor mentioned it would be fun to read about a wedding that gets called off in the beginning of the story instead of the end. What would the fallout be? How would relationships be tested? Who would end up together in the end?

I fell in love with those questions and set out to answer them all. I hope you enjoy seeing where my romantic imagination took me.

You can find out more about me and my books at amyvastine.com or on my Facebook page Facebook.com/amyvastineauthor. Hope to see you all there.

xoxo,

Amy Vastine

HEARTWARMING

A Bridesmaid to Remember

—

Amy Vastine

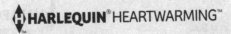

Recycling programs for this product may not exist in your area.

ISBN-13: 978-1-335-88954-6

A Bridesmaid to Remember

Printed in U.S.A.

www.Harlequin.com

Amy Vastine has been plotting stories in her head for as long as she can remember. An eternal optimist, she studied social work, hoping to teach others how to find their silver lining. Now she enjoys creating happily-ever-afters for all to read. Amy lives outside Chicago with her high school sweetheart husband, three teenagers who keep her on her toes and their two sweet but mischievous pups. Visit her at amyvastine.com.

Books by Amy Vastine

Harlequin Heartwarming

Grace Note Records

The Girl He Used to Love
Catch a Fallen Star
Love Songs and Lullabies
Falling for Her Bodyguard

Chicago Sisters

The Better Man
The Best Laid Plans
The Hardest Fight

The Weather Girl

"Snow Day Baby" in *A Heartwarming Thanksgiving*

Visit the Author Profile page
at Harlequin.com for more titles.

To my awesome bridesmaids, none of whom tried to steal my husband away. Tricia, Cheryl, Jennifer and Leslie—love you, ladies!

CHAPTER ONE

IT WAS INCREDIBLE the kind of wedding that could be thrown when money was no object. This wasn't something Bonnie Windsor would have ever discovered by planning her own wedding, but since her best friend was Lauren Cole, she got a front-row seat to the most lavish wedding Blue Springs, California, had ever seen. The Cole family was like royalty around these parts, and Lauren loved the idea of being a princess. With dark hair styled exactly like Kate Middleton's was on her wedding day, she sported a sparkling tiara that rivaled the one worn by the duchess.

"We are gathered here this lovely afternoon to celebrate with Mitchell and Lauren as they proclaim their love and commitment. We are gathered to rejoice, with and for them, in the new life they will begin together today," the minister proclaimed.

Dressed in a custom-made Elie Saab that

she had flown back and forth to France to be fitted for, Lauren was absolutely stunning. The strapless satin princess ball gown was cinched at the waist by a thin belt and had tulle and gemstone embroidery on the bodice as well as floral appliqués. Bonnie didn't know for sure how much it had cost, but Lauren had hinted that it was over ten thousand dollars. Ten grand was more than Bonnie's dad could afford for an entire wedding someday.

Mitch tugged on his shirt collar. He had some sweat beading on his forehead. It was warm outside for late May in California, and there were more people in the church than showed up on major religious holidays. He had to be overheating in his tuxedo. He fidgeted with a handkerchief in his hands. Mitch was a big guy. He had played football at Stanford and spent more time in the gym than he did at the office. He "worked" for his father and hopefully would be as good at spoiling Lauren as her parents were.

"Marriage is not about putting on a fancy dress or a tuxedo. Nor is it about having a lavish party with friends and family," the minister continued. He obviously didn't know

Lauren very well. This wedding was all about the spectacle. She loved the limelight. Lived for it. "That might be what we think of when someone says there's a wedding, but marriage is about living your lives as one. Finding a way to work together for the success of your family. Your new family."

Bonnie smiled. Lauren would always be a Cole, even if she planned to take Mitch's last name. The Bennetts were a prominent family in Blue Springs. They, of course, had lots of money and plenty of influence, but they weren't a founding family like the Coles. Lauren's ties to her father's name would always be stronger than her ties to his.

Bonnie glanced out at the guests as the minister continued on. The church was filled to capacity, and someone had said there were people who hadn't been invited to the wedding gathering outside the church hoping to catch a glimpse of the happy couple after the ceremony.

Bonnie still had to pinch herself. Was she really the maid of honor at a wedding like this? When she befriended Lauren back in elementary school, she'd had no idea what being the friend of a Cole would entail. There were definite advantages to being her side-kick growing up, but at the same time, Lauren didn't exactly make it easy to be her friend, either.

No one had been safe from Lauren's wrath during the wedding planning. "Bridezilla" could describe Lauren on a good day. She was a woman who knew what she wanted and would not stop until she got it. No matter whom she had to run over. She had wanted everything to be perfect, and as far as Bonnie could tell, she had made that happen.

The church aisle was lined with bunches of pale pink and white roses. A giant halo of those same roses, as well as orchids and hydrangea, hung above the bride and groom. Lauren carried a ballerina bouquet of pink peonies and cascading white orchids. Bonnie knew this was nothing compared to what awaited them at the reception at the Cole Winery after the ceremony. Lauren had wanted a secret garden theme, and her father had spared no expense. The reception flowers had been delivered by the truckload.

"If any of you has a reason why these two should not be married, speak now or forever hold your peace."

Bonnie wasn't sure why Lauren had left this part in the ceremony. Maybe she wanted to make sure there weren't any ex-boyfriends still pining away for her. Even if there were, it wasn't like anyone would dare to disrupt this moment for her. No one was that self-destructive.

"I do," Mitch choked out.

There was a quiet rumble of laughter through the church. Lauren let out a nervous giggle. "Not yet, honey," she whispered to him. "Wait until our part."

Bonnie exchanged looks with Cheryl Cooper, the bridesmaid on her left as they faced the congregation. Leave it to Mitch to be so worried about what he was supposed to say that he prematurely gave his consent to be married. Lauren had been so hard on him last night at the rehearsal, threatening to make him sleep alone on their wedding night if he messed up his vows.

Mitch dabbed his forehead with the handkerchief. "No, I mean that I object."

Silence fell over the church like a heavy blanket. It was as if everyone was holding their breath in shock. Bonnie locked eyes with Aaron, Mitch's best man and Lauren's older brother. Had Mitch just said what they thought he said? Did he have a death wish no one was aware of?

"What?" Lauren asked, her tone disbelieving.

"I'm so sorry, Lauren. I know that you put a lot into planning all this and you've been waiting impatiently for today to come. I know we talked about being together forever, but I wasn't being honest with you or myself."

Bonnie braced herself for the complete meltdown Lauren was about to have. It was unbelievable that something like this could happen to someone like her. Never in a million years was this how anyone could have imagined this was going to go. No one told Lauren no. No one.

"I need you to stop and think about what you're doing right now, Mitchell. You have been in love with me since high school. You wanted to marry me almost immediately after we started dating."

"I was infatuated with you back in high school. Who wasn't? You're Lauren Cole. But I'm not in love with you. I'm in love with someone else," he admitted, causing everyone in the church to gasp.

Red alert! Bonnie could imagine the heat building inside Lauren's body. She was about to explode. Who in the world could Mitch be in love with if it wasn't Lauren?

Curiosity coursed through Bonnie's veins. There had never been any doubt that he'd had a crush on Lauren since they were teenagers. Lauren had always said so. They hadn't dated in high school but were friends. After college, he'd spent a few years backpacking all over Europe before coming back to Blue Springs to work for his dad. Soon after that, Lauren had decided he was the one for her. And what Lauren wanted, she got. No one really thought about what Mitch wanted. It was assumed that he wanted Lauren.

Bonnie was kind of proud of him for getting out from under Lauren's thumb before it was too late. If he wasn't in love with her, he shouldn't marry her, for his sake and hers. She did wish he had thought to speak his piece before today, though. This was no way to break up with anyone, especially Lauren.

"Bonnie," Mitch said, stepping around Lauren.

Why was he talking to her? Maybe he was

going to ask her to take care of Lauren. That had to be it.

"Bonnie?" Lauren screeched. "Are you kidding me?"

No. He wasn't in love with her. She wanted to believe that, but he looked at Bonnie like he only had eyes for her. She felt like all the blood had drained from her face. *No, no, no, no, no.*

"You are the most incredible woman I know. Mostly because you don't even realize how amazing you are. I've fallen in love with you, and I can't deny it anymore."

Lauren's worst nightmare had suddenly turned into Bonnie's. She had never picked up any vibes that Mitch had feelings for her. He was nice to her and she was kind in return, but love? That had never crossed her mind.

"Mitch—" Bonnie had no idea what to say to him. She couldn't string any words together. This was surreal, and she prayed it was some sort of horribly realistic dream she was about to wake up from.

"Have you two been running around behind my back?" Lauren asked.

"No!" Bonnie couldn't believe she had to

answer that question. "I don't even know what's happening right now."

"I know all this is crazy, but I want you to give me a chance. I can't imagine my life without you," Mitch said, taking her by the hand.

"I can't believe you would do this to me, Bonnie! You're supposed to be my best friend. You ruined my wedding. You ruined my life!" Lauren threw her bouquet and it hit Bonnie smack in the face. She ran off down the aisle with her parents following behind her.

"You are a horrible person," Wendy Hillbrand, Lauren's college roommate and one of the other bridesmaids, said, brushing past her to follow after Lauren.

The other bridesmaids began to chime in with their misplaced disgust, each one following the next back down the aisle.

"I sure hope he's worth it," Theresa Gilmore said with a shake of her head.

"How could you?" Jeanne Watson asked with teary eyes. She idolized Lauren and would have done anything to be her maid of honor. She was the one who had questioned everything Bonnie had planned for the bachelorette party.

"I never understood why she considered you her best friend," Kathy Cole, Lauren's cousin, said with sneer. Kathy was a couple years younger than Bonnie and Lauren and had a love/hate relationship with her cousin. Apparently, today she was in love.

"She is never going to forgive you for this. Ever," Cheryl said.

Mary James was as much Bonnie's friend as she was Lauren's. They had known each other their entire lives. She walked past with pity in her eyes but no words. She was the one person Bonnie thought would know she was innocent. There were no secrets between them.

"Mary! You have to believe me. There's been nothing going on. I swear!" The church went from silent to a cacophony of chatter. All eyes were on Bonnie and Mitch. She pulled her hand away. "What have you done?" she asked him.

"Don't listen to them. They can't understand because they are all under Lauren's spell. Give me a chance. Please. I know we can be happy together."

The very thought of having a relationship with him was ridiculous. She had no intentions of being romantic with Mitchell Bennett in this lifetime.

"We need to get you out of here," Aaron said to Mitch. "Before my father sends someone in to assassinate you."

Aaron tugged Mitch away and out of the back of the church, leaving Bonnie alone at the altar with no one but the minister, her horror and an invisible target for town gossip on her back.

"HAVE YOU LOST your mind?" Aaron asked his best friend as they made their way to the nearest exit. He had to get Mitch away from this church before something terrible happened. He didn't really think his father would have the man killed, but if that was what Lauren wanted, anything was possible.

"I know I should have said something earlier."

"You think? That would have been preferable."

"I didn't know how to tell her. You know your sister. She runs the show. We're all just here to do as she says. She said we're getting married, so I bought a ring and proposed. I didn't want to propose. I wanted to tell Bonnie that she looked gorgeous the night of the Fourth of July fireworks. I wanted to tell her she has the prettiest smile and that her laugh makes me want to kiss her. I want to take her to Paris and I want her to not be afraid of being with me because of Lauren. Lauren doesn't get to decide who we love."

All that might have been very true, but there wasn't time to discuss how to appropriately handle Lauren's autocratic ways. Aaron was also taken aback by how strong Mitch's feelings for Bonnie really were, but one thing gave him pause. "Are you telling me that Bonnie has no idea you felt like this until right now?"

"When was I supposed to tell her?"

Aaron pinched the bridge of his nose. Not only had Mitch committed social suicide in there, he had brought Bonnie down with him. "How could you do that to her before you even know how she feels? Lauren thinks you two have been messing around. That there's been something going on between you guys."

Mitch grimaced. "I didn't mean it to sound like that. I panicked. The minister was talking about starting our lives together and how our two lives become one now. We would have been forever linked. Me and Lauren. The rest of my life spent doing what she says. I looked over at Bonnie, and she flashed me that smile. You know, the one that makes you feel like everything is going to be all right?" He didn't wait for Aaron to reply, but Aaron knew that smile. Bonnie had always been a calming presence in Lauren's drama-filled existence. "I just had to tell her how I felt. I needed her to know I'm in love with her."

Aaron didn't understand how he could be in love with someone before he even had a real relationship with that person. What he did know was that Mitch needed to get out of Blue Springs immediately. Just then, Mitch's parents came out the back door.

"Son, what have you done? Do you have any idea what it is going to take to clean up this mess?" his father asked.

"Mitchell, you have to reconsider," his mother said. "You need to go back in there and tell Lauren you blacked out and you have no idea why you said all that. You need to marry that woman right now."

Mitch shook his head. "I can't marry her, Mom. I'm sorry. I'm in love with someone else."

"Bonnie Windsor? The woman sells houses for a living. Houses on the north side of town," his mother said with a touch of disgust, as if the people on the north side were all living in cardboard boxes.

"I don't care what she does for a living. I love her, and I won't marry Lauren."

Mrs. Bennett seemed a bit hysterical. Her eyes were wild and her voice shrill. "You will marry her, or else!"

Mr. Bennett put a hand on her shoulder. "Meredith, relax. We can't force the boy to marry someone he's not in love with, and we sure as heck can't waltz back in there and act like nothing happened."

"No offense, Mrs. Bennett," Aaron chimed in. "But I can't pretend that I don't know Mitch does not want to marry my sister. I don't want Lauren or Mitch in a loveless marriage."

"Your father will destroy us. Do you understand that?" Mrs. Bennett clutched the pearls around her neck.

"We need to get Mitch out of town," Aaron suggested. "Today. He needs to disappear while Lauren pulls herself together. Once things have calmed down, I truly believe level heads will prevail. No one will be destroying anyone."

Mr. Bennett nodded. "Good idea. You have your bags packed for your honeymoon. You should go as planned and extend your stay until the smoke has cleared."

The Bennetts had gifted Lauren and Mitch a two-week honeymoon in the south of France. That was definitely a safe distance away, and there was no reason he couldn't stay all summer if that's what it took.

"I'm going to ask Bonnie to come with me," Mitch said, heading back inside the church.

Aaron grabbed him by the arm and pulled him back outside. "You are going to leave Bonnie alone. Now is not the time to bring her into this. You just dropped the bomb that you don't want to marry Lauren. My sister needs to get over that before she can handle you wanting to date her best friend." Which she would absolutely *never* get over. Therefore, it was never going to happen. Bonnie wouldn't do that to Lauren. Not the Bonnie Aaron knew.

The Bennetts adamantly agreed and managed to get Mitch into a car and as far away from the church as possible. Aaron went back in to check on his baby sister. There was no way this day would end well. Lauren had basically never been told no her whole life. Things always went her way, so she had no idea how to cope with something like this.

Bonnie sat on the floor in the back hallway, her knees pulled up to her chest and her face hidden behind her hands as she cried. Her long sandy-blond hair fell like a curtain, shielding her face from view as well.

"Hey," he said, taking a seat next to her. "You're going to get mascara all over your pretty pink dress. And I heard that's not easy to get out."

Bonnie lifted her head and wiped her cheeks. "Mary made us all wear waterproof mascara in case we cried during the ceremony. I didn't think I needed to worry about that." She sighed and sniffed. "I hope you believe me when I say I have never done anything with Mitch. Nothing is going on between us. I don't know why he thinks he's in love with me when he was about to marry Lauren."

Typical Bonnie. She was the most humble person in all of Blue Springs. That was probably why Lauren was friends with her. His sister never had to worry about Bonnie trying to steal the limelight or balking at Lauren taking all the credit whenever they did something together.

"I believe you. Mitch told me he hadn't said anything to anyone about how he felt until today. Bad timing, huh?" he asked, trying desperately to get her to smile just a bit.

Her expression remained somber. "Can you please tell your sister that? I don't want her to think that I was running around with her fiancé behind her back. It wasn't like that."

"We'll talk to her together. Come on." He stood up and held out a hand to help her up. All of the bridesmaids had worn the same blush-pink color, but each dress was styled a little bit differently. Bonnie's was strapless and had crystal beading on the bodice. He'd known Bonnie since they were little kids—it was strange to think of her as stunning, but that was what she was today, all done up like this.

Together, they headed through the doors to the hall that led to the bridal suite. The rest of the bridesmaids hovered outside the room while Lauren could be heard ranting from inside.

"She shouldn't be here, Aaron," Kathy said, scowling at Bonnie.

"We need to clear things up with Lauren. She needs her best friend more than ever today," he replied, giving Bonnie's hand a reassuring squeeze. Her shoulders straightened a bit, and she smiled up at him in appreciation.

"She doesn't need a best friend like her." Cheryl stood in front of the door. Theresa folded her arms across her chest and stood on Cheryl's right. Wendy flanked her on the other side, effectively blocking them from getting inside the room.

"Come on! Bonnie had nothing to do with this. This was all Mitch. Move so we can talk to my sister."

The women refused to budge. "You can go in, Aaron, but she needs to stay away."

This was ridiculous. Aaron couldn't believe how quickly everyone had turned on someone who they would have all sworn was their sweetest friend thirty minutes ago.

"Go without me," Bonnie said, dropping his hand. "Seeing me will only make things worse. You can convince her there's nothing going on between me and Mitch better than I can right now."

Aaron couldn't really argue with that. The ladies moved aside for him. Inside the suite, their mother was crying right along with Lauren, who sat on the floor in the middle of a massive pile of satin and tulle. Their father was pacing around on the phone barking orders at whoever was on the other end of the line.

"I don't care how long it took to set up. I want it all gone before I get there," he said. "I don't know what to do with all the food. Maybe we can donate it or something."

Aaron could only imagine how many heads had exploded when they heard the news over at the winery, where the reception was planned. They had to break down a party for five hundred guests after spending all day setting it up.

"Are you here to tell me Mitchell's ready to apologize?" Lauren asked when she noticed Aaron was in the room. She wiped her wet face with the back of her hand. "I bet he's trying to figure out what to say to me after you talked some sense into him."

He was surprised she still had hope Mitch would come around. Leave it to Lauren to refuse to believe she'd been dumped. "Mitch is gone. He's leaving town for a while to give you some space."

"What do you mean he's leaving town?" their mom shrieked. "He needs to fix this. He needs to get in here on his hands and knees and beg her to take him back."

"So I can tell him to jump in a lake. I wouldn't take him back if his parents paid me."

"Of course you wouldn't, sweetheart, but he deserves to have his heart ripped out when you reject him." Elizabeth Cole did have a flair for vengeance. This was exactly why Aaron suggested that Mitch take off.

Their dad hung up the phone and said, "I'm going to go out there and tell everyone to go home. Once I get rid of them, we'll take Lauren home."

"Make sure there's no one waiting outside," their mom said. "People were lining up earlier."

He rubbed the back of his neck, the stress evident on his face. "I'll take care of it," he said as he slipped out the door.

Aaron got down on the floor and climbed over the poofy skirt to get to his sister. He wrapped an arm around her. "I'm sorry he did that to you. You didn't deserve to be treated that way. He's a fool. But you knew that when you agreed to marry him."

"You can't be friends with him anymore," she said, resting her head on his shoulder. "You have to hate him with me."

"Let's talk about another friend. Bonnie is out there and wants to talk to you."

Lauren straightened. "You can tell that back-stabbing cheater that she is no friend of mine."

"This was all Mitch, Lauren. Bonnie had no idea he felt that way about her."

There was a fire in her eyes that Aaron had never seen before. "I don't believe that for a second. You can't be friends with her anymore, either. No one can. Bonnie Windsor is dead to me."

CHAPTER TWO

Two weeks later

"GOOD AFTERNOON, THIS is Bonnie."

"Um, hi, Bonnie. This is Carly Spaulding."

"Carly, how are you?"

There was a bit of a pause. "I'm fine. Listen, I'm calling because my husband and I were talking last night and we've decided to take the house off the market."

"Oh, I know it's been a quiet month, but I have a feeling that things are going to pick up here real soon. A lot of people want to buy before school starts in the fall, making July a busy house-hunting month."

"I understand that. It's just…we aren't planning to give up trying to sell it. We…ah… think it might be better to try another Realtor."

Bonnie sat back in her chair. She'd had an open house planned at the Spauldings' and had spent the last hour creating an updated advertising brochure. Time now wasted. "I'm sorry to hear that I haven't met your expectations. I will take the house off the market and send someone over to get the sign within twenty-four hours."

"Thanks, Bonnie."

It wasn't unusual for clients to become impatient when a house didn't sell after some time. Although five weeks wasn't a very long time for a house to be on the market. It was a bit concerning that there hadn't been any showings in the last couple weeks. The Spauldings weren't the first clients to part ways with Bonnie this month after only being on the market for a short while. The Carters fired her last week. The Mayers, who were looking for a house, had called, claiming they no longer needed her help.

She clicked and dragged the open house brochure into her computer's trash. She dreaded what she had to do next—call her office and let them know another client was backing out. She worked for Blue Springs Realty, where there were three other broker agents working under Gordon Harrison, the broker manager. Gordon had been friends with Bonnie's parents since she was a baby. He'd happily agreed to be her mentor when she decided this was the career for her. He wouldn't be angry with her, but disappointed in losing more business.

"Hey, Gordon. It's Bonnie."

"Tell me something good, Bon Bon," he said. She could picture him sitting at his desk, leaning back in his chair with his legs stretched out in front of him crossed at the ankles.

"I wish. I just got a call from Carly Spaulding. They want to pull their house on Elm. I'm sorry, Gordon. I don't know what's going on."

"I think I might. Can you come to the office? We need to have a chat." He didn't ask her to come in unless he needed to talk serious business.

"Sure. I can be there in a couple minutes."

A sense of dread tightened her shoulders. Grabbing her purse and car keys, she went out the front door. As she walked to her car, she noticed Becca Valentine, her neighbor, standing on her front porch.

"Hi, Becca." Bonnie waved hello.

Becca turned her head and cringed. That

was when Bonnie noticed the workman busy digging a hole for a new For Sale sign. Becca and Jon had mentioned a couple months ago that they were thinking about upsizing and promised to call Bonnie when the time came to put their house on the market. Apparently, they had changed their minds.

"Making the big move, huh?" Bonnie tried to hide the disappointment in her voice even though she felt it so strongly in her chest.

"I'm really sorry, Bonnie. We need this place to sell before summer is over, and with everything that's going on…you know…the face on our sign matters."

Bonnie felt her forehead crease. "Everything that's going on?"

"You can't ruin someone's wedding day and think there won't be consequences. Especially when that someone is Lauren Cole."

Bonnie's stomach dropped. Lauren still wasn't talking to her. She had heeded Aaron's warnings and backed off, giving Lauren some space to clear her head and come to her senses. None of their mutual friends were talking to her, either, but that was expected. Of course they were going to side with Lauren until Lauren realized Bonnie had had nothing to do with what happened. She understood being shut out socially, but Lauren wouldn't mess with her livelihood.

Would she?

Bonnie got in her car and drove straight to the office in downtown Blue Springs. Main Street was lined with quaint local shops and restaurants. There was Patches From Heaven, a tiny quilting store, to the right of Blue Springs Realty and Sweet and Savory, a café and sweet shop, on the left. Across the street was the Cole Market. One block north was the Cole Theater. Two streets south was where the Cole Family Library was located. Just seeing their name made her blood boil a bit.

Gordon was on the phone when she got to his door. He waved her in and motioned for her to take a seat. "Thanks for being honest. We'll talk soon." He hung up the phone and adjusted his tie, which was tied much too short. "I think I know what's happening."

"It's Lauren," they said at the same time.

"You knew?" Gordon asked.

"I just found out. My neighbors put their house on the market today with another Realtor after promising they would come to me when the time came. She said this is a consequence of ruining Lauren's wedding."

"That's what I'm hearing, too," Gordon said sadly. "Word around town is that you've been blacklisted."

"Blacklisted?"

"No one is supposed to do business with you."

It felt like the world had stopped turning. How was Bonnie supposed to make a living if the entire town had her blacklisted? It was one thing to push Bonnie away as a friend— it was another to push her out of town.

"I had nothing to do with that wedding being canceled. I have never had any kind of relationship with Mitch Bennett. There is no reason for Lauren to be doing this to me. To you. Does she not understand she's hurting more than me by messing with clients?"

"Lauren Cole doesn't think about anything but Lauren Cole." Gordon placed his elbows on his desk and clasped his hands in front of him. "Let's not get too worked up. There are plenty of people who seek out our business who aren't from Blue Springs. Those are the clients I will funnel your way until this all blows over."

Bonnie was so appreciative of Gordon's cool head. She was ready to storm over to the Cole Winery and give Lauren a piece of her mind. The smarter thing to do was to carry on with her head held high. Lauren could try to blacklist her, but Bonnie wasn't going to roll over. Those days were done.

On her way out, she decided some comfort food was in order. Sweet and Savory had the best Monte Cristo in all of California and chocolate chunk cookies that were to die for. She'd buy some cookies and bring them over to her dad's. They'd had dinner together once a week since her mom died five years ago. It was their chance to catch up and for her to make sure he was taking care of himself.

Sweet and Savory smelled the way love felt when she walked through their door. It was like a warm hug on this frustrating day. She purchased half a dozen chocolate chunk cookies, because one each for her and her dad would never be enough. The only thing that would make the cookies better was milk. It was unlikely her dad had milk in the house, so she crossed the street to the Cole Market to snag a half gallon.

It was annoying that markets always put

the milk in the back of the store so there was no easy in and out. It was also annoying that a half gallon of milk cost two-thirds as much as a full gallon.

"Hey, Bonnie." Cal Fullerton was the manager of Cole Market. He'd gone to high school with Lauren and Bonnie.

"How's it going, Cal?"

"I'm doing all right. How are you?"

"I've been better, actually. But hopefully these cookies from Sweet and Savory and this milk will turn my day around." She smiled, hoping that was possible.

Cal's expression was grim, and suddenly Bonnie felt an uncomfortable tingle in her chest. "I'm real sorry, Bonnie, but I can't sell you that milk. I'm going to have to ask you to leave the store."

Bonnie could feel her heart beating in her chest, thumping hard against her rib cage. Her face flushed with the heat of her embarrassment. "You're refusing to sell me milk?"

Cal averted his eyes. "Like I said, I'm real sorry."

"She banned me from the market? Can I not go to the movies anymore or borrow a book from the library? Have I been banned from everything that has the Cole name on it?"

Cal shrugged. "I don't really know about the other businesses, but I'd probably drive over to Morris to see a movie if I was you. Save myself the trouble of being asked to leave."

Bonnie could feel her eyes getting wet. She handed Cal the milk and clenched her jaw so she didn't let out the sob that was building. Without a word, she left the store and headed straight for her dad's house. She would not cry about this. She would not give Lauren the satisfaction, even though she couldn't possibly see her right now anyway. Lauren could be mean, but this was beyond mean. This was cruel.

Bonnie was surprised to see her dad's truck already in the driveway when she pulled up. He usually got home around five. She had planned to tidy things up for him before he got there. Good thing the Coles didn't own the local pizza delivery place, because that was what was on the menu for family dinner this week.

"Dad?" she called out as she entered the small bungalow.

"In here, Bon Bon," he shouted from the kitchen.

Dirty dishes from the previous week were piled in the sink. Her dad wasn't good about keeping up with the day-to-day chores. "What are you doing home already?"

He took a seat at the tiny café table in the breakfast nook. "What's in the bag? Something I can eat?"

The fact that he was avoiding her question made her nervous. She glanced at the calendar hanging on the fridge. There was nothing noted on today. He hadn't just come from the doctor or something. Her father was meticulous about writing all of his appointments on the kitchen calendar.

"Cookies for dessert, but I bought some extras, so maybe they can be an appetizer, too." She joined him at the table and slid the bag of goodies his way. "I wanted to bring some milk, but that didn't work out."

"These babies don't need milk," he said before taking a bite. He pushed the bag back her way.

"Why are you home so early?"

Her dad took his time eating his cookie. He

stared down at the table and up at the wall and everywhere but at Bonnie.

"Dad. What's going on?"

"They let me go today."

"They let you go home early?"

He shook his head. "They let me go. Permanently."

Bonnie set her cookie down. The bite in her mouth tasted like sand. She managed to swallow it down. "They fired you?"

"Mr. Cole came by the job site and did it himself. Said they needed to trim some fat and figured I was close to retirement anyway."

Bonnie's dad wasn't anywhere near retirement. He had spent much of his retirement money on her mother's medical bills when she was sick. They'd had to refinance the mortgage on the house and dip into his 401(k). He'd been working for Cole Construction his entire adult life. He had helped make lots of money for Lauren's father and had been underpaid for all that hard work. They weren't trimming any fat. This was about Bonnie.

"I won't let them do this, Dad."

"There's nothing you can do about it. I'll figure something out."

Bonnie stood up. There was something she could do about it. She was going to stand up for herself and her dad. She hadn't done anything wrong. Even though she hated confrontation, Mr. Cole was about to get an earful.

"Dad, I don't want to work for Cole Industries." Aaron stared hard at his reflection in the mirror. Had that been firm enough? He needed it to sound final, like there was no way to talk him out of this decision. He tried again. "Dad, I am not going to work for Cole Industries. I want to work with my hands, not sit behind a desk all day."

He had to be careful about sounding like a willful child, which his father would probably accuse him of being regardless. Aaron straightened his tie and adjusted his suit coat. He had to put his foot down and state his case. His father wouldn't like it, but that was the way it had to be.

He stepped out of the men's restroom and made his way to his father's corner office. Patricia, his father's administrative assistant, smiled with sympathy as he walked by. She had no idea what he was about to say, but every conversation with his father lately led to Aaron storming out of his office in frustration.

He took a deep breath and knocked on his dad's door, pushing it open at the same time. "Got a minute?" he asked when his father looked up.

"Half of one." Walter Cole was always busy. Day or night. Workday or weekend. Regular day or holiday. The man was always working.

"I needed to talk to you about something," Aaron said, entering the enormous office. "I'll talk fast." He sat down and mustered up the courage to repeat what he'd rehearsed in the bathroom. "Dad, I'm leaving Cole Industries. I want to work with my hands and not sit behind a desk all day. I appreciate the opportunities you've given me, but I think it's time for me to try something on my own."

"I want to build a rocket ship and be the man who colonizes the moon," his father replied. Aaron stared blankly back at him. He hated when his father used sarcasm to belittle his feelings. "We all want things, Aaron. Sometimes we get them, and sometimes we do not. I paid for your Ivy League education and sent you to a very expensive and very prestigious business school so you could work for me. I suggest you get back to that work."

Just like Aaron knew he would, his dad treated this as something he had final say over. "I appreciate everything you've done for me, Dad."

Dismissively, his father waved a hand at the door. "Good, now get back to work so I can get back to mine."

Before Aaron could reply, Bonnie Windsor burst into the room. "Mr. Cole, I need a word with you."

Patricia followed her in. "I am so sorry, Mr. Cole. She wouldn't listen when I told her she needed an appointment. She just let herself in."

His father sighed with frustration. "Call security, Patricia."

"How dare you fire my father because of what happened at Lauren's wedding? Don't even think about telling me that's not why you fired him. It's one thing to let Lauren ban me from your market and your movie theater or to blacklist me so people won't let me sell their houses, but to fire my father, who has dedicated his life to your construction company, is…" She seemed to struggle with finding a harsh enough word for his father's actions. "…heartless."

Aaron eyes were wide. He couldn't believe what he was hearing. Mr. Windsor was a foreman at Cole Construction. He was an incredibly hardworking employee and an amazing craftsman.

"Well, some would say that it's heartless to have an affair with their best friend's fiancé, Miss Windsor."

Aaron couldn't stay silent. "Dad, she wasn't having an affair with Mitch. I told you this."

Bonnie had tears in her eyes. "I never had anything to do with Mitch. I have done nothing but be a loyal friend to Lauren since we met. You have known me since I was a little girl. How could you think I would do something like that to her?" Aaron's father didn't bother to reply. "Please don't do this to my dad. Hate me. Ban me. Run me out of town. I don't care, but don't do the same to my father. Blue Springs is all he knows."

"The Cole family has decided to cut all ties from the Windsors. You have wreaked havoc on my daughter's life, and we choose to no longer associate with you or anyone related to you. That is our choice. And it's non-negotiable."

Two brawny security officers entered the room. "We need you to come with us, miss," one of them said.

The other one put his hand on her arm. Bonnie pulled away. Aaron got on his feet.

"Don't touch her," Aaron said, feeling protective. "I'll see her out." He got in between Bonnie and the security guard who dared to put his hands on her.

Bonnie didn't fight about leaving. She stormed out the way she had stormed in. Aaron had to jog to keep up with her. "Bonnie, wait." He caught her right when they got to the bank of elevators. Tears were streaming down her cheeks. "I am so sorry. I don't know what's going on, but I will do whatever it takes to make this right."

She shook her head. "There's nothing you can do. Your sister always gets her way. She wants to destroy me, and she knows that the best way to get to me is through the only family I have left in this world. Your sister is the worst."

"My sister is not at her best right now, but she's hurting. I'll talk to her. I thought she was coming around. She's been less agitated lately."

"Yeah, well, I'm sure she's been very pleased about successfully ruining my business and humiliating me in public in front of people we've known for years. I can't wait to see what she has up her sleeve next."

Lauren didn't make it very easy to defend her. Still, Aaron was struck by a sense of family loyalty. "I don't condone anything that's happened, but let's remember she was publicly humiliated in a way neither one of us would wish on anyone."

"I was mortified for her that day. What Mitch did was terrible, but Mitch did that to her, not me." The elevator opened and Bonnie stepped inside. "Why am I the only one being punished?"

The doors began to close, and Aaron didn't have a good reply. It was unfair, plain and simple. Lauren was taking out all of her anger on Bonnie because she was an easy target and Mitch was out of the country. Aaron loved his sister, but this was wrong. The Windsor family didn't deserve to take any of the heat.

Aaron went back to his father's office, where the elder Cole was busy signing his name to a stack of papers. "You can't fire Mr. Windsor because Lauren has decided that Bonnie is the bad guy. Mitch told me himself that he hadn't even shared his feelings with Bonnie, let alone had an affair with her."

"If there are things I can do to ease your sister's suffering, then I'm going to do them. When you have children, you'll understand."

Anger affected Aaron's ability to see straight. "So Lauren's feelings matter, but mine don't? You're going to ruin an innocent woman's reputation and take away her father's livelihood because of Lauren's irrational feelings, but I tell you I want to do something different with my life for completely valid reasons and I'm told to be quiet and do as I am told? None of that makes any sense, Dad."

His father set down his pen and glared at Aaron. "I can only deal with one child's drama at a time, and your sister is draining every ounce of patience I have left. If you want to work with your hands, get a hobby. You need to take a vacation to go build houses for some charity, go ahead. But I need you to do your job for this company. You are a Cole, and you need to start acting like one."

"If acting like a Cole means mistreating people because of Lauren's childish whims, maybe I'll change my name."

Aaron left and walked down the hall to his office. He shut the door and sat at his desk. He hated everything about this job. The long hours, the business trips, crunching numbers, answering emails and spending a ridiculous number of hours on the phone. Aaron's passion had always been building things. He'd had enough Lego kits as a kid to open his own store. He loved how it felt to take a bunch of pieces and make them whole. He enjoyed taking something old and worn down and cleaning it up and giving it a face-lift.

He had spent every summer during high school working for Cole Construction, and it had been the best time of his life. His father had thought doing manual labor would teach him to appreciate his opportunities to go to college and follow the path of being a white-collar worker instead. What he missed was that Aaron was in his element when he had a hammer in his hand.

If this was not the life Aaron wanted, he only had one option.

He opened his laptop and hit Print on the

letter of resignation he had already written up. As much as he loved his family, he was embarrassed to admit that sometimes they acted like nothing more than entitled bullies. His father thought he could tell Aaron what to do. He wouldn't like that Aaron was leaving, but he would have to get over it.

Right now, given how horrible his family was being to the Windsors, Aaron was fine with taking somewhat of a stand against his father. He was going to do some honest work that would at least make him feel proud of who he was and what he was doing.

letter of recommendation, he had already written up. As much as he loved his family, he was embarrassed to admit that sometimes they acted like nothing more than entitled bullies. His father was always telling Maxon what to do. He wouldn't like that Maxon was leaving, but he would have to get over it.

CHAPTER THREE

"WE COULD HIRE an attorney. We'll have to find one who has no connections to the Coles. I'm sure they've told everyone they know to not do business with me. I can't believe I managed to buy cookies. What if Sweet and Savory started refusing me service?" Bonnie rambled as she washed her father's dishes. Soap suds flew around the kitchen as she waved her hands in the air.

"Bon Bon, you need to take a breath," her father said, putting his hand on her arm to stop her from flailing. "We're not going to hire an attorney. There's no way we can fight the Coles. Their attorneys would keep us in court until I ran out of money. It wouldn't be worth it. I can find work. I'll just have to find it somewhere other than Blue Springs."

"That's not fair! Why should you have to?"

Her dad ran his hand over his balding head. "Life isn't fair. We learned that when we lost your mom. You gotta roll with the punches sometimes."

It felt like she'd been punched a hundred times today. She couldn't roll with all of them. She was ready to fight back. "Sometimes we have to stand up for ourselves."

"I'm not hiring an attorney, Bonnie," he replied gruffly, walking out of the room. "Drop it."

She pulled her hands out of the dishwater and gripped the edge of the sink. She loved her father, but he had this belief that life happened to him and he didn't have much control. Bonnie was guilty of feeling that way as well. When she was in Lauren's good graces, bad things didn't often happen to her, making it easier to not worry about who was in control. Now, things had changed, and bad things were happening much too often. Bonnie didn't want to roll with the punches. She wanted to believe she had some control over what happened to her.

Talking to Mr. Cole hadn't done her any good, however. Maybe it was time to go to Lauren and confront the beast.

Bonnie finished her dad's dishes and practiced in her head how she would tell Lauren to stop her madness. The doorbell rang, and her dad shouted that he would get it. Bonnie dried her hands off and went to see who it was. She couldn't take any more disappointment today.

Aaron Cole stood in the foyer with her father. He shook her dad's hand, and it made Bonnie's blood boil.

"What are you doing here?" she asked, suspicious of his intentions.

"I wanted to apologize for what happened today. First, to you, Mr. Windsor. You have been a valuable part of Cole Construction for as long as I can remember. You were an incredible mentor to me when I worked under you all those summers in high school."

"I appreciate that, Aaron. And call me David. We're all adults here."

"I'll try to remember that," he replied with a grin.

"Are you here to offer him his job back?" Bonnie asked. She stood next to her dad, arms folded across her chest. There was nothing to smile about today.

"Seeing that I no longer work for Cole Industries, I wouldn't be the one to talk to about that."

Bonnie felt her eyes go wide. "What do you mean, you don't work there anymore? Did your father fire you for defending me?" How far would the man go to do Lauren's bidding?

Aaron shook his head. "No, I resigned. I left the company on my own."

Bonnie almost fell over. How many bombs were going to get dropped today? "You quit your job? What did your dad say? Can you even do that?"

Aaron shrugged his broad shoulders. "I did, so I guess I can. My dad can't force me to work for him."

Bonnie's dad placed a hand on Aaron's shoulder. "I hope you've thought this through, son. Your father has always wanted nothing but the best for you. He was thrilled when you came to work for him. I would hate to see this come between the two of you."

Leave it to her dad to be worried about the father/son relationship of someone who'd just fired him for no good reason. The man didn't have a mean bone in his body. She could understand why her dad sounded so surprised. For as long as Bonnie had known Aaron, it had been his destiny to take over Cole Industries. He had been groomed for it.

"I've done nothing but think about this for a long time. I've wanted to do my own thing for a while. I finally decided to take the plunge, but I'm not here to talk about me. I'm here to let you know that I don't agree with what my sister is doing. I plan to talk to Lauren and convince her to back off."

It was tempting to let someone else fight Bonnie's battles for her, and for a minute, she considered letting him do it. She'd never been very good at getting Lauren to see different perspectives. She usually let her best friend have her way, but Bonnie needed to handle Lauren on her own.

"I was going to talk to her myself. I don't need you to intercede on my behalf."

Aaron chuckled. His laughter at her expense raised her hackles. "I don't think I have ever seen you stand up to my sister," he said. "I can remember all the way back to when you two were little girls. Lauren always called the shots. Remember when you played house and she always had you be the maid?"

Bonnie straightened her shoulders and lifted her chin. That might have been true back in the day, but things were different now. "We're not little kids anymore."

"No, you aren't," he agreed. "But how far did you have to drive to pick up those bridesmaids' gifts? Is it normal for the maid of honor to pick up and wrap her own gift?"

"He's got you there, Bon Bon," her dad said.

Bonnie let out a frustrated huff. "They couldn't ship them on time, and she had to be at the winery for that hospital fund-raising event. I had the time to do it and she didn't." That was a lie. Bonnie had told Lauren she had a showing and couldn't go, but Lauren convinced her to call and reschedule so she could do her bidding. Bonnie tried to rationalize it. "It's called being a good friend."

Aaron nodded in agreement. "You're absolutely right. You have always been a good friend to my sister, but she doesn't always return the favor, and you never say a word. No offense, but being assertive is not your superpower. I, on the other hand, have been telling my sister what I think, good or bad, for her whole life. Let me talk to her."

He made it difficult to argue with him. Bonnie couldn't change Lauren's mind. If she couldn't stand up to Lauren when they were actually friends, how was she supposed to successfully defend herself now?

"If you think you can sway her, go for it."

"I thought she was going to come around. It's not like you and Mitch have been talking since the wedding." He paused a second and bit down on his lower lip. "I mean, you haven't, right?"

Bonnie refused to dignify that question with an answer. She opened her father's front door. "Have a good day, Aaron. Good luck in your newest endeavor."

Chagrined, he nodded and headed out the door.

"I'd turn my phone off tonight if I was you," her dad said before Aaron left. "Your family isn't going to accept your resignation easily."

"You're probably right about that, Mr. Wi—I mean, David."

Bonnie shut the door behind him and pressed her back against it.

"You stand up to him pretty well. Maybe you need to pretend you're talking to him when you talk to Lauren," her dad said.

"It's your fault that I'm a pushover," she whispered as he walked away. She'd definitely inherited it from him. She loved her father more than anyone, but he was too nice for his own good.

SEVENTEEN TEXT MESSAGES and thirteen voice mails. Aaron's family was relentless. His plan, however, was to avoid their calls and texts until the morning. He decided he'd heed Mr. Windsor's advice—*David's* advice—and shut his phone off.

He sprawled out on his couch. Feet up, cold drink in one hand. Remote control in the other. He had some binge-watching to do. Usually when he got home from work, he had about three more hours of work to do on his computer. He'd end up too tired to do anything other than go to bed when he was finished. Then he'd wake up the next morning and do it all over again.

Just another reason that wasn't the life he wanted to live. There was no real living going on. He crunched numbers that meant nothing to him. Aaron wanted to have a purpose.

Before he could even choose which show he wanted to watch, his sister unlocked his front door with the key he should never have given her years ago. She threw her purse down on the coffee table.

"What are you doing? Trying to give Mom and Dad a heart attack?"

"What would you recommend I start watching? *Game of Thrones* or *The Office*?" he asked, ignoring her question altogether.

Lauren sat next to him. "I'm serious, Aaron. Is this your way of getting Mom and Dad's attention? Have you been feeling neglected or something?"

"You got me. I couldn't stand all the attention you were getting, so I decided to stop working where I got to see Dad every day."

His sister frowned. "You know what I mean. Is this some kind of stunt to get them all riled up? You're not usually this rebellious."

No, he wasn't. Aaron usually did as his dad said and what made his mother happy. He was easygoing about everything and never made much of a fuss about anything. That had always been Lauren's job. Maybe he was a bit more like Bonnie than he thought.

"I decided that it was time to do something I want to do instead of what I'm expected to do. There's no other hidden agenda."

"What exactly could be better than working for Daddy and making tons of money? You think I run the winery because I love wine? Wait, I do love wine, so that's a bad example. What I'm saying is that people do things they don't love all the time. At least you don't have to break your back to make ends meet. Imagine how miserable those people are."

Aaron actually couldn't wait to be sore after a hard day's work. He wasn't going to argue with her about this, though. She couldn't understand because she always got what she wanted, not what their parents wanted for her. She didn't have to live up to expectations. She demanded others live up to hers. Maybe it was a good time to remind her that she should try a little harder to be the person she thought she was.

"How about we change the subject. Like, when are you going to stop this ridiculous campaign against Bonnie?"

"Who? I don't know anyone named Bonnie."

Aaron rolled his eyes. "Come on. Don't be like that. Mitch was wrong to break things off on your wedding day. He's the one you deserve to be mad at."

"Mitch will rue the day he embarrassed me like that. He will pay, along with everyone who loves him."

"Bonnie does not love him. Bonnie loves you like a sister. Or at least she did before you asked Dad to do all those terrible things to her and her dad. I can't believe you went after her family. David has never been anything but kind to you."

"David? Really? Since when do you call Mr. Windsor by his first name?"

"We're all adults now."

"Too bad his daughter is a spoiled brat who thinks she can ruin people's lives and get away with it."

"Lauren," Aaron said with a sigh. "Mitchell told me that he hadn't even told Bonnie how he felt until he professed his love at the wedding. She wasn't in on it. Is there a reason you aren't willing to accept that?"

Lauren stared straight ahead at the television. He could see her clench her jaw. She tucked some of her mahogany-colored hair behind her ear.

"Your best friend in the entire world would not go after your fiancé, especially when that best friend is Bonnie."

"But my fiancé would choose to embarrass me in front of the entire town by announcing his secret love for my supposed best friend, who was completely oblivious to his feelings? I'm supposed to believe that?"

This was what Lauren was struggling with the most. Embarrassment was an emotion that didn't sit well with anyone, but Lauren even more so. She couldn't imagine Mitch would dare to humiliate her without knowing for sure he was going to get what he wanted.

"Come on, Lauren. Mitch's ego is big enough that it's completely plausible that he didn't think for a second that she wouldn't want to be with him." He decided to try a little sarcasm. "Someone as humble as you might not get it, but there are people who assume everyone is secretly in love with them."

She side-eyed him, jaw still tense. "She probably has been secretly in love with him this whole time. She's always been jealous of me," she said, refusing to go down without a fight.

"I love you, little sister, but you're going to regret letting your anger blind you. When you realize you were wrong and Bonnie doesn't forgive you for what you've done, you'll be the one ruing the day."

Her head snapped in his direction. "You are the one who is going to regret walking away from Cole Industries and defending the indefensible. I came here to try to talk some sense into you, but I guess you just want to self-destruct." She stood up and started for the door. "Don't come crying to me when Dad doesn't let you have your job back and whatever you're planning on doing fails."

"Thanks so much for your support!" he called after her. The front door slammed shut. He was never going to go crawling back to his dad. Before he quit his job, he'd been thinking of a way out. And he'd come up with a plan to flip houses. He was determined to succeed. He had a huge to-do list to start working on in the morning.

He also hoped that he'd at least planted a few seeds of reality in Lauren's brain. She had to see that Bonnie had had nothing to do with her wedding nightmare. That would ease some of this guilt he was feeling. It wasn't like any of this was his fault, but he still felt terrible that he hadn't been paying better attention to what Mitch was thinking and feeling. The guy was his friend. His best friend. He should have picked up on the signals when Mitch decided he wanted Bonnie instead of Lauren. He could have saved both his sister and Bonnie from all this hurt and pain.

He pinched the bridge of his nose. Sleep was calling his name. Aaron had a big day ahead of him tomorrow. It was the first day of being his own boss, and it was going to be amazing. He fell asleep the moment his head hit the pillow.

The next morning was full of promise. He'd never had such a good night's sleep. It was as if a huge weight had been lifted off his shoulders. No more waking up and dreading the day. No more putting on a suit and tie. No more sitting in morning meetings.

This morning, he made himself some coffee and pulled out his to-do list. First things first, he needed to find some people to help him make his dream a reality. He wasn't going to be able to flip houses on his own. As soon as he found the perfect house to buy, he needed some contractors to help him make it beautiful.

He spent the first hour of his day searching the internet for a house to buy. He hadn't realized how hard it would be to find his dream flip. He had so many questions—was he picking a good neighborhood? Did other houses in the neighborhood sell for more money? Everything on the Realtor websites looked too nice. Where were all the run-down shacks that needed a face-lift? Didn't they list them on these sites?

He decided he might need some help. Finding an easier way to locate the right kind of houses was added to his list. Maybe he should start with something easy, like calling a few of the contractors from around town to see if they were interested in teaming up. He knew who was the best of the best, and he couldn't wait to get them on board. Networking was something he was good at, something beneficial he'd learned working for his dad. A couple calls and he'd have the best flipping team ever assembled.

Except that wasn't what happened. Instead of hearing how excited these guys were about the opportunity to work together, they all said no. Every single person he called. No one was interested in working with him.

Aaron had a sinking feeling that there was a reason why, and it wasn't because these guys were too busy, like they claimed. Someone had gotten to them before he did. Someone who was already at the office at the crack of dawn and was smart enough to know exactly where Aaron would look for help first.

His father had effectively shut him down before he even got started. This must be how Bonnie had felt when she figured out she'd been blacklisted. Bonnie, Bonnie, Bonnie.

Inspiration struck. He grabbed his keys and got in his car. This was going to take a face-to-face meeting to pull off.

CHAPTER FOUR

"IF I GO TALK to Lauren today, I think you
need to go talk to Mr. Cole. We can both
practice being assertive."

"I'm not talking to Mr. Cole," her dad said,
setting down his coffee cup. "I already talked
to him when he let me go. Trust me, there's
nothing I can say that's going to change that
man's mind. You, on the other hand, haven't
even tried to talk to Lauren."

This morning's pep talk was not going the
way Bonnie had planned. She had come over
to her dad's to motivate him to fight for his
job. Instead, he was pushing her to do what
Aaron had basically talked her out of doing
yesterday.

"Aaron said he was going to talk to her.
Let's see if that changes anything." She didn't
have high hopes. Once Lauren got stuck on
an idea, there was little that could veer her off
course. Right now, she wanted to run Bon-

nie out of town and was working overtime to make it happen.

The doorbell rang, and her dad got up to answer it. Aaron's voice caught her attention right away. She hurried over to the front door.

"I stopped by Bonnie's and she wasn't there. I hoped I'd find her here, which is perfect, because I want to speak to both of you."

Had he performed a miracle? He was smiling. That was a good sign. "You talked to Lauren?" Bonnie asked, knowing he must have and that was why he was here.

The corners of his mouth fell, and Bonnie's heart sank. "I did." His gaze dropped to the floor. "Her wounds are still so raw, but I think I started to create some doubt in her conspiracy theory."

No miracles. Lauren still believed Bonnie was the bad guy. Maybe he was here to share good news about her dad's job. "Did you get my dad's job back?"

Aaron's eyes lifted. "Not exactly, but I am here to offer him a different job. Both of you, actually."

Bonnie tilted her head. "You want to offer me a job? I already have a job, Aaron. I know your sister is trying to get me fired, but that's not going to happen. I don't need a job from you or anyone with the last name Cole."

Aaron shook his head. "That's not exactly what I meant. I need to hire both of you. You, Bonnie, to help me buy some houses and you, Mr. Windsor, to help me flip them."

Bonnie's dad turned and looked at her, but if he was hoping for her to understand why Aaron Cole was involving them in this scheme, he was sorely mistaken. It made no sense to her why Aaron would come to them.

"You quit your high-paying job to flip houses? That was your plan? Are you sure you've thought this all the way through?"

"Like I told you yesterday, I've done nothing but think about it. This is what I want to do, and you two are exactly what I need to get started."

"Your family hates me. Why would you hire me to find you houses?"

"Because I trust you. You're smart and know this market." He sounded so sincere, but there was something else going on. He continued, "And I don't know anyone better at general contracting than you, David. You could teach me how to do things and eventually we could have multiple projects going at once. I think it could be a profitable business."

"Flipping houses can be high risk as well as high gain. More people lose money than make it, despite what they show you on all those television shows," Bonnie warned.

A grin spread across Aaron's face. He had the most perfect teeth. "I've got the money to risk. What I need is you. You can help me choose the best houses, and your dad can help me make them amazing."

It sounded too good to be true. A member of the Cole family helping the Windsor family after Walter Cole had stated very clearly that the Coles were no longer going to associate with the Windsors?

"And what are your parents going to say? What about Lauren?"

Aaron slid his hands into his pockets and shrugged. "We won't tell them. I think we can keep them in the dark for a little while, at least. The longer they don't know, the less likely they are to sabotage what I'm trying to do."

Would his family really do that? Sabotage his new career because he chose to work with her and her father? That might be too much pressure. Bonnie also hated the idea of sneaking around. Lauren was bound to find out, and it would give her more reason to hate Bonnie when she did. Although, after everything that had happened, she wasn't sure she wanted to be friends with Lauren anymore.

She had no reason to believe Aaron wasn't being earnest, but every reason to believe the rest of the Coles would do everything in their power to bring Bonnie down. Staying away from everyone with the last name Cole seemed like the best idea. Their answer most likely had to be a solid no.

"We'll do it," her dad said.

"What? No, we need to talk about this." Bonnie wasn't ready to give him an answer on the spot.

"What's there to think about? I lost my job, and he's offering me a new one."

"Dad, it's not that simple."

"I told you, we have to roll with the punches. And it looks like we rolled right into this." Her dad waved a hand toward Aaron.

"How about you two talk it over and get back to me. No pressure to decide right now. I do need an answer, though. I'd like to start flipping houses sooner than later."

"We will talk it over," her dad replied.

The two men shook hands, and Bonnie opened the door. "I hope you know what you're doing."

Aaron flashed her that smile. "Me, too."

"Well, that was interesting," her dad said once Aaron was gone.

"Interesting? That was an invitation to go poke a bear. Two bears. Two huge, powerful bears with lots of other bear friends who would love nothing more than to tear us to shreds."

Her dad chuckled as he made his way back to the kitchen. "Oh, Bon Bon, I have never heard you be so dramatic. I think Aaron is right—this is a match made in heaven. He wants to start this business, I need a job, you need some commissions. We all win."

"Until we lose."

"What can the Coles really do to stop us?" he asked. She could tell he legitimately couldn't think of anything. That was because her father was a good man who didn't think of ways to destroy people. Ever.

Bonnie knew better. She had no doubts the Coles would find lots of ways to make this impossible once they found out the Windsors were teaming up with their son and brother. "'What wouldn't they do' is a better question."

AARON WENT HOME and decided to enjoy an extra day off before his real work began. Hopefully, the Windsors would agree to work with him. If David didn't help him, he wasn't sure how he was going to make this dream a reality. He cleaned his house. He rearranged the books on his bookshelf, putting them in alphabetical order by title and then switching it to grouping books by the color of the cover. He watched a few cooking shows and decided to make himself lunch and dinner. He surfed the internet for a few hours, took a nap and organized his shoe collection. After watching three episodes of *The Office*, his doorbell rang. Couldn't be Lauren. She would have barged right in like she did last time. There was no way his dad would have come. He'd be waiting for Aaron to come to him. His mother would probably try to reach him by phone for at least another day before coming over to check on him. This had to be someone outside the family.

He opened the door to find Bonnie on the other side. It was late, and she had obviously been unable to sleep. Her long hair was pulled up in a ponytail. She had on flannel pajama shorts and a Blue Springs High School T-shirt. She was all kinds of adorable, something he'd been thinking with way more frequency lately.

"If this is some sort of game, we don't want to play," she said.

Aaron had to ease her mind. "I'm not playing any games. I can write up a business plan if that will prove to you how serious I am. I want to do this because it's something I am truly passionate about."

Her eyes narrowed in doubt. "If this makes my family a bigger target for Lauren, we're out."

He smiled. Maybe there was hope. "Does that mean you're in?"

She worried her bottom lip and closed her eyes. All he needed was for her to give him a chance to prove himself. That was more than anyone in his own family seemed willing to give him.

"We'll do one house with you," she finally replied. "If all goes well, we will consider doing more, but for now, we only agree to one."

One was better than none. Aaron would

take it. "You have yourself a deal. Thank you for letting me prove myself."

"Don't make me regret it," she said, stepping off his front porch and taking off toward her car.

She wouldn't regret it. Not if he had anything to say about it. Aaron would do whatever it took to make this work.

CHAPTER FIVE

"WHAT HAVE I GOTTEN us into?" Bonnie poured herself and her dad another cup of coffee. He had brought over doughnuts for the two of them to enjoy while they waited for Aaron to show up.

"Hopefully you got us into a profitable business deal." His optimism was admirable but possibly quite misguided.

"With a Cole, when I am currently blacklisted in the community by his sister. You do know that as soon as Lauren finds out, he will be pressured into cutting us loose. Maybe she already did. Maybe that's why he isn't here yet."

Her father finished chewing his bite of apple fritter. "Lauren will come around. You two have been best friends since you were little girls. She's always acted entitled, but underneath all her self-absorbed nonsense was someone who always looked out for you."

Bonnie wasn't too sure of that. How could someone be a good friend and do what Lauren had done over the last couple weeks? Bonnie had done nothing to deserve being outcast, and there was no one who could prove she did. Mitch had even admitted to his fantasy being one-sided. Of course, his trip to France made it difficult to do much defending of her honor.

"She's not looking out for me anymore. Now she's out to destroy me, and she has the power and influence to do it."

He wiped his hands on his napkin. "No one is going to destroy my girl. You are unbreakable. And she might have money behind her, but you have me and all the other people who love you in this world."

That list didn't seem very long at the moment. Anyone who was friends with both Bonnie and Lauren had sided with Lauren, most likely out of fear. Bonnie had her dad and Gordon, at least.

The doorbell rang, and Bonnie could see Aaron standing on the porch from the side window.

She opened the door. "I thought maybe you changed your mind." Hoped was more like it.

"Nope. More excited about this venture today than I was last night," he said with that crooked smile of his. Dressed in cargo shorts, a T-shirt and flip-flops, he looked like he was ready to go to the beach instead of house hunting.

Bonnie stepped aside to usher him in. Aaron Cole on her front porch would definitely raise some eyebrows, and word would get back to Lauren or their father. As much as she feared what a bad idea this was, her father needed the work.

"I took the liberty of pulling up a few listings for you to review," she said as she led him back to the kitchen.

"Morning, Aaron," her dad said, lifting his coffee cup in greeting. "Doughnut? I bought enough for everyone."

"Good morning, Mr. Windsor. I'd love a doughnut." Aaron took a seat at the kitchen table and lifted the doughnut box lid, perusing his options.

"I thought I made it clear that you're to call me David."

"Right. Old habit. Harder to break than I thought." He took the chocolate long john. "Thank you for the doughnut, David."

"So, like I said, I pulled a couple listings for you to review." Bonnie grabbed the listing sheets off the table. "I wasn't sure how big you wanted to go with your first flip, so I have them sorted into three levels. First would be the houses that need some cosmetic work, maybe a bathroom update. Second would be houses that need a bit more love. Kitchens are outdated, major cosmetic changes are needed, like this one." She handed him the listing on Mulberry Road. "All the flooring will have to go, and there's wallpaper in almost every room."

"What's level three?" Aaron asked, looking over the listing.

"Total gut. Probably not the place you want to start for your first flip. Much more risk involved."

Aaron set down the Mulberry listing. "I want to look at those. Why not go big with our first flip? More opportunity for me to learn."

"More opportunity for you to lose money. You could end up having to put more into it than you can get out," Bonnie argued.

"Sure, but if we start small, I only learn to do whatever we're working on. I'd have to flip ten houses to do it all. You and your dad have only agreed to help me with one. Why not buy a house that needs a little bit of everything? If it doesn't make a profit, at least I will have gained the experience needed to do the next one."

"The boy's got a valid point there," her dad chimed in.

Of course, money was no object for a Cole. To Aaron, this was playtime. A break from his real job. A new worry blossomed in the pit of her stomach. What if after flipping one house, he decided to go back to his job at Cole Industries? She had been the one to agree to only work on one house, but she knew her dad was hoping for consistent work. Where would that leave her dad if Aaron decided flipping houses wasn't for him? Suddenly, she wasn't sure which way to push. Something too easy might bore him to death and he'd lose interest. Something too hard could overwhelm him and cause him to throw in the towel as well.

"Come on, Bonnie. I'm up for a challenge, and I've got your dad here to guide me through it all. I couldn't ask for a better teacher."

Her father chuckled. "Give the man the

level-three listing, Bon Bon. It's his money and I get paid by the hour, not by the house."

Aaron smirked up at her. Thick eyelashes framed his brown eyes. "Level three, please."

With a sigh, Bonnie pulled out the listing on Greenbriar. It was a foreclosure. The bank wasn't going to negotiate. Not that the price mattered to Aaron. "Can we at least look at a couple of the level-two houses? Maybe my dad will notice there's more to be done than I did by looking at pictures online."

Aaron scanned the listing sheet before glancing back up at Bonnie. "We can look at whatever you want to look at, Bon Bon."

"Please don't call me that," she snapped.

"But it's so cute. I can't believe I didn't think of it."

"I've been calling her that since the day she was born," her dad chimed in. "It is pretty cute, isn't it?"

"Makes me think about chocolate," Aaron said, taking a bite of his chocolate long john.

"I love chocolate bonbons," her dad mused aloud.

"Can you two stop?" Bonnie begged. "Seriously, I thought we were going to be professional."

Her dad set down his coffee. "You want professional? I can be professional. Right after I drop the kids off at the pool." He stood up, grabbing the newspaper before heading for the bathroom. Bonnie covered her face with her hands. She should have been used to it by now. The man had been embarrassing her this way her entire life.

Aaron almost did a spit take. "Oh my gosh, I love your father."

Bonnie sat next to him and broke off a piece of blueberry doughnut. "He has no filter sometimes."

"My father's filter is so strong, sometimes we sit in the same room for hours and he doesn't say a single word. I would much prefer to be around someone like your dad over mine."

Mr. Cole wasn't exactly the warm-and-fuzzy type. Bonnie had been over at the Cole house enough to know that. He showed his affection for Lauren by spending his money on her, but she could never tell him her problems or go to him for advice like Bonnie could with her dad. David might have said things that made Bonnie cringe, but her dad was always there to give emotional support whenever she needed him.

"Speaking of your father, how do you plan to keep it from him that you're working with me and my dad?"

"I figure it will take a little while for the Blue Springs gossip machine to get the word out. Hopefully, we'll get a lot done before I have to deal with the fallout."

"And when Lauren tells you that you have to choose between working with me and being her brother, what will you do then?"

Aaron shook his head. "Lauren is going to come to her senses. I know she's wreaking some havoc on your life, but if you can wait her out just a little bit longer, I know she'll see the light."

Bonnie felt the fire in her chest. "Wait her out? Wreaking *some* havoc? She has destroyed my reputation, got my father fired from the job he's had since way before we were born and basically made it her life's mission to run me out of town. Your sister has turned into a hateful beast. I don't think she can see light. She has been permanently blinded by her misplaced rage."

With a deep sigh, Aaron placed a hand on

top of Bonnie's. "I didn't mean to downplay any of the terrible things my sister has done. I know she's been completely unfair. That's why I tried to stand up for you. I told her you're the same old Bonnie she has known her whole life. She has to realize she's done you wrong, and I believe she will do everything she can to make amends."

Bonnie pulled her hand out from under him. She wasn't the same old Bonnie. Not after everything Lauren had put her through. "Maybe I don't want your sister to make amends." She pushed her chair back and stood. "Even if Lauren does realize she's been wrong, I don't know that I will forgive her. Maybe it's time Lauren learns she can't treat people like they're gum on the bottom of her shoe and then apologize, believing that makes everything all right. It's not all right. It will never be all right."

Aaron held his hands up in surrender. "Let's agree not to talk about Lauren. I think it's clear we will not see eye to eye when it comes to her."

"I think that's a great idea. My concern, however, is that once Lauren puts pressure on you to stop working with me and my dad, what's going to stop you from giving in to her? You have to realize that the only ones taking the risk here are me and my dad. She isn't going to come after you—she's going to work harder to take me down. Period."

"What do you want from me, Bonnie? You want me to sign something that says I'll finish this project with you guys or at least pay you whatever if I back out? Is this about money?"

Only a Cole would wonder why someone else was worried about getting paid. They didn't have a clue what it was like to survive paycheck to paycheck, to live on a budget, to save up to be able to afford something they really wanted.

"Yes, Aaron, this is about money. My dad lost his job. He needs to pay his mortgage the first of the month and his other bills that will still keep coming in even though he doesn't have an income anymore. My dad needs to have money in the bank so he can buy his prescription heart and blood-pressure medication. If he's working for you, he won't be able to look for another job. So, yes. This is about the money."

AARON TRIED NOT to let his feelings be hurt. He knew what had happened to the Windsors was wrong. He was trying to do right by them, yet he still was greeted with so much mistrust. He took a deep breath.

"I understand you two are in a difficult position. I want to believe that the house we pick today is the first of many that your dad and I flip. I hope to keep your dad busy until he's ready to retire. I don't know how to prove that to you other than to do what I say I'm going to do."

Bonnie crossed her arms across her chest and chewed on her thumbnail. Her green eyes scanned his face as though she thought she could tell he was being honest with her if she looked hard enough.

"I really need you to think about the flak you're going to get for including me. It's not going to be easy to go up against your family. You know what a force of nature they can be. I can't have you be flippant about how you're going to handle it."

Aaron knew what they could do. He couldn't admit they had already interfered. It was embarrassing to say aloud. He wanted to prove to his father that he could handle anything his family threw at him. Lauren could pout and threaten to disown him. She wouldn't really mean it. He needed to be prepared for his mother to cry and try to lay a guilt trip on him because how could he do this to poor Lauren? His father's only concern was getting Aaron back on board, back under his thumb. That would be the easiest to resist.

"You're going to have to trust me, Bonnie. Let's go look at these properties and buy me a house."

She still looked skeptical, but Bonnie picked up the listings on the table and began sorting them in order from closest to farthest. She found her phone and called the listing agent on the first house.

"Hello, this is Bonnie Windsor from Blue Springs Realty. I have a client interested in looking at your property on Willow Road." She paused to listen. "Yes, Bonnie Windsor," she repeated, looking over at Aaron. "They put me on hold."

Aaron leaned against her kitchen counter, waiting with her for the person on the other end of the line to come back. "Do they play Muzak? Or is it an annoying advertisement? I hate when you get put on hold and have to listen to a commercial for the place that has so annoyingly put you on hold."

Bonnie flashed him a smile. Finally, something other than that scowl on her face. He felt a twitch in his chest. She had such a beautiful smile.

"Yes, this is Bonnie Windsor from Blue Springs Realty. Oh, from the pictures online it didn't look like anyone was living there right now. When is the next open appointment?" The way her forehead scrunched up gave Aaron a sinking feeling. "To whom am I speaking? Well, Harry, I don't know that I have ever called a Realtor and been told you don't know when I can see a property. I have a client here, ready to make a cash offer on a house. If we can't see it, he can't decide to give your client that money. Now can he?"

"Tell him I have every intention of making an offer on something today," Aaron whispered.

"You'll call me? Hello?" She pulled the phone away from her ear. "How exactly is he going to call me back when he didn't even ask for my number? Those homeowners need a new Realtor. That guy was terrible."

"I'm not a big fan of that neighborhood, and that was a level-two house anyway. Call on the level-three house." Aaron wanted something he could take from rags to riches.

"Well, luckily, I actually know the person selling the house on Greenbriar. I'll call him on our way over there. It's definitely abandoned."

David rejoined them in the kitchen with his newspaper tucked under his arm. "I feel like a new man. Where are we going first?"

"To the house that's a handyman's dream," Aaron replied, pulling his car keys out of his pocket. "I'll drive."

As soon as they were buckled in, Bonnie made her phone call from the back seat. Aaron slipped on his sunglasses. Blue Springs should have been named Blue Skies, given the disproportionally high number of sunny days its residents enjoyed. It was a beautiful town in Northern California, just south and west of some of the most gorgeous national parks the state had to offer. It was the perfect location, which was why he wanted to fix up houses in this area.

"Brad, it's Bonnie Windsor. I have a client who wants to see your house on Greenbriar." She paused. "What? It's a foreclosure, Brad. Why in the world would you need to talk to the bank about a showing?"

Aaron made eye contact with her in the rearview mirror. Her face flushed red.

"This is about Lauren Cole, isn't it? You know it's unethical for you to prevent a showing that could result in a sale for your client. What? You're telling me that the bank told you they wouldn't sell to anyone being represented by me? Are you serious?"

Aaron shouldn't have been surprised that Lauren's influence had been so far-reaching, but this was ridiculous. "Hang up," he said and kept driving until he turned on Greenbriar. He had to figure out a way to make this work, no matter how hard Lauren and his father had worked to ruin Bonnie.

"Give me the number for this Brad guy," he said. Bonnie rattled off the number, and Aaron prayed his father hadn't added his name to the no-sell-to list. "Brad? This is Aaron Cole. I am prepared to pay cash for the house on Greenbriar. Can I get in there today?"

"Absolutely, Mr. Cole," Brad replied, and Aaron sighed with relief. "I can meet you over there in an hour. Does that work for you?"

"I'm actually sitting outside it right now

with my Realtor. Can you give us the code to get in?"

"I need to speak with your Realtor to give out that information, Mr. Cole."

Darn it. Of course he did. "Yeah, hang on one second." He put Brad on mute. "He needs to talk to my Realtor. David, can you pretend to be Gordon?"

David shrugged. "Why not?"

"Dad, I don't know if we should do that. It's unethical."

"It's unethical for him to refuse to give you the code," David was quick to reply. Aaron wasn't the only one in the car feeling angry about the way people in this town were treating her. "There's no way Gordon wouldn't give us his blessing to do this."

Aaron put David on the phone. "Hi, Brad. Gordon Harrison from Blue Springs Realty. Can I get that code?" He was quiet for a minute and then thanked Brad. Aaron motioned to get the phone back.

"All set?" he asked Brad.

"Yeah, I'm glad you're dealing with Gordon. A little surprised to hear you're working with Blue Springs Realty since...you know.

Not to mention she called here a couple minutes ago."

"Right. Well, I'm only working with Mr. Harrison, so no big deal."

"Yeah, the bank was specific about not selling to Bonnie Windsor, but they didn't say anything about the company she works for."

Aaron hated that he couldn't express how he really felt about this discrimination. His stomach turned at the reality of what his dad and sister were capable of doing. "Which bank am I dealing with here?"

"Golden State Bank. Jeff Caplan is in charge of this property."

Cole Industries did plenty of business with Golden State Bank. Jeff Caplan had gone to high school with Lauren and Bonnie. His father played golf with Aaron's father all the time. His mother participated in the planning committee for the Cole library gala every year. Clearly, Jeff had already received a call from someone in his family, but he was about to get another.

Aaron finished up with Brad and found the contact number for the bank. He had to make sure Bonnie could get the commission on this sale while keeping her name from getting back to his father. If not, there was no reason to even look at the house.

"I can't believe your sister has even gone as far as calling the banks in town." Bonnie was understandably livid. "Will anyone give clients of mine a loan? Is it even legal for them to refuse services to people because of whom they associate with?"

"Let me handle this," Aaron assured her. Someone from the bank answered the call, and Aaron got straight to the point. "Aaron Cole for Jeff Caplan, please."

After a short wait on hold, Jeff picked up. "Aaron! How are you? I don't think I've seen you since that scramble at the club a month ago."

"Hey, Jeff. It's been too long."

"We should get out there again soon. What can I do for you today, though?"

"I'm interested in buying the house that foreclosed on Greenbriar, but I have a question."

"Awesome," Jeff said, his fake enthusiasm gross. "Although I can't imagine what you'd want with that dump."

"I need to know that I can trust you to be discreet about my business with you if I do make an offer."

"Of course."

"Even if Bonnie Windsor was the one who submits the offer to your Realtor."

"Excuse me?" Jeff's shock was evident in his tone. "I'm not sure I understand. We were told it was in our best interest to not work with anyone associated with Bonnie if we wanted to keep our business relationship with Cole Industries. Why are you working with her if that's the message we got?"

"Jeff, you've known Bonnie and my sister for a long time, correct?"

"I don't know, maybe since grade school."

"Have you ever known Bonnie to be anything but a kind and good-natured person?"

"Bonnie's always been a real sweetheart. I was shocked to hear that she did what she did. I felt terrible for your sister."

Aaron pinched the bridge of his nose. He couldn't believe how easily people would believe a rumor even about someone they had known their entire life. It was incredible that so many of them would quickly choose a side without getting all the facts first. "Bonnie didn't do anything to my sister. Bonnie is and always has been one of the sweetest people in all of Blue Springs. She is kind and generous. She doesn't gossip about others or put people down. She has the patience of a saint. She is a good person, Jeff. That is why she is my Realtor, and that is why you should tell Brad that the bank will sell to anyone willing to buy the house."

"Does your dad know about this?" Jeff asked a bit warily.

"Jeff, I am a twenty-nine-year-old man. I do not have to get my father's permission to do anything. You are a twenty-seven-year-old man—do you need your father's or my father's permission to do your job?"

Jeff was quiet on the other end, and Aaron feared he had blown everything before he had a chance to see the first house Bonnie had found for him.

"I will let Brad know to send me your offer when it comes through."

Aaron let out a relieved breath. "Thank you, Jeff. Way to man up." He hung up and pulled back onto the road.

"Thank you for what you said." Bonnie's voice was much calmer. "About me."

"I appreciated that as well," David said.

Aaron made eye contact with Bonnie in the rearview mirror. She had the most beautiful eyes. They were the softest green and reminded him of spring. "It was the truth. More people need to know the truth."

CHAPTER SIX

IT HAD BEEN a long time since someone said that many nice things about Bonnie to her face. She tried to be a nice person. She did her best to treat people the way she would want them to treat her. It was something her mother had not only preached but practiced as well.

Aaron had definitely given her the warm fuzzies. It was especially appreciated after all the negativity she had experienced this morning. It was still baffling that he was being so good to her. She understood why Jeff was confused about Aaron working with her.

Why would he risk so much potential backlash from his family for her? She still couldn't wrap her head around it. He could have used any Realtor to find him houses. Bonnie wasn't sure what she could offer that someone else couldn't.

"I don't think I've ever been on this side of

town. It's nice," her dad said as they pulled up to the house on Greenbriar.

She had made an effort to find Aaron houses that had more to offer than just a chance for him to remodel. She also took into account that the properties were in areas where some teardowns had already begun popping up.

"I do love the location of this one," she said. "It's at the quiet end of the street. The lot is one of the biggest in the neighborhood."

Aaron pulled into the driveway and put the car in Park. "I knew you would think this through, Bonnie."

She punched in the code and retrieved the key while her father and Aaron walked around, inspecting the outside of the ranch home. It was built in the 1950s, and everything outside looked like it was original. The bushes were overgrown, and there was garbage scattered all over the front yard.

"Gonna need new gutters, and Lord only knows what the roof looks like up close," her dad said. "Brick is in good shape. We could paint it to give it a face-lift."

"Is that pile of bricks on the roof a broken chimney?" Aaron held a hand over his eyes to block the sun as he stared up at what did appear to be a crumbling chimney.

Bonnie unlocked the front door that was painted two different shades of blue. "I told you this place needs a lot of work. You two might be biting off more than you can chew with this one."

"I don't see anything that scares me away," Aaron assured her.

"You haven't even been inside yet." She stepped back as she was hit by a horrific stench. It smelled like a mix of death and rotting food.

"I have a feeling I'm going to love it." His grin was wide and toothy, forcing her to smile back. Heat warmed her neck and cheeks. An unfamiliar tingle danced across her skin. Aaron was proving himself to be more than she'd expected.

"Well, after you then," she said, waving him in ahead of her.

Aaron waltzed into quite possibly the narrowest foyer on the planet and was quick to cover his nose and mouth with his hand. "Oh my goodness, did something die in here?"

Bonnie followed him in, plugging her nose and stepping over the pile of newspapers on the floor. There was no room for her dad to come inside until she moved into the living room straight ahead. Things weren't any prettier in there. The former tenants must have left in a hurry. That or they realized all their stuff was trash. A broken, ripped-up couch was in the living room, along with piles of garbage. Old soda cans, more newspapers and fast food wrappers were scattered all around, along with one of the reasons it smelled the way it did. "I don't know about something dying, but I'm pretty sure the last people to live here had a dog that wasn't potty trained. At least, I hope it was a dog and not something else."

"I hope I can take this wall down," Aaron said, running a hand across the floral wallpaper on the wall to his right. "What's on the other side?"

Bonnie moved farther into the house. She peeked her head into the room Aaron was curious about. "I'm guessing it's the dining room. There's a hideous chandelier hanging in here."

Walls would have to come down to give the place a true open concept. The kitchen was tiny, less than half the size of the dining room, and seemed like some kind of after-thought. It was as if the designer had realized they'd forgotten the kitchen and plopped it and a breakfast nook at the far end of the decent-size living room. Cabinets separated the two rooms instead of a wall. If she stood in front of the stove, she could look out into the living room. Bonnie hated everything about this layout.

"These guys really liked wallpaper," Aaron noted as he joined her in the living room. "But I like the windows on either side of the fireplace."

"Gives this room some good natural light," her dad added. As if immune to the smell, he walked around like normal. He had his notebook out and a pencil behind his ear. He grabbed his pencil and started jotting down some notes. "We could take out all these walls and open this up. I would knock out this side of the kitchen and put in a large island."

"Let's check out the bedrooms." Aaron's excitement was as contagious as his smile. He took off for the other side of the house and came back shaking his head. "Master bath is way too small. And the fourth bedroom is the size of my walk-in closet. How terrible would it be if we got rid of the supersmall bedroom and made the master huge? Would people be happier with having three good-size bedrooms compared to four small bedrooms? Or is it more desirable to have more bedrooms regardless of size?"

Bonnie made a note on her phone. "I can run some comps in the area and compare the two. Generally, the more bedrooms you can list, the more you can ask, but if you give people three amazing bedrooms, the wow factor might pay off."

Bonnie and her dad went back there to check it out. The bathroom and the closet each took up a corner of the far end of the bedroom, with a gap in between that served little purpose. There was a window there, looking out to the backyard, but it certainly didn't add anything significant to the room.

"I think you could definitely knock down this wall, get rid of this little hallway going to the master and make all this a giant master suite. Blow out the wall of the bathroom, make that whole area back up to the closet en suite. We could even come this way into the room and make more space in the closet and bathroom if we're going to add square footage on this end by adding the fourth bedroom and hall to the master."

It was hard to picture what he was saying. Bonnie didn't have the ability to envision changes the way her dad did, but Aaron was nodding along like he could see it all.

With one hand on his hip and the other covering his nose and mouth, Bonnie could see by the way the skin around his eyes crinkled that a grin was back on his face. "I want this house," Aaron said.

How could he fall in love with this pigsty? What did he see that she didn't?

"You should really have my dad look at things a bit more, let me check some of the comps in the area and run some numbers for you before you jump all in, Aaron. I know money is no object, but the point is to make a profit so you don't have to spend your savings on the next house as well."

"What do you think, David? Do you think we could handle this?"

"I think Bonnie's right about looking at the numbers. I can do the work, but it's going to cost a ton. We'd be gutting the place. Who knows what the electrical looks like. We should get a better look at that roof."

Aaron seemed to hear something completely different than Bonnie did. "There you have it," he said. "Your dad can help me with everything. This is the house I want. I don't need to see any others. Its potential is huge, and I can't wait to get my hands dirty to make it beautiful." He strode confidently past Bonnie and her father into the living room.

Bonnie wasn't sure why she hadn't expected him to act like a typical Cole. Coles got what they wanted because they didn't take no for an answer. They didn't have to worry about being wasteful with their money. This was exactly what Bonnie had been worried about—that Aaron would make decisions based on his emotions and she'd have to stress about him walking away if things went badly, leaving her dad high and dry.

"You really should let me run some comps at the very least." As she followed him into the trash-littered living room, some kind of vermin came running out of the kitchen. Bonnie did what any self-respecting woman in that situation would do. She screamed bloody murder and practically climbed onto Aaron's shoulder.

BONNIE WINDSOR WAS afraid of mice? That would have been hilarious if Aaron wasn't equally terrified of those disease-carrying creatures. There was something about them that gave him the creeps. They were so small and quick. It was like they had no bones in their bodies, because they could squeeze themselves through something as tiny as a buttonhole. Not to mention they did freakish things like run up pant legs or nibble on people if they get too close.

Aaron somehow managed to hop up on the dilapidated couch with Bonnie on his back. "Are there more?" he asked David, who seemed completely unfazed by the possibility that this house was infested with rodents.

"You two going to be all right over there?" David said with a chuckle. "Two grown adults afraid of one teeny mouse."

"I am not coming back inside this house until you two have finished remodeling it," Bonnie said. She set her feet down on the couch as well.

Aaron turned to face her, holding her waist to steady them both. "So you'll put in the offer for me?"

"If you still want this house after you see

the numbers, I'll put in the offer. It's your money." Her tone made it clear she thought he was foolish.

As much as his sister would hate him for thinking it, he couldn't help but notice how pretty Bonnie was, even when she was being a little sassy. "As long as you and your dad get paid, you couldn't care less, right?"

"That's why we're here," she said, pushing him away and getting off the couch. "Because my dad and I need to work. Something your family has made it almost impossible for us to do."

"Hey," her dad snapped. "Aaron is not responsible for what the other people in his family have done. He's as much to blame for what is happening to us as you are for Lauren and Mitch not being married. Remember that."

Aaron was impressed with David's level head. He was grateful the man could see him as more than a last name.

"This house is going to be the first of many your dad and I are going to flip in Blue Springs. I'd say trust me if I thought there was any chance of that happening."

"Well, there's not."

"Bonnie!" David was visibly disappointed.

"Dad, I heard what you said. I don't blame him for what's happened, but that doesn't mean I trust him to do right by us. I have no idea what we're getting ourselves into. Right now, all I know is that he wants to buy this pit. I know when Lauren finds out that he hired me to find this house for him, she'll do whatever she can to make me pay for it. And when his dad finds out he hired you to help him remodel this house, he will also make me pay for it."

Aaron got off the couch. It was clear that Bonnie's fear of his family was greater than their fear of mice. He needed to squash some of that right now. He took his phone out of his pocket and dialed Lauren and put the call on speaker.

"Aaron," Lauren said, answering the call.

"I need you to hear something, and I need you to hear it from me first." Aaron took note of how wide Bonnie's eyes got in that moment. She shook her head. He mouthed to her that it was fine. Everything would be fine. He wasn't going to tell her everything, just enough to make Bonnie relax.

"Oh, I can't wait to hear this. Why do I

fear you have done something that is going to make Daddy even madder than he already is?"

"I am sure the fact that I am not coming back to work for him will make Dad mad, but that is not going to deter me from following my own path."

"And what path is that, dear brother?"

"I am going to flip houses. In fact, I have already found the first house I want to buy and flip."

Bonnie had her hands over her ears and continued to shake her head from side to side.

"You're going to flip houses?" his sister replied in disbelief. "What in the world do you know about flipping houses?"

"I know a little, but I've hired someone who knows a lot so he can teach me as I go along."

"Oh, really?"

"I hired David Windsor." Silence came from the other end. Bonnie not only had her ears covered, but now she turned her back as if not being able to see would prevent what came next. Unfortunately, he had to come clean about something else. "Dad contacted every contractor in town. No one would work with me, so I had no choice but to work with David since Dad let him go the other day."

Still nothing from Lauren. It was quite possible, given how quiet it was on the other end of the line, that she had put him on mute while she screamed. Or maybe she was taking it better than he thought she would. The former being the most likely. Bonnie's eyes were on him now. She looked just as mad as Lauren probably was.

"I know you're probably angry," he said to both of them. "But I need you to understand that Dad backed me into a corner and I didn't have any other options. I'm not doing this to hurt you and really do have a lot of respect for David. He's a good man, and I'm grateful to him for working with me."

The call disconnected.

"I'm dead," Bonnie said, throwing her hands in the air. "I thought it was bad when I couldn't buy milk. I'll probably get stoned in the middle of the street now."

"She's not going to have you killed. Come on. She only knows I'm working with your dad. Not you."

Bonnie walked away, just like everyone in Aaron's life seemed to do when they disagreed with him. "I was trying to prove that I'm not afraid of Lauren and that she shouldn't be, either," he tried to explain to David.

"You're not afraid because you and your sister have an equal share of influence in this town. Bonnie, on the other hand, feels like she has none."

"Well, if Lauren tells everyone in this town to shun Bonnie and I ask everyone to be nice to her, maybe she'll have at least half the town on her side."

"Heck, why do you think I agreed to work with you in the first place, boy? I'm banking on the fact that you'll change a bunch of minds and my daughter can keep doing what she's doing in the town she loves." David took his pencil from behind his ear and flipped open his notebook. "I'm going to go check the fuse box. See what kind of electrical mess we might be dealing with before we go."

"I'm sorry I wasn't honest about why I came to you for help."

David seemed unfazed. "I figured that had something to do with it. Your father wants you by his side. He doesn't give up what's his real easily."

Aaron heard newspaper crinkle behind him

and spun around, looking for a mouse. He didn't see anything, but that didn't mean it wasn't there, lurking, waiting for him to turn his back so it could attack. Aaron raced for the front door. After he talked to Bonnie, he was going to call someone to get rid of all the mice in this house.

Bonnie was leaning against his car, her phone in her hand. Everything he had done so far made her feel worse. That was not his intention. It was time to find out what she thought was the best plan of action.

"I give up," he said. "Tell me what you need me to do."

"I don't need you to do anything."

"Wrong. You need someone to hire you to help them buy a house or to sell their house. Your dad needs a job. You need these things, and I can give them to you. I want to give them to you, because I think it's terrible that my family had everything to do with why you need them."

Bonnie looked up from her phone. "Lie. You need us as much as we need you, apparently."

"You have a right to be mad about that. I should have been honest with you."

"It's also not your responsibility to make up for their wrongdoing. Like my dad said in there, this isn't your fault. You aren't to blame. Why should you have to make things better?"

"I don't have to. I want to. And some of that…correction, most of that is me being selfish." He came up beside her and leaned against the car like her. "I need help, as you can see, and your dad is the best. Ten years ago, when I worked on Cole Industries' construction sites in the summer, I learned your dad is amazing at what he does. He knows better than anyone how to manage a project. He also isn't afraid to do the work. Even when he was the boss, he would be in there, working side by side with whoever needed help at the moment. If my dad is dumb enough to let someone like your dad go, I am going to be smart enough to snap him up."

"So you aren't really doing this to make amends to me, you're doing this because you have a man crush on my dad?"

Aaron laughed. She was funny on top of everything else. David wasn't the only Windsor Aaron could quite possibly have a crush on. "I guess you could say that. I'm also trying to put my fancy business school knowledge to good use. That's why I hired you."

"Your fancy business school taught you it made good business sense to hire the town pariah?"

"It makes sense to hire someone who can give you their full, undivided attention. It also makes sense to hire someone who is personally invested in your business's success."

Bonnie's head tipped back and her lips parted slightly as she realized what he was saying. "And because my dad's livelihood is dependent on your success, I am motivated to do my best for you as well."

"Exactly. I want to help you because, in the end, it helps me. I need you to let me help you. Tell me what I can do to put you more at ease, because I need you to do your best work and I don't think you can do that when you feel like your head is constantly on the chopping block."

Bonnie kicked a rock off the driveway. It skittered to a stop in the overgrown grass. "I think when it comes to Lauren, I need you to stop defending me. The more you try to convince her that I'm not to blame, the more she's going to blame me. It would be better for me if you never mention my name to her again."

If anyone knew Lauren better than he did, it was Bonnie. If she thought less was more, she was probably right. "I can do that."

"I'm sorry that your dad tried to blacklist you, too. I know that has to hurt."

Before he could share with her just how much, David came running out of the house with his arms flailing.

"Wasps!"

CHAPTER SEVEN

BONNIE WOULD BE sure to note that Blue Springs Hospital was thankfully only five miles away from the house on Greenbriar if she listed it for Aaron after the renovation. It also only took eight minutes to get there when the person driving went a tad over the speed limit. Had it been any farther away, things may have ended much differently for her father, who had gone into anaphylactic shock in the car.

"Can I get you something to drink?" she offered Aaron once they got her dad back home. She pulled a can of soda out of the refrigerator for her dad. "He's got some soda and lemonade in here."

"I'll just have some water," he replied. "Which cabinet houses the glasses? I can get it myself."

Bonnie pointed at the right one before running the can of soda out to her dad, who was resting on the couch in the living room.

Aaron handed her a glass of water when she returned. "Thanks," she said, grateful that he'd thought about her. She drank the glass down. Who knew that fearing for her father's life would make her so parched?

"I never would have guessed that your dad would be the first one we'd have to run to the hospital. My money was definitely on me."

Bonnie let out a soft laugh. "My money would have been on you, too."

Aaron placed a hand on her shoulder. "I'm glad he's okay. That was more intense than I was prepared for. I can only imagine how scary it was for you."

"Way too intense for me. Maybe a power higher than Lauren was trying to tell me something. Maybe we shouldn't go into business together." Bonnie had never experienced such panic. The helplessness she had felt when her dad's lips swelled and he could barely breathe was like no other. All she could think was that this was some sort of bad omen.

Tipping his chin down, Aaron frowned. "A wasp nest is not a sign. It's a nuisance like the mice. That house needs us. I mean, first, it needs some other people to come in and get rid of the mice and wasps, but then it needs us."

He was funny, so gorgeous, and he'd been so sweet to her. Still, there was this lingering feeling of dread in the pit of her stomach. There were so many reasons not to work with Aaron.

"I can't get this darn thing off," her dad said, walking into the kitchen tugging at his hospital bracelet. His gray comb-over was sticking up instead of slicked down.

"Here, let me get it." Bonnie retrieved the kitchen shears from the wood block on his counter. She snipped off the plastic band, and he rubbed his wrist.

"What house are we going to go look at after lunch?" he asked.

"Dad, you almost died. You're staying home."

He hitched up his pants and shook his head. "Relax, Bon Bon. I'm fine. A couple bee stings aren't going to take me out."

"That doesn't mean you don't need to take it easy."

"I'll take it easy when I'm six feet under," he argued.

Bonnie could feel her blood pressure rising. "Do you want that to be sooner or later?"

"I already decided I'm putting in an offer on the Greenbriar house." Aaron stepped between the bickering father and daughter. "We don't need to look at anything else, David. We can spend the rest of the day brainstorming ideas from the comfort of your living room."

"Okay, sounds good. What's for lunch?"

Taking a deep breath, Bonnie let her fists unclench. Her father was so infuriating and stubborn. She could have pleaded with him to rest until she was blue in the face and he still would have refused. Thankfully, Aaron was here to save the day.

"Should I run out and pick something up?" Aaron asked.

"We have plenty of food here." Bonnie couldn't allow herself to depend on him to always swoop in. Even though it was nice to have someone supporting her when it seemed like the rest of the world had turned their backs on her, she couldn't count on it to last. Lauren would see to that at some point.

Aaron let out a slight snicker.

"What's so funny?"

"Nothing. I just thought of something Lauren used to say."

"About?"

"About how she liked to come over to your house when you guys were little because your mom always made all your meals. She said you guys never went out, even on special occasions."

Bonnie suspected that Lauren didn't say she liked coming over to eat her mom's food but rather shared how sad it was that the poor Windsors lived the way they did. Bonnie had never felt embarrassed to have Lauren over until they were teenagers and she could truly appreciate how different their life situations really were.

The Windsors did not live like the Coles. There hadn't been a room in her house that Bonnie would've called formal. Her mom had never asked anyone to take off their shoes when they came inside because a little dirt never hurt anything. A white-glove test would have revealed some dust for sure. And unlike at Lauren's house, where they'd had a personal chef make all of their meals, Bonnie's mom had always done the cooking.

"I'm sure Lauren loved to tell you all about

how she used to have to slum it over at my house growing up."

Aaron's brows pinched together. "Slum it? Are you kidding me?"

"You guys had Byron, who had cooked for the queen of England. I don't think my mom's chili really competed."

"He may have cooked for kings and queens, but Byron wouldn't make something called a PBM sandwich, though. It was Lauren's absolute favorite, and not a fluffernutter sandwich as I wrongly assumed once."

Bonnie's heart ached a bit at the memory. Her mom had made peanut butter and marshmallow sandwiches quite often, because they were a family favorite. Her mom would use her cookie cutters to make them into different shapes depending on the time of year. Hearts in February, shamrocks in March, pumpkins in October.

"PBM sandwiches are the best," her dad chimed in. "You got any marshmallows at your house, Bon Bon? I could really go for a PBM for lunch."

She did not have any marshmallows, and seeing that she was banned from the local market, she had no desire to drive to the next town over to get some. She was hungry now. "I'll try to remember to pick some up the next time I'm in Morris. You've got plenty of turkey here to make a few sandwiches."

"Why don't we go grab some marshmallows downtown?" Aaron asked naively. "We can be back in minutes."

"Because your sister has informed all Colerun businesses to refuse me service."

Aaron's eyebrows shot up. "What?"

Bonnie shrugged. Did he not understand the extremes to which Lauren was willing to go?

He took her by the hand and tugged her out of the kitchen toward the front door. "We're going to change that right now."

"Aaron—"

"Bonnie. That's wrong. I will not allow my family's businesses to start discriminating against people."

"Stop," she said, trying to hold her ground but losing. "Are you planning on accompanying me everywhere I go so that you can order people to do the opposite of what your sister and father told them?"

"If I have to."

It was sweet of him to offer, but unrealistic. It was clear that he wouldn't be deterred today, however. She got in the car and let him drive her over to the market. She followed behind him, waiting for someone who worked there to notice her and alert the manager. Aaron had been walking with such purpose until they got inside.

He turned around with a chagrined expression. "Honestly, I have no idea where anything is in this store. Do you know where the marshmallows are?"

Cooking the food wasn't Byron's only responsibility. The Coles didn't shop for groceries.

"Aisle four," she replied, trying to hold back her smile.

He took her by the hand and led her to aisle four. Scanning the shelves, he grabbed two bags. "Miniature or jumbo size?"

"Miniature."

He tossed her the correct bag and set the other one back on the shelf. "Let's check out. I dare someone to say something to you."

Just as they exited the baking aisle, Cal was heading their way. The look of determination on his face when he saw Bonnie quickly morphed into one of confusion when he noticed Aaron by her side.

"Bonnie. Aaron."

"Cal," Aaron said with a tilt of his head. "How's it going?"

"It's going. Is there anything I can help you find today?"

Aaron shook his head. "I don't need anything. Bonnie's here to get some marshmallows."

"I see that," Cal said, seemingly torn about how to handle this. "I thought we talked about the predicament I'm in here, Bonnie."

"Oh, you made yourself very clear," she replied. "But Aaron really wanted me to buy these marshmallows here, so…"

The three of them stood in the middle of the main aisle in some sort of weaponless standoff. Bonnie wasn't sure if she should simply walk past him or wait for him to take the marshmallows away. No one seemed to know what the next move was. The tension made Bonnie's stomach ache. She wasn't good with confrontation, and she hated the fact that Lauren was forcing people to do just that to her on the regular now.

Aaron broke the silence. "Well, her dad is

waiting for his lunch. It was good to see you, Cal." He placed his hand on Bonnie's back and gave her a gentle push forward.

Bonnie stepped forward, maintaining eye contact with Cal the whole time. She tightened her grip on the marshmallows, certain he would snatch them if given a chance.

"Does your sister know you two are shopping together?" he asked as they moved past him.

"Does that matter?" Aaron asked, his tone challenging Cal to say yes.

"Honestly? I'm not sure. All I know is I have clear instructions when it comes to Bonnie, and you being here with her makes it difficult for me to know what to do."

"I wish doing the right thing wasn't difficult with or without me here," Aaron said. "Refusing to provide service to a perfectly upstanding member of our community isn't right. You should feel more conflicted about which tie to wear in the morning than if Bonnie should be able to buy these marshmallows."

Bonnie stared at Aaron's handsome face and a rush of those feelings she'd been having earlier hit her with even more force. He made her feel warm from the inside out. The way he defended her so effortlessly made her almost believe that everything might be okay one of these days. Her gaze shifted to poor Cal. It had been difficult for him to turn her away yesterday, but the man had a family to support and a boss who was telling him to shun her. She didn't hold him responsible for Lauren's maliciousness. People did what Lauren told them to do. It had been that way the entire time they had been friends.

In sixth grade, Lauren had told everyone in the entire school to wear pink on her birthday because it was her favorite color. Boy or girl, it didn't matter—the expectation was to wear pink. Every single one of them showed up to school wearing something pink. That was the kind of social power Lauren wielded.

Nothing had changed all these years later. People did what she asked them to do. They didn't ask why they had to do it, they simply obeyed.

Everyone except Aaron.

As LONG AS Aaron had anything to say about it, Bonnie was not walking out of this store without those marshmallows. He understood that Cal was only doing what he was told, but didn't people have a conscience? Was there anyone in this town willing to push back against something so unfair and ridiculous?

"Maybe you could be the one to buy the marshmallows instead of Bonnie," Cal suggested as they made their way to the checkout.

Aaron hated that idea, but Bonnie clearly wanted to avoid any more attention. "Smart," she said, slapping the bag against his chest for him to take.

"No," he said, handing them back. "The whole point of coming here was to show them they shouldn't discriminate against you."

"Let's not make a scene and let's not make things harder for Cal, who has a family to support and can't afford to lose his job because someone, otherwise known as your sister, finds out that he sold me marshmallows."

"Yeah, let's not do that," Cal said, anxiously tugging on the blue-striped tie around his neck.

Cowards. They were all cowards. Lauren wouldn't do that. She was using fear to control, but Aaron knew deep down that she was harmless. "She's not going to fire anyone over marshmallows."

"Are you very handy, Cal?" Bonnie asked, her hand on her hip and her head cocked to the side. She held the bag of marshmallows out. "Because if you sell me these, you could end up like my father, who Mr. Cole fired for basically being related to me. Thankfully, Aaron is here to hire anyone his dad and sister fire to help him renovate houses, but you need to be handy. Are you handy?"

Point taken. Maybe his family wasn't as harmless as he thought. He snatched the bag out of her hand. "Fine. I'll buy them, but I want everyone in this store to know these are for Bonnie Windsor, because she isn't the reason my sister didn't get married."

Several shoppers stopped and stared as he strode to the front of the store and checked out. He had to end this nonsense and the only way to do that was to talk to Lauren. After he ate lunch with the Windsors, he was going to do just that.

"Did you bring a reusable shopping bag, sir? Or did you want to purchase one?" the young man bagging the groceries asked.

Aaron seized the bag of marshmallows

from the boy. "She doesn't need a bag." He handed the cashier a five-dollar bill and tossed the marshmallows to Bonnie while he waited for his change. The least she could do was carry them out of the store.

"Good job not making a scene," she said as they exited the store.

"This better be the best sandwich I have ever had in my entire life."

Bonnie's laughter was almost worth his frustration. "I fear that expectations may be too high at this point."

She was wrong. PBM sandwiches were the greatest invention known to man. It was like a s'more with peanut butter instead of chocolate that was smashed between two slices of bread instead of graham crackers. They were broiled in the oven just long enough to toast the layer of mini marshmallows and begin to melt the thick layer of peanut butter Bonnie had spread on there. Aaron and her dad both ate two.

"I completely understand why Lauren loved these," he said, taking his last bite. At least Aaron could relate to his sister on this one particular subject.

Bonnie shook her head. "I can't believe she

actually talked about PBM sandwiches. I always assumed nothing compared to what you ate at home. I remember thinking the best thing in the world were the sundaes we used to eat at your house that were served in those huge glass bowls."

"Those were good, and I'm sure Lauren enjoyed them. I think she loved PBM sandwiches so much more because they were made with love by your mom. Everything Lauren does is because she desperately wants people to love her. Byron could add sprinkles to ice cream sundaes, but he never added any love."

He watched as Bonnie let that sink in. Truthfully, he was trying to make her feel a little bad for his sister. No one knew better than he did that they hadn't exactly grown up in the most emotionally warm family, and that had affected Lauren more than him. Based on her expression, he could see there was still some hope Bonnie might find it in her heart to someday forgive his sister for what she'd done.

She wiped a bit of peanut butter from the corner of her mouth with her napkin. "Lauren may want to be loved, but she needs to learn that you have to give to receive."

"True." He couldn't disagree. Lauren was much better at getting than giving. Aaron still wanted to believe that Lauren loved Bonnie even if she had a terrible way of showing it.

Aaron's phone rang. Caller ID told him it was his father, who only called for one of two reasons: to tell Aaron to do something or to tell him to stop doing something. Given Aaron's life choices recently, either reason had potential today.

"Dad?"

"My office in fifteen minutes, or else." That was all he said before hanging up. He didn't even give Aaron a chance to respond.

"Everything okay?" Bonnie asked as Aaron slid his phone back into his pocket.

"I have been summoned to my father's office. ASAP."

Bonnie gave him a sympathetic smile. "There are so many things you could be in trouble for doing today. I tried to warn you."

"It'll be fine," he said, more to convince himself than her. "Maybe I won't go. What can he do to me?"

David chuckled at Aaron's unconvincing

bravado. "I don't think you want to find out, son. If I was you, I would go."

Internally, Aaron groaned. He knew he would have to face the music at some point. It was discouraging that it hadn't taken very long.

"I guess we'll discuss plans for the house when I finish having a very grown-up conversation with my father about how I am an adult who can make his own decisions." Aaron placed his plate by the sink. "I wish he'd just chastise me over the phone rather than make me drive over there and back."

"Good luck," both Windsors said as he reluctantly left.

He hated how little impact asserting himself had on his father. It didn't matter that he'd quit and no longer worked for him—if Walter Cole wanted Aaron in his office pronto, Aaron was expected to be there. It was going to take some practice saying no when being the cooperative child had been his MO for so long.

His father's assistant gave him the same sad smile Bonnie had. "He's ready for you."

Of course he was. He probably had scheduled this ten-minute tirade into his day between brokering a deal with some foreign investors and a call to someone on his board of directors. Aaron stepped into the massive corner office. The views from his dad's office were some of the best in all of Blue Springs. It was too bad the old man never took a moment to appreciate it.

The elder Cole sat behind his immense mahogany desk. Everything about the office screamed power and wealth. His chair was more like a brown leather throne on wheels, which sat much higher than the stationary ones on the other side of the desk. Pictures of Walter with important people hung on the walls alongside the awards and achievements he had earned over the years. Aaron realized there wasn't one photo of the family.

"How's it going, Dad?" Aaron took a seat across from his dad. "Did you need my help hiring my replacement? You do know I don't work here anymore, right?"

"I don't have time for your smart mouth. You need to call off whatever deal you made with David Windsor. You are not going to work with him. It upsets your sister, who in turn upsets your mother. I don't want to deal with your mother being upset. I have enough on my plate since you decided to abandon the family business."

Aaron tried not to laugh. It was hilarious to hear his dad speak about him as if he was so essential to the company's success. "Well, maybe it's time Mom stopped letting Lauren dictate how she should feel. Just because Lauren is deflecting her anger onto Bonnie instead of onto Mitch, doesn't mean we all have to follow in her foolish footsteps."

His father slammed his fist down on the desk. "I don't care who you think or don't think is to blame. Your sister was humiliated in front of everyone she knows in the most egregious way possible. You act like it's no big deal and she should just get over it."

"I'm not trying to downplay what happened." He hadn't meant to come off as dismissive of Lauren's feelings. It was everyone's lack of care for Bonnie's. "I understand that what Mitch did was terrible. But do you get that it was Mitch who did this to Lauren, not Bonnie? Have you blackballed the Bennetts as well? When Mitch comes back from France, will he not be able to buy bread at the market?"

His father leaned back in his chair. "You will not do business with either of the Windsors. I have a call with New York. You can go now that we're clear."

Aaron could feel his heart thumping in his chest. He had to remind himself he didn't work for his father anymore. "Or what?"

His dad set his phone down. "Excuse me?"

"I won't do business with them or what?" Aaron couldn't imagine what threat his dad could actually pose.

His father simply answered, "Or you'll force me to choose between your happiness and your sister's."

Aaron would have asked what that meant, but his father was clearly finished with him. He picked up his phone and dialed someone in New York.

Reasoning with his father was pointless. This wasn't only about the Windsors and Lauren's hurt feelings. This was about getting what he wanted. His father wanted him to come back and work for Cole Industries. Instead of supporting him in what he wanted to do with his life, Aaron's father was willing to go out of his way to see to it that his son failed. The reality of that was worse than anything he could actually do to him.

CHAPTER EIGHT

"No, I UNDERSTAND, BUD. You have to do what's right for you. I'll see you around." Bonnie's dad ended his call.

Aaron had closed on the house exactly one week ago. He and her dad had spent the first week planning, cleaning up all the garbage in the yard and securing the permits they needed to get started. Bonnie had a bad feeling that these first few things would be the last ones to go smoothly during this flip.

Her dad had been trying to put together a team of subcontractors to help. He'd reached out to everyone he knew, hoping some of them would be interested in some side work. Thus far, no one had taken him up on his offer. It didn't even help to throw around Aaron's name. Bonnie was certain he was now just as blacklisted as she was.

"Another no?" she asked.

Her dad nodded. "It's clear they've all been

told not to associate with me or Aaron. That boy doesn't realize how much work he's going to have to do if we can't find a few extra hands."

"I have hands." Bonnie held hers up.

"Yeah," her dad said with a laugh. "We need hands that know how to do things like lay tile and hang drywall, however."

Unfortunately, she was not skilled in that kind of work, but she had to be good for something. "I can help with demolition, at least. I know how to swing around a sledge-hammer."

"You sure you want to go back into that big scary house full of mice?" he teased her.

Bonnie shivered at the thought. "I said demolition, not extermination. Please tell me you were able to hire an exterminator." The Coles had a lot of influence, but they couldn't possibly have all the exterminators in the area in their back pocket. At some point, there had to be an end to their sphere of influence.

"Yes, dear. The exterminator has already been through the house. There shouldn't be any mice in there."

"Or wasps?"

"No wasps," Aaron announced as he walked

out of the house. He was dressed exactly like her father—jeans, plaid flannel shirt. He even had safety glasses resting on the top of his head like they were Ray-Bans. "So when's the demolition crew getting here?"

"You're looking at it," David said, opening the tailgate of his pickup. "Unless you have some buddies who can give us a hand."

Aaron took a deep breath and closed his eyes for a second. When his eyes opened, a look of determination fell over his face. He strode over to the pickup and helped unload the tools they were going to use. "I'm here to learn, and I've got you to teach me. We don't need anyone else."

"What about me?" Bonnie asked. "You sure you don't need a scrappy, five-foot-four powerhouse who's ready to knock down some walls?" She picked up the sledgehammer, but it was heavier than she expected, and the head of it thunked on the ground as she lost her grip.

Aaron and her dad both chuckled.

"Careful, Little Miss Scrappy," Aaron said, taking the sledgehammer from her. "Don't hurt yourself."

Bonnie flexed her nonexistent biceps. "I

have so much pent-up frustration, I need to do something destructive."

"I thought you were here to find out if we wanted anything to eat or drink," her dad said as he buckled his tool belt around his waist.

"I did." That had been the original plan before she found out that the only ones working were these two. She could be put to better use if they needed the help. "But it seems like you need more than food and coffee."

"I disagree," Aaron said, stepping around her. "I would kill for a large coffee with cream and sugar right about now."

"Fine," she relented. "I'll get coffee, but when I get back, I'm putting a hole in something."

Her dad gave her a peck on the cheek. "I'll take a large black coffee and an apple danish if you can find one, Bon Bon."

"I hope there's no mice in there!" she shouted.

Aaron smiled over his shoulder. "If there are, I'll be sure to introduce them to my new friend," he said, holding the sledgehammer above his head.

Happy to not have to see that, she got in her car and headed into town. The Bean was a small coffee shop at the north end of Main Street. The roar of a motorcycle caught her attention as she got out of her car. A man the size of a small giant parked right in front. Dressed like he was a card-carrying member of a real biker gang, he got off his bike. The pink teddy bear strapped to the back made Bonnie do a double take.

The biker was at least two feet taller than her, and he had a reddish-brown beard that came down to his belly button and long hair pulled back into a ponytail. His black leather vest had various patches on it, and chains hung from his belt. As intimidating as he looked, he kindly held the door open for her.

"Thank you," she said with a smile. "Are you and your bear visiting or just passing through town on to somewhere more exciting?"

He grinned back as they both got in line for coffee. "Well, I don't know. If I can find some decent work, I may stay for a bit. Right now, I'm just here to visit my sister and brand-new baby niece. The bear and I got into town late last night. I figure my sister and brother-in-law could use some caffeine. I hear new parents don't get much sleep."

"I have heard that, too. You're a good brother."

"I try. This is the first baby in the family. I hope I'm a good uncle as well."

This guy was as sweet as the teddy bear on the back of his motorcycle. "What's the baby's name?"

He leaned forward. "Now, I am in no place to judge someone for an unusual name, but I think this one is kind of weird. They named her Winter, but she was born in the summer. I don't get it."

"Oh, I think it's a beautiful name. Maybe they were trying to be ironic?" Bonnie offered.

He guffawed. "Maybe. That's nicer than saying they were being weird."

"I can't believe you still dare to show your face in this town." Jeanne Watson and Kathy Cole appeared out of nowhere. Bonnie had been so distracted by her new friend she hadn't scanned the place for unfriendlies.

"Why should I hide when I've done nothing wrong?"

"Nothing wrong?" Kathy scoffed. "Having an affair with Lauren's fiancé and ruining her wedding isn't wrong? Wow, that's news to me. Did you know that's not wrong, Jeanne?"

"I always thought that was literally the worst thing a person could do to someone they claimed was their best friend. Maybe we were both wrong."

Bonnie could feel her face flushing red at their sarcasm. For almost a month, she'd wanted to be able to clear her name with these women, but she hadn't expected them to be so mean. "I didn't have an affair with Mitch. I had no idea he had feelings for me until the same exact moment you two did."

The bells on the door chimed, and Bonnie made eye contact with Mary as she stepped inside The Bean. Mary had been one of Bonnie's closest friends up until the wedding-that-wasn't. Bonnie had tried multiple times to reach out to Mary over the last month, but sides had been chosen and Lauren had won everyone's support, even though everything she believed was a lie.

Jeanne wouldn't stop. "I can't believe you're still trying to sell that story to everyone. Why didn't you just go to France with Mitch? Wouldn't that be so much easier for you and all of us?"

"Doesn't it make sense that I'm not in France with Mitch because I want nothing to do with him? He and I were never a thing. His feelings are completely one-sided."

"Hi, ladies. Maybe we should find a table instead of making a scene in line," Mary suggested to Jeanne and Kathy as she approached.

"I don't know if I can stay with her here. I think we should leave," Kathy said.

"Why should we leave?" Jeanne questioned. "She should leave. She's the one no one wants to be around."

Bonnie was doing everything in her power not to burst into tears. This was more humiliating than the two incidents with Cal at the market combined. "I'm not staying. I'll be out of here as soon as I get my coffee."

The woman in front of her in line finished giving her order and stepped aside. It was Bonnie's turn, and she was more than ready to grab her coffees and leave. Connie Wheeler, the owner of The Bean, was behind the counter.

"Hi, Connie. Can I get a large coffee black, another large coffee with cream and sugar, and a medium iced coffee with cream? Oh, and if you have an apple danish, can I get one of those, too?"

"Are you seriously going to serve her?" Jeanne asked. "If you serve this backstabber, not only will we not spend another dime here, I will be sure to let Lauren know so she can steer clear of here as well. I sure hope The Bean can withstand the negative Yelp reviews we're all sure to write."

"Jeanne," Mary said in a scolding tone. "No one needs to get Lauren all riled up."

Connie paused, and Bonnie could see it in her eyes. The fear of Lauren's retribution had her frozen in her spot. Bonnie couldn't ask Connie to go up against Lauren any more than she could have asked Cal last week. There was a gas station down the road that served coffee and most likely wouldn't be the gathering place for Lauren's friends. Bonnie could go there and get what she needed.

"Never mind, Connie. I'll go. I don't want to cause you any trouble." She glanced at Mary, who seemed more sympathetic than she'd expected. Jeanne and Kathy, on the other hand, were both thrilled with themselves. They would be sure to tell Lauren how they trampled all over Bonnie today at The Bean.

Bonnie turned to leave, but a hand fell lightly on her shoulder. "Hang on a second," the biker said. He stepped forward and spoke only to Connie. "I'll take two large caramel frappés, a large black coffee, a large coffee with cream and sugar, and an iced coffee with..." he looked at Bonnie "...cream?"

She nodded as a tear escaped and ran down her cheek. His kindness was overwhelming given the hateful things the women had said.

"Cream," he said to Connie. "And an apple danish. Make that two. Heck, make it three."

The smug expressions on Jeanne and Kathy's faces slipped away. Bonnie couldn't look at Mary for fear that she'd really lose it and be a blubbering mess.

"I'll be outside," she said, heading for the door. It seemed best to wait for her new friend outside, where things would hopefully be less hostile.

Another hand touched her arm, this one not so big. "Hey," Mary said. "I'm sorry."

"Are you?"

Mary glanced over her shoulder at the other

two and gave Bonnie a nudge out the door. She followed and waited for the door to close. "I am. They shouldn't treat you like that or force other people to treat you badly, either."

"Well, it's becoming a regular thing round this town. I'm getting used to it. I mean, I can't go to any Cole family businesses without being treated like a criminal. It's like they have wanted posters hung up everywhere to warn everyone and anyone not to do business with me. And the people who I thought were my friends don't answer any of my calls or texts."

"She's really upset about what happened, Bonnie. Her dream wedding became her worst nightmare. I would bet that Lauren didn't even know that was her worst nightmare until it happened, because she never in a million years would have thought Mitch would do that to her."

"Thank you for saying what Mitch did to her and not what Mitch and I did to her, because I didn't do anything, Mary. You have to believe me. You know me. When would I have ever run around with Mitch behind Lauren's back?"

"I know you didn't, but it doesn't matter what I know or think. You know how she is when she's hurt. She needs me around because otherwise all she has is those two and Theresa and Wendy, who are equally over-joyed with the possibility of moving up the ranks in Lauren's friendship circle."

That was a frightening thought. They were all vying for the best friend spot without a real care for Lauren or what happened. Bonnie couldn't feel bad for Lauren and her lack of quality friends right now, though. Not when she didn't even have one person in her corner.

"You have to convince her of the truth. I can't keep living like this. Did you know she got my dad fired? She's out of control, Mary. She's even making things hard for Aaron because he's being nice to me."

The lack of surprise on Mary's face spoke volumes. She probably knew everything Lauren was doing and had done. "Keep your head down a little bit longer. The less of a target you are, the less she'll come gunning for you. I have to go or they'll tell Lauren I was talking to you." Mary pushed the door open at the same time the biker was backing out of it.

"Sorry," they both said at the same time. Mary went in and the biker handed Bonnie a tray of three drinks. "I forgot to ask for two bags," he said.

"Please, bring those danishes to your family. How much do I owe you for the coffee?" Bonnie asked, fumbling to open her purse while holding on to her coffees.

"You don't owe me anything," he said, strapping his frappés into cup holders attached to the saddlebag on the side of his motorcycle. "Anyone with the patience to deal with those awful women in there deserves a few free coffees."

Bonnie felt the swell of gratitude inside her chest. "Thank you," she managed to choke out. "You have no idea how much your kindness means to me. I wish there was a way to repay it."

"Do you know how many strangers strike up a conversation with me? I'll give you a hint—zero. People tend to judge me the minute they see me. You, however, treated me like I was like everyone else in there. I know good people. *You* are good people, no matter what those harpies in there had to say."

"Thank you," she repeated. There was no way she could possibly convey how much he had turned this horrible experience into a positive one. "My name is Bonnie, by the way."

"Nice to meet you, Bonnie. My name's Sasha." Bonnie's face must have registered her surprise. "I told you I shouldn't judge anyone's name. I used to hate it until my mom sat me down and told me my name means *defender* and that people named Sasha tend to be leaders who show great bravery. After that, I felt a little bit like I had a responsibility to live up to my name."

"It fits you perfectly, Sasha. I hope you enjoy your visit with your sister and niece." She started for her car when a thought popped into her head. "Hey! Any chance you have any construction experience?"

DAVID AND AARON had established a strict timeline for this flip, and it already felt like they were behind schedule. Time was money in this business, and with only two people doing all the work, this job was going to cost more than he'd like. Since Bonnie had left to get coffee, they'd only cleared out two rooms. At this rate, the house would be finished in two years instead of two months.

After tossing the disgusting broken couch into the dumpster in the driveway, David pushed his dust mask down over his chin. "We may need to rethink our game plan. We should think about what changes are musts and which ones we can cut to save time."

Aaron didn't want to give anything up. The plans they'd drawn up were perfect. Maybe he would have to hire people from farther away. His father didn't control the world, only his little slice of it.

He slipped off his dust mask. "We aren't giving up anything. If I have to fly guys in from Portland, I will."

"And eat up all your profits?"

The idea was to make a living doing this, but if he had to take a loss on this first flip, he would. Aaron was willing to do it to prove to his dad that he couldn't stop him from doing what he wanted to do.

"Whatever it takes to get this project done on time."

David shook his head. "It's your money, kid."

Bonnie's car pulled up in front of the house, followed by a guy on a motorcycle. They both walked up the driveway together.

"Not only did I get you guys some coffee, I found some extra hands that actually know what they're doing and will have no trouble picking up a sledgehammer." She looked up at the man next to her. "Sasha, meet my dad, David, and my...friend, Aaron." The way she paused made Aaron wonder why she wasn't sure what to call him. "Guys, this is Sasha."

Sasha was a mountain of a man. It was a bit confusing how someone like Bonnie goes to the coffee shop and comes back with someone with tattoos and chains.

The three men exchanged greetings. Sasha's huge paw engulfed Aaron's when they shook hands. Only Bonnie would make friends with someone who not only looked like he could ride with the Hell's Angels, but also could be a lineman for any professional football team.

"I thought it would be a good idea for him to see what he was getting himself into before he actually commits," Bonnie said.

"Well, then, come with me, Sasha," David said. "I can show you what we're dealing with and go over what we're thinking of doing here."

They went inside, and Aaron helped Bonnie with the coffee. "Look at you, making friends wherever you go."

"He really just came to my rescue, and I realized I could repay the favor."

Aaron's eyebrows pinched together. "You needed to be rescued? What happened?"

She shook her head and handed him his coffee. "It's not important. Let's focus on the fact that I found you a helper."

"Bonnie, what happened?" he pressed.

She rolled her eyes and tried to come off like it was no big deal. "I guess there was a bridesmaid reunion at The Bean this morning, and they were not happy to see me."

Nowhere in this town was safe for poor Bonnie. "I'm sorry."

Bonnie shrugged. "It is what it is. They are all loyal to Lauren, and as long as she hates me, so will they."

"She doesn't hate you. She thinks she does because she's hurting."

"You've said that before. Saying it again doesn't make me believe it." It was clear that Lauren wasn't the only one hurting. He wanted to wrap her up in his arms and convince her that he wasn't only planning to fix up this broken-down house, but he was going to fix her broken relationship with his sister as well.

"I would love to work on this house," Sasha announced as he and David rejoined them outside. "When can I start?"

"You can start whenever you want," Aaron said. "We're going to be here every day until it's done."

"I will not be here on Sundays," David added.

"You're only going to take off Sundays?" Aaron asked. He didn't expect David to work on the weekends.

"Do you want to finish this place before the end of the year?"

"We'll have this house ready for sale before you know it," Sasha said. "I will be here tomorrow. What time do you two start?"

"I'll see you tomorrow at eight." Aaron extended his hand. The two men shook on it. He wasn't sure how Sasha had rescued Bonnie, but he knew he owed this man a debt.

It was also a huge relief to know they'd have one more person on their crew. Aaron would find more. He had to if he wanted to finish this house in a reasonable time frame. Just another reason for him to fix things between Bonnie and Lauren. If he could do that, he would be helping himself as much as Bonnie.

David clapped his hands together. "Break time is over. Let's get back in there and get this place cleaned out before lunch. Bon Bon, you staying or going? Because if you're staying, you're working."

"Put me to work. I can stay until lunch."

David threw his arm around her. Father and daughter led the way back inside. Aaron had to keep his envy in check around them, but it was difficult not to feel jealous of their close relationship. Aaron dreamed of having something like that with his dad, but all he got from his father were high expectations and lectures about not living up to them.

Bonnie got suited up. Even in rubber gloves and a dust mask, she was adorable. She picked up a garbage bag and got to work cleaning up the mess in the living room. Lauren wouldn't have stepped foot in this house, let alone touched someone else's garbage. Bonnie wasn't like Lauren, which was why she was the best kind of friend for his sister. Lauren needed people like Bonnie. He would make sure she remembered that.

"You can't go in there," he heard Riley, Lauren's assistant, say as he walked into his sister's office. She wasn't going to be happy to see him regardless of how he looked, but she would especially be perturbed by the fact that he smelled and was covered in grime. He only had an hour to get this chat over with, so there was no time to go home to shower first.

Lauren sat behind her desk, typing on her laptop. Her eyes lifted, and her neutral expression changed to a scowl instantly. Her gaze returned to her screen.

"Leave," she said. "I'm never talking to you ever again."

Aaron loved his sister. He didn't always like her, but he loved her. He almost sat in the chair across from her before deciding he probably shouldn't touch anything in his condition. "Good. I don't want you to talk— I want you to listen."

She had to be struggling to stay quiet. He could see her clenching her jaw.

"I came to tell you that you were right," he said. That piqued her interest. She stopped typing and looked at him through narrowed eyes. He knew she was hoping for something she wasn't going to get. "PBM sandwiches are the bomb."

Lauren groaned and went back to whatever she was doing on her laptop. Her office was so tastefully decorated, Aaron paused to take it all in. The walls were a soft gray with white trim. The wood floors were also stained gray, with a huge white leopard-print rug covering them. Her blush-pink chair was armless and on wheels. Pink peonies sat in a crystal vase on her desk. Every accessory had been carefully chosen. When he ended this feud between her and Bonnie, he was going to have Lauren help him decorate his house.

"Seriously. They are the best. I see why you loved them when Mrs. Windsor used to make them for you."

She folded her arms across her chest and changed the subject, a clear sign that he had struck a nerve. "Why do you look and smell like you've been sleeping in a garbage dump for the last week? Is that what happens when Daddy cuts you off?"

"I've been working at my house. You know, the one you and Dad are trying to keep me from flipping."

"I'm not trying to do anything to you but get you to leave. You're gross and I don't want to talk to you."

"I don't care if I smell. I need you to hear me out. You and Bonnie have always been like sisters. I've always felt like I grew up with two annoying little sisters, not one."

"I won't talk about her with you," she interrupted. "I told you, she is dead to me, and if you keep this up, you will be, too."

"You know who's dead? Mrs. Windsor is. And I know Mrs. Windsor was basically like a second mom to you. I don't think I have ever seen you cry as hard as you did at her funeral. Your best friend, the woman who welcomed you into her family, would not betray you the way you have convinced yourself she has. You know Bonnie better than anyone. You know that's not who she is. She's a good person who goes grocery shopping for her widower dad once a week and makes friends with scary-looking biker dudes while in line for coffee. She has been more worried about how my working with her dad is going to impact my relationship with you than how it could make things worse for her. She does those things because she's thoughtful and kind. She's not some minx who knowingly lured Mitch away from you. Mitch probably fell in love with her because she's clueless about how attractive those qualities are."

Lauren stood up and slammed her palms on her desk. Her face was flushed red with her anger. "Do not talk about Mitch, and do not tell me Bonnie didn't know what she was doing! Do you really believe Mitch would leave me for her without some conniving on her part? Theresa was right. Bonnie has been jealous of me our entire friendship. She has always wanted what I have. It's obvious she finally decided to try to take something that was mine."

"You're wrong," Aaron asserted. So were all her other "friends," who weren't half the friend Bonnie had been. Lauren shook her head. "You are so wrong. The saddest part of all this is that you're the one losing the most because you refuse to admit that maybe, just maybe, someone liked Bonnie more than they liked you."

"Get. Out," she said through clenched teeth.

Aaron didn't have anything else to say anyway, but he did notice this weird feeling in his chest. It had started as soon as he had begun defending Bonnie. Maybe Mitch wasn't the only one who had fallen under Bonnie's spell.

CHAPTER NINE

"REMIND ME TO never make you mad," Sasha said, taking a step back.

Bonnie gripped the sledgehammer a little tighter and took another swing like it was a baseball bat, smashing it into the wall separating the living room from the dining room. Demolition was way more fun than cleaning up garbage and ripping up stained carpet.

"She's got lots of pent-up frustration," her dad said, standing beside Sasha with his arms folded across his chest. "I can't wait to see how long it takes her to tire out."

Bonnie whacked the wall again. "Are you two going to just stand there watching me or are you going to get to work?"

"I could use some help over here," Aaron called from the kitchen. "We need to take out the counters and knock down cabinets."

Bonnie rested the sledgehammer on her

shoulder. "Oh, I want to knock down cabinets."

"You can't stop in the middle of a job to do another one," her dad said. "Nothing will ever get finished."

Sasha punched a hole in the drywall underneath one of Bonnie's, then ripped a chunk off with his bare hand. "She got it started. I can finish it."

Bonnie and her dad exchanged a look. Sasha was a one-man wrecking machine and worth every penny that Aaron was paying him. She lugged the sledgehammer over to the kitchen, excited to break something rather than just put holes in the wall.

"Can I smash them?" she asked Aaron, winding up to take a swing.

He grabbed the sledgehammer and pulled her closer to him. "Whoa, slow down there, Rosie the Riveter. Maybe we should unscrew them from the wall."

He smelled too good to be working construction. He was supposed to stink like sweat, not expensive cologne. Bonnie found herself momentarily intoxicated by him. It wasn't only his scent that had her captured, but the way he gazed into her eyes made her weak in the knees. Since when did Aaron look at her like she was something other than his little sister's friend? He was like family. She shouldn't be feeling *things* when he was near.

Pretending she was completely unfazed, she pulled away. "Well, that's no fun. I'm going to go back to knocking down walls, then."

He was quick to stop her from going. "Fine, you can sledgehammer a couple, but let's start with the counters."

Bonnie needed to shake off whatever just happened between them in those few short seconds and get back to taking out a few weeks of frustration on this house. She could only wrestle with one emotion at a time.

Aaron showed her how to hit the overhang from underneath it rather than from above. As hard as she tried, she wasn't strong enough to pop it off. After half a dozen attempts, her forearms were burning.

"Maybe we should take turns. That way we won't tire out," he suggested, kindly not making her feel like a failure by simply taking over.

She handed over the sledgehammer. In two

hits, he detached the counter from the cabinets. "You loosened it up for me."

He was too nice. Bonnie snatched the sledgehammer away. She wasn't cut out for removing the counters—she was better when she got the help of gravity when she swung this thing. "You are in charge of counters, and I am going to get rid of these horrible floating cabinets."

Without missing a beat, she spun around and attempted to hit the cabinets separating the kitchen from the living room. Only instead of hitting the cabinets, the sledgehammer slipped right out of her hands and went flying right into her dad, who had come over to see what they were doing.

"Dad!"

It was a total knockout. Everyone ran over to where he went down. Blood flowed from his head like a river. Bonnie felt herself get a little woozy. She wasn't used to seeing so much blood. Her dad opened his eyes and put his hand over his wound. It didn't do much to stop the flow.

"This is not good," Aaron said.

"Do we have anything for him to hold on that cut?" Sasha asked.

There was nothing in the house that was clean enough to put on an open wound. Aaron didn't hesitate. He lifted his shirt off his head and folded it up so her dad could use it to stop the bleeding. A shirtless Aaron would have been the distraction of a lifetime if Bonnie wasn't feeling so panicked about her dad.

"We need to get him to a hospital," Bonnie said. He probably couldn't get up off the floor. Calling 911 might have been her only option.

"I'm fine," her dad protested, trying to sit up. "I don't need to go to no hospital. Head wounds bleed a lot."

Aaron and Sasha helped him to his feet. "David, you just got knocked over by the flying handle of a sledgehammer. Let me see that cut." Bonnie's dad pulled his hand away. The blood was still pouring out. The cut on his forehead was deep. There was no bandage that was going to hold that together successfully.

"You need stitches, Dad. It's not good."

Her stubborn father shook his broken head. "I just need to sit down for a minute."

"Dad."

"You can rest for a minute in my car," Aaron said. Bonnie was about to start a fight when he added, "But I'll be driving you to the hospital while you do it."

Her dad started to protest when he lost his balance. Sasha scooped him as though he were a child. "Don't worry, Dave. I'll keep tearing stuff down while you guys are gone," he said. "We won't get too behind. I promise."

Bonnie was so grateful for these two men who had her father's back. She relaxed enough to appreciate the way Aaron looked from behind without his shirt on. In one day, she'd almost killed her dad and was suddenly both hot and bothered whenever Aaron was near. Things were so confusing, it was like she had been the one hit on the head.

NOT ONLY WOULD she mention how close Blue Springs Hospital was to the house when she listed it, Bonnie would also talk up how amazing the ER staff was. After the doctor stitched up her less-than-cooperative father, Bonnie sat with him until they brought him his discharge papers. Thank goodness the Coles didn't own the hospital.

"I am so sorry I wasn't paying attention to what I was doing."

"I'm sorry that I thought I was safe around

you and weapons of mass destruction," he said with a chuckle.

Bonnie tipped her chin up. "Weird, your head injury somehow made you less hilarious than usual."

"How are we doing in here?" Aaron popped into the room. He had a soda in each hand and one tucked under his arm. The nurse had given him some scrubs so he didn't have to sit in the waiting room half-naked. "I wasn't aware of the fact that you were such an injury magnet, David. Your luck has not been very good lately."

He handed them each a soda and sat on the doctor's stool. He spun around in a couple circles. Bonnie smiled at his silliness. She felt bad that he'd stopped working to accompany them to the hospital, but he'd been adamant that he would drive them.

"I think we need to be honest about the bad karma coming from us working together," Bonnie said. Her dad had worked for Cole Construction for years and never had to be rushed to the hospital. He worked for Aaron for a couple weeks and he'd become a regular in the ER.

"I don't know why you'd say I'm unlucky,"

her dad said to Aaron. "And I don't know why you think this was bad karma, Bon Bon. Things could have been much worse."

"That is true. It was actually very lucky that you hit him with the handle of the sledgehammer instead of the head."

"Right," Bonnie said. Emotion began to tighten her throat. "Unlucky would have been dying from a massive brain bleed. Killing you would have been worse than slicing your head open."

He reached for her hand. "It's going to take more than a swarm of angry wasps and a fly-away sledgehammer to take me out, sweetheart."

It was dumb to be upset. He was fine. She hadn't done any major harm, but her dad was her person. He was the one who loved her unconditionally. He was the only family she had left. Their bond had only gotten stronger when her mom died, and losing him was completely unthinkable.

Aaron wheeled himself over to her. "I know you're letting yourself doubt why you agreed to take this on with me, but I promise I'm going to make sure that we are safe moving forward. It's my responsibility to make sure there are no more injuries."

"Don't beat yourself up, kid. If anyone is to blame, it's me. I should have known something like this could happen. I mean, I'm the one who coached her when she played T-ball and usually threw the bat farther than she hit the ball."

Aaron laughed while Bonnie narrowed her eyes. "Wow. There's that terrible sense of humor again. That hit on the head really messed up your ability to tell a funny joke."

Her dad smiled and gave her hand another pat. "I love you. You know that."

The lump in her throat was back. She did know.

AARON DROPPED THE Windsors off at David's house. Bonnie was going to stay with him overnight, since he had been diagnosed with a concussion. Even when she nearly took his head off, their love for one another shone through. He wasn't so sure his dad would have been so forgiving.

"How's the patient?" Sasha asked when Aaron got back to the job.

Sasha the Giant had single-handedly bulldozed everything in the living room and kitchen. He'd seriously finished more on his own in a few hours than Aaron would have hoped the four of them could accomplish all day. He had knocked down the wall between the living and dining rooms. The countertops were gone, and the cabinets were all removed.

Aaron's jaw dropped. "You are the hardest-working man I have ever met."

"It wasn't that much. The hanging cabinets our little firecracker was trying to hit fell down with nothing more than a tap. Had she hit her mark, those things would have gone flying at her dad like the hammer did. He's probably lucky she lost her grip."

His use of the word *lucky* made Aaron laugh. Bonnie would most likely disagree that any of this was lucky. She didn't realize what a good-luck charm she was. She was the one who'd found Sasha, and he was more than Aaron could have asked for.

Aaron inspected the work that had been done. It looked like nothing had been holding the cabinets to the ceiling, but the paint under them was a completely different color than the rest.

"It's going to look so good in here when

we're finished," Aaron said. "I love how open this space is now. If we could just find a way to get some more light in here, it would be perfect."

There was a sharp knock on the door. Aaron felt his brow furrow.

"Sounds like you have a guest," Sasha said.

That was strange. Aaron hadn't given this address to anyone. "I don't have any friends who would come looking for me here."

"Maybe it's a neighbor."

Aaron would need to be neighborly while he was working on the house, but he didn't need people nosing around until they were closer to being finished. He made his way to the front door. "Are there still door-to-door vacuum-cleaner salesmen? I'd rather deal with that."

"Oh, what if it's a little girl selling cookies?" Sasha's eyes got big. Aaron could only imagine how many cookies Sasha could eat.

He opened the front door to find out if either one of them was right. Two Blue Springs police officers were on the other side. They were a huge letdown after the mention of cookies. "Good afternoon, Officers. What can I do for you?"

"Are you the owner of this house?" the burly officer in sunglasses asked. He wasn't exactly Officer Friendly.

"I am."

"We've had multiple complaints from your neighbors that there is excessive noise coming from your house that is disturbing the peace and quiet in the area," the officer explained.

Aaron tipped his head to the side. "During the day? People can complain about noise in the middle of the day?"

"They sure can. When it's excessive," the lanky, bearded officer replied.

Aaron looked over his shoulder at Sasha. "Were you doing something *excessively* loud while we were gone?"

"I don't think so," he said with a shrug. "Nothing that would have woke the neighbors."

The first officer put his hand on the door-jamb. "I sure hope you have all the proper permits for the work you're doing here. I would hate to have the city come out and shut you down."

Suspicion set in. That sounded much more like a threat than a warning. Something was not right here. "We have all the permits."

Aaron folded his arms across his chest. "Who exactly called about the noise? I would love to apologize and let them know we'll keep it down moving forward?"

"We aren't at liberty to give out names, Mr. Cole. How many people do you have working here?" The officer took off his sunglasses and tried to see around Aaron, who quickly blocked the doorway with his body the best he could.

"How do you know my name? I don't remember giving you my name."

Officer Big Mouth glanced back at Officer Lanky, who answered for him. "The person who made the report gave us your name."

Unlikely, since he had yet to introduce himself to any of the neighbors. This had his dad and sister written all over it. "So, am I getting some kind of ticket or citation for being 'too loud,' according to this anonymous neighbor who knows my name?"

"No citation. Just a warning," Officer Lanky said. "Of course, if we have to come out again, we might need to shut this down."

"'Shut this down'? You mean the renovations on the house that I own? You're going to stop me from remodeling my own house because someone says that one man—" he pointed back at Sasha "—disrupted the entire neighborhood in the middle of the afternoon? I'm not sure you can do that, Officer. I think that my lawyers would have a thing or two to say about that."

Officer Big Mouth slipped his sunglasses back on. "Well, we might not be able to shut you down, but like I said, I sure hope you have all your permits in place, because the inspectors sure can."

"Bring them on down. I have all the permits. If that's all, I think we're done here." He shut the door and pressed his back to it. "Can you believe that?"

"What did you do to make the police hate you so much? Rob a bank or something?" Sasha asked.

It was so embarrassing to admit the truth. He didn't want Sasha to think he came from some evil family that would sic the police on their son or brother because he was nice to Bonnie. "I didn't rob a bank. I just made some powerful people unhappy."

"You and Bonnie have a lot in common, huh? That poor girl got run out of a coffee shop yesterday by a pack of angry women accusing her of all kinds of wild things. I didn't realize this town was full of so many cutthroat individuals."

Cutthroat was a good way to describe the Coles these days. Thank goodness Bonnie wasn't here for the shakedown by the police. She would have thought she was headed for jail in the near future for sure. He'd have to warn her to be careful not to go over the speed limit in town. Something told him they wouldn't let her off with a warning if his family truly had gotten to the police.

He'd tried talking to his dad. That had been miserably unsuccessful. His chat with Lauren had accomplished nothing. There was only one Cole left for him to try to reason with. He needed to corner his mother. She was the last hope for stopping this madness.

AARON PULLED INTO his parents' horseshoe-shaped driveway and parked his car right in front of the door. It was before five o'clock, meaning there was no way his father was home yet. He rarely left the office before six.

This house always made Aaron smile. They had moved in when he was in high school, and his mother had been very involved in the design. He remembered her having blueprints spread open on the dining room table and listening in on her conversations with the architect. That may have been when he developed his love for house design.

The arched front door of their gorgeous Mediterranean-style house was surrounded by windows. He peered inside and tried the door. Thankfully, it was unlocked. He pushed it open and stepped into the massive two-story foyer.

"Mom?" he called out. The house was too huge to go room to room looking for her.

"Aaron?" Her voice came from the living room, which was unmatched in size and volume. They could host a party for the whole town in it and no one would feel crowded. The high ceilings were accented with wood beams. That was something Aaron would love to do in his house.

His mom was relaxing on the cream-colored chaise lounge that sat in front of the glass french doors that looked out to the patio and swimming pool. She lifted off it and sashayed over to him with the grace of the ballerina she'd been before she got married and had children. She greeted him with a hug. At least someone in this family still loved him.

"What are you doing here?"

"I came to talk to you."

"Well, it's about time," she said, pulling back. Her hands rested on his shoulders and gave him a little shake. "I have only left you a million messages that were never returned."

"I know. I apologize. I guess I just didn't want to hear you tell me that I shouldn't be doing what I'm doing when I feel so strongly that I am doing exactly what I should."

She dropped her hands to her sides. "Why? Sweetheart, your sister needs you now more than ever. She needs to know you have her back."

"Mom, Lauren is being unreasonable. The reason I am standing with Bonnie is because that is what is best for Lauren. She needs to see that if she doesn't end this attack on her innocent friend, it's going to be her downfall."

His mom shook her head. "No, it won't. It makes her feel better. And she deserves to feel better right now. What those two did to her was unforgivable. She needs to show the world it cannot treat her like that."

Aaron was all for Lauren standing up for herself. He was not okay with her trampling all over Bonnie to do it. "Mom, listen to yourself. What did those *two* do? From where I was standing, only one of them humiliated Lauren, and that was Mitch. He is the only one responsible for how bad Lauren feels right now."

She waved that thought off. "You're telling me that Bonnie, Bonnie Windsor, didn't do a single thing to lead him on so he would be daring enough to do that to your sister? No one in their right mind would take a chance like that if he didn't already know he was going to get what he wanted."

How could he explain that was the beauty of Bonnie? She was completely clueless that she could win someone over by simply being herself. She didn't have to do anything but smile and treat people with kindness. That was what had him caught in her web right now. He could understand exactly why Mitch wanted to be with Bonnie instead of Lauren. Aaron would have liked his best friend to find a better time and place to tell Lauren he had changed his mind about getting married, but there was no ill intent on Bonnie's part.

"I know you're wrong. I know Lauren is wrong. But I'm not going to waste my breath trying to convince you that you are. Instead, tell me this. What if you are wrong? What if Bonnie had no idea what Mitch was going to say that day? What if Bonnie doesn't even like Mitch? Can you live with yourself if her life is turned upside down because of Lauren's hurt feelings?"

His mom sat on the enormous sectional in the middle of the room. She let her head fall back. "You know I have always liked Bonnie. She's always seemed like a nice girl."

Aaron felt a surge of hope. He sat next to her. "She is a nice woman, Mom. She always has been and will continue to be. Can we say the same about Lauren?"

His mom frowned. "Don't talk about your sister like that. She is a nice person."

"She's not acting like it."

"I'll talk to her about backing off Bonnie a little bit. I'll point out that she hasn't had anything to do with Mitchell since the wedding. Can you imagine what your sister would have done if they were together right now?"

That was never a possibility, a reality Aaron

would never have to consider. "Thank you for trying."

"Now you have to do something for me," she said, crossing her legs.

Aaron's shoulders tensed. Nothing good was going to follow that sentence. She was going to ask him to go back to work for his father or something equally impossible.

"Mom—"

"Hear me out," she said. "The library gala is coming up, and I need you to do me a favor."

"What kind of favor?" he asked hesitantly.

"The kind that includes you accompanying Fred and Ingrid's daughter to said gala."

A date? That was unexpected, but still not something Aaron wanted to entertain. He wasn't sure he was even invited to the gala this year, considering his father had basically banished him from the kingdom.

"Did you run this one by Dad? Because I am fairly certain that I am not on his list of favorite people right now. I doubt he wants me traipsing around his gala showing my traitorous face."

"Well, if I get you out of hot water with your sister, that will get you out of half the trouble with your father. When you come to your senses and go back to work for him, you'll be fully reinstated to favorite son status."

"I'm his only son," he reminded her.

She pinched his cheek. "Exactly. You need to remember that."

He wasn't going to argue with her about why he was not going to go back to work for his father—ever. He agreed to take Fred and Ingrid's daughter to the library gala. It was a couple months away. By then, he could either be completely disowned or back in everyone's good graces. Either way, he'd get out of going somehow.

He decided to change the subject to something they would both rather talk about. "Do you want to see the plans for the house I'm flipping? I could use your advice on something I'm thinking about doing to the living room."

His mother's eyes lit up. As much as she wanted him to go back to work for his dad, her love for design would always win out in the end.

CHAPTER TEN

"I VOTE THAT anyone but my father goes up in the attic."

Bonnie's dad glared at her as he unbuckled his tool belt. "Don't start with me. Why don't you go sell houses to someone and let us work in peace?"

Well, for one thing, there was no one in town willing to let her sell them a house. Secondly, she was not going to let anything happen to him today that might send him to the hospital.

"I'm not spending another afternoon in the ER, so let Aaron go up there."

"I can go up there, David. It's fine."

"Are you kidding me? Both of you need to get out of my way. I am going up into the attic, and no one is stopping me."

Bonnie wasn't moving from her place in front of the pull-down attic stairs. "Dad, you have a concussion."

He rolled his eyes as if he was the child in this relationship. "Let me do my job. Move. Now." He may have looked childish, but he sounded very parental.

"He'll be fine. What could happen up there?" Aaron asked.

He could fall through the ceiling, there could be a rabid raccoon hiding up there, maybe he'd trip and hit his head. The possibilities were endless. This job was a magnet for trouble.

"Nothing bad is going to happen. I'm going to inspect things and come back down. That's what's going to happen." Her dad wrapped his arms around Bonnie, picked her up and moved her out of his way.

"Dad! Stop. I was going to move."

"Next time, do it when I tell you to." Up he went.

Aaron covered his mouth to hide a grin. It wasn't funny. The corner of her mouth curled up, but she fought a full-blown smile. Okay, it was a little funny.

"You look pretty today," Aaron said while they waited in the hallway by the bedrooms.

Bonnie fidgeted and tugged on the pale pink blouse she had put on today. She purposely didn't dress to work today, because she was clearly not cut out for construction. "Thanks."

"You should wear pink more often. It complements your complexion."

"My complexion?" This time she smiled without restraint.

He ducked his head, his cheeks pink like her shirt. He gripped the back of his neck with his hand. "I don't know. I've heard my mom say that before. It looks good on you, that's all I'm trying to say."

She could feel her forehead crease. Since when did Aaron Cole get so easily flustered? The Aaron she knew was full of confidence. There was no way she could throw him off his usual game.

"You assured me there weren't going to be any more accidents on this job. You better make good on that promise."

"I'll make sure. We aren't doing anything dangerous today and you're not going to be wielding any sledgehammers, so I think we're in the clear."

She put a hand on her hip and tipped her head to the side. "Really? You're going to go there with me?"

His laughter caused her stomach to do a little flip, and the way he looked at her sometimes made her wonder if he saw someone different than she did when she stared into a mirror. Someone *more*.

"If the butterfingers fit," he said with a shrug.

"Oh, really?" She was smiling so much her face hurt.

"Really." His swagger was back, and it was even more attractive than his adorable sheepishness.

"You two done flirting? I could use some help in here," Sasha said, coming out of the master bedroom.

"We aren't—" Bonnie started to say.

"Coming," Aaron said, slipping past her to help Sasha.

Flirting? Bonnie was not flirting with Aaron. Aaron was like a brother, and he thought of her as an annoying little sister. He dated people like Caroline Gilbert, Miss Blue Springs 2012, or Sylvie Washington, who modeled part-time and ran her own cosmetic company. He'd never been interested in women like Bonnie.

Her dad's feet appeared as he climbed

down the ladder. She came over to hold it steady for him even though it was attached to the ceiling.

"Where's Aaron?"

"Helping Sasha."

"What's the good word?" Aaron asked, coming out of the bedroom.

"Well, the only good news is that the attic does extend over the living room, so it is possible to take down the ceiling and really open up that room."

"Yes!" Aaron fist pumped. "It's going to look amazing. Wood beams, maybe a couple skylights. It will sell the house."

"The not-good news is that it looks like that roof is a problem. There was leaking at some point. I can see the water damage on the attic ceiling. I'm surprised we couldn't see water damage in the living room. I fear you need a new roof."

"How much is that going to cost?"

"Around four thousand. The other problem is you might have asbestos wrapped around some pipes up there. I can't say for sure, but you need to get someone in here to check it out. If it is asbestos, removing it is going to be costly."

Aaron's face fell. "How costly?"

"I can't say for sure, but I'd estimate it around seven, maybe eight thousand."

Bonnie felt that in her chest. Twelve grand was a lot of money. Of course, Aaron had plenty to go around.

"We have to take care of it no matter what, right?" Aaron asked.

"You have to take care of it no matter what."

With his lips pressed tight, he squeezed his eyes shut for a moment. "Well, there goes more of our profits."

"Disappointing, I know," her dad said. "But it's a good thing we checked up there and found it. I'll call around and find someone to remove it."

Her dad picked up his tool belt and walked back out to the living room. Aaron leaned against the doorjamb. "You warned me," he said to Bonnie.

"I warned you about what?"

"You said I might be getting in over my head with this house. You were right."

"I love being called right, but I'm sorry I was right about this. Hopefully, this is the worst of it. Giving the living room high ceilings is going to be awesome. We can make that a huge selling point."

"Can you get me an extra twelve thousand because of it?"

Bonnie scrunched up her face. "Probably not that much, sorry. I'll do my best, though."

"I know you will. I'm pretty sure if you flash that smile at someone, they'll buy this house for top dollar."

She appreciated his faith in her. Although she didn't have many people wanting to buy houses from her at the moment, so they'd have to pray someone from out of town, with no knowledge of who the Coles were, came in to buy. "I will do everything in my power to make you money."

"Well, this is still an excellent learning experience even if I only make a hundred dollars, right?"

"You are learning a lot. And I'm going to work hard to make you more than a hundred dollars."

"That's sweet of you."

Sasha appeared behind him, a towering giant filling up the entire doorway. "You know what would be sweet of you? Coming back in here to help me instead of once again flirting with the pretty lady."

"He's not—"

"I'm coming," Aaron said at the same time.

"Thank you," Sasha said. "And yes, he's flirting with you. Has been all day."

Bonnie needed to get out of there. She was supposed to be watching her dad to make sure nothing happened to him, not chatting it up with Aaron and Sasha.

"Why does Sasha keep complaining about you two flirting?" her dad asked when she got out into the living room.

"How did you—"

"Voices carry in an empty house, my dear," her dad explained. "Is there something going on that I need to know about?"

"Between me and Aaron?" she whispered, because if voices carried, she did not want Aaron or Sasha to hear this conversation. "There's nothing going on. We were talking about whether or not he was going to make any money off this place."

"And how pretty you look in pink."

Could he really hear that up in the attic? Her face burned. "Stop talking, please."

"I like him, but until you work out things

with Lauren, I wouldn't suggest getting too friendly with our friend in there." Her dad nodded toward the hallway.

"I am not getting too friendly with anyone. And I will not be working anything out with Lauren." Not that she had much of a choice, since it was highly unlikely that Lauren would ever admit she was wrong and try to make amends for all the terrible things she had done.

"It's really sad that the two of you would walk away from so many years of friendship. Your mother would have been very disappointed."

That was a low blow. Bringing up her mother was unfair. He wasn't wrong about what her mother would think about all this, though. Of course, she would have confronted Lauren a long time ago. There was no way her mom would have allowed no contact between Bonnie and Lauren to go on for this long.

Her dad winced and touched the bandage on his forehead.

She moved closer and placed a hand on his arm. "Are you okay?"

"I'm fine. Just have a bit of a headache."

"See? Concussion. You should be taking it easy. I think that you can call asbestos removers from home."

"I'm not going home," he said, stepping away. "We've got lots of wallpaper to remove today and lots of work to do on that master bedroom."

He wasn't going to budge. It didn't sound like peeling off wallpaper could be too dangerous. Both she and her dad needed groceries, and since she had to drive to another town to buy them, she had things to do.

"Promise me you'll be careful and I'll go buy us some groceries," she said, giving up.

He pulled his car keys from his pocket since they had driven over together and tossed them to her. "I'll be fine. Go, be free. Shop till you drop."

Bonnie shouted goodbye to Aaron and Sasha. When she opened the front door, the last person she ever imagined being on the other side stood there with a scowl on her face.

"Lauren." Bonnie couldn't manage anything else. She was so shocked, she had to wonder if she was seeing things.

"You have to be kidding me," Lauren

sneered. "I knew this was a mistake." She started to back away.

"I'm leaving," Bonnie said, wishing she would have left about five minutes ago. "If you're here to see Aaron, you won't have to worry about me."

Lauren shifted her oversize designer purse in front of her like it could act as some sort of shield to protect her from getting too close to the person she hated the most in the world. "I don't know why I came here."

Bonnie wanted to say the same thing. She was so taken aback by Lauren's presence that she didn't notice her father had come up behind her until he made his presence known.

"Aaron! Your sister is here!" he shouted, making Bonnie nearly jump out of her shoes. "Hello, Miss Lauren. Would you like to come in?"

Bonnie couldn't believe her dad could speak so civilly to someone who basically was the reason he was fired from the job he'd had all of his adult life. He was way too nice.

Lauren seemed equally surprised that he was being congenial. She pushed her chestnut hair back over her shoulder. "If she's leaving, I'll come in."

Now that the shock had worn off, there were a million things Bonnie wanted to say. None of them would go over well, however, so she bit her tongue. Instead, she stepped onto the porch with Lauren.

"I'll be back later to get you, Dad."

Lauren moved aside so Bonnie could step off the porch. Never in her life had she looked into eyes that were so cold. To think almost two months ago, the two of them had had weekly dinners together and giggled over glasses of wine. They'd made plans to take a girls-only weekend trip this summer. There were no doubts they would keep each other's secrets, and they had discussed the possibility of their future children being best friends.

How quickly things could change. Bonnie's anger had been so strong the last few days, but today, she realized how depressing it was that this friendship was over. Sadness was the only thing Bonnie felt as she got in the car and drove away.

"LAUREN." AARON COULDN'T believe she was actually standing inside his house. Had his mom worked a miracle so quickly?

"I need to talk to you." She glanced at David. "Alone, if possible."

"I'll let you two catch up, but I want you to know that I've been praying the good Lord heals your heart, Lauren. Hatefulness is an ugly disease I wouldn't wish on anyone," David said before retreating back to the living room.

Lauren folded her arms across her chest. Aaron could tell that she wanted to say something but didn't. It was one thing to allow Mr. Windsor to be collateral damage in this war against Bonnie—it was another thing to face him and own her vengefulness. David was like Aaron; he knew she was better than this. They just needed to convince her.

"I'm guessing you talked to Mom," Aaron said.

She had no problem unleashing her wrath on Aaron, however. "I don't know why you thought going to Mom was going to help this situation. You don't get to tell me who to forgive or when to forgive them. If I want to stay mad at you-know-who for the rest of my life, that's my choice."

He noticed she had lowered her voice and made sure not to use Bonnie's name. "And that's why Mr. Windsor keeps praying for you. For someone who cares so much about being pretty, you should remember what he said about hatefulness."

She glared at him. "I don't need anyone's thoughts and prayers. And my hate is justified, so it doesn't hurt me at all."

"Did it feel good to see Bonnie or her dad? Because I'm going to bet it didn't. What has to happen to convince you that Bonnie didn't do anything to you? When does she get the benefit of the doubt? Because it's wrong to hold this against her forever when you have no proof she did anything in the first place."

"Wrong. I have plenty of proof. My real friends have told me about several times they saw her and Mitch talking a little too close, times she was being a little too friendly."

"Ooh, Bonnie was friendly? How strange! I mean, she's not friendly to anyone else. That's so out of character for her." Aaron's sarcasm was biting. Was she really going to buy in to these ridiculous accusations? "Come on, Lauren. Don't tell me your proof is exaggerated gossip."

"I know you think she's so innocent, but you're wrong."

"Because Theresa Gilmore told you she saw her talking to Mitch one night? Or because Wendy Hillbrand said she saw them standing next to each other at the engagement party? Bonnie is here. Mitch is in France. They haven't spoken. They aren't having some torrid affair behind your back."

Lauren jutted her chin out. "How could you possibly know they haven't spoken? Do you monitor all her calls, day and night?"

"I know because I talked to Mitch the other day." Mitch had called to get Bonnie's phone number, which Aaron refused to give him, but he wasn't about to mention that part to his sister. Unfortunately, being away had not lessened Mitch's feelings for Bonnie. His infatuation was something they would have to deal with eventually. All Aaron could do was hope Mitch stayed away long enough to fall for some French beauty and forget all about Bonnie. "He doesn't even have her number. How could they be carrying on a relationship before the wedding if he doesn't even have her phone number?"

He watched as she mulled that over. That little nugget was difficult to dispute. There was no way that fit into her Bonnie-is-evil theory.

Sasha appeared, carrying the toilet that needed to be thrown away in the dumpster outside. "Do you want to salvage any of the shelving in the master closet?"

Lauren's eyes went wide and her jaw dropped at the sight of him.

"No, I'm going to put in a whole new closet system, so all that can be trashed."

"Did you hire another person to add to our humble crew?" Sasha asked, nodding at Lauren and giving her a big ol' grin. "Is she better with a sledgehammer than our little Bonnie was?"

"Sasha, this is my sister. Lauren, this is Sasha. He's helping us out, since everyone else who works the trades in this town is suddenly unavailable."

"Lauren." Sasha got a perplexed look on his face. "Where have I heard that name before?"

Aaron realized Sasha had no idea that Lauren was *the* Lauren who was causing Bonnie all her trouble. "We'll get out of your way so you can throw that out. It looks heavy," he said, trying to move Sasha along.

"It's not that heavy," he said, shifting it into the crook of one arm. "See? Oh, I remember now. There's a Lauren in town trying to take down my girl Bonnie. Can you believe anyone would have beef with someone like Bonnie? Blows my mind. That woman is one of the nicest people I have ever met. Bad Lauren better hope we never cross paths, but it was nice to meet you, Aaron's sister Lauren." He walked out the front door with the toilet.

Lauren paled and looked like she needed to throw up.

"He didn't really mean anything by that," Aaron said, trying reassure his sister. "He wouldn't actually do anything if he knew who you were."

Her fear was evident on her face. He wouldn't doubt she had the sudden urge to flee.

"I know he looks scary, but he's actually a really nice guy. He was at the coffee shop the other day when your so-called friends attacked Bonnie while she was out buying me and her dad some coffee."

Lauren hugged herself tightly and closed the front door. Again, lowering her voice, she said, "So because other people were mean to her, I'm the bad guy? Does he even know what Bonnie did to me?"

"How many times do I have to remind you that she didn't do anything?" His sister was exasperating. "She didn't even give Mitch her phone number!"

"Help!" David called out from the living room.

Aaron didn't hesitate. He raced into the living room. He had promised Bonnie there would be no accidents involving her father, and he'd meant it.

David was on a ladder in the center of the room, holding a piece of the ceiling that was falling down while the ceiling fan he'd apparently decided to take down by himself dangled by its wires. He had leaned forward to keep the ceiling from crashing down on top of him, and the ladder was ready to tip over.

"What is going on?" Aaron went to steady the ladder. "Lauren, come help."

"I don't know what happened. I was trying to take this fan down, and when I pulled the wires out to detach them, I must have pulled on the electrical box and this section of drywall just started to collapse on top of me. Where's Sasha?"

"Lauren! Come hold the ladder so David doesn't fall." Thankfully, his sister did as he asked. He heard the front door open, and a second later, Sasha was there to help as well. He was tall enough to help David hold up the sheet of drywall while Aaron detached the fan from the electrical box. Once Aaron could help Sasha with the drywall, David was able to climb down the ladder safely.

David grabbed his utility knife and went back up to cut away the part of the drywall that was still hanging on so the other two could carefully set it on the ground.

"I made your daughter a promise I wouldn't let anything else happen to you on this job. Are you trying to get me in trouble?" Aaron asked.

"I've never had anything like that happen before. I'm guessing that's where the roof leak was and they painted over the stain instead of fixing the problem, compromising the drywall."

"Good thing we had Nice Lauren here to help," Sasha said. Aaron prayed David wouldn't ask what that was supposed to mean and make everything ten times more awkward.

"Absolutely. Thank you for helping out, Lauren," David said. "I don't think I've had a ceiling-fan incident like this since you and Bonnie decided to use the one in her bedroom as a cat toy."

Lauren actually started to laugh. *Laugh.* That was something Aaron hadn't heard her do since her canceled wedding.

"Oh my gosh, Buttons loved it at first."

"Yeah, until she got tangled up in that yarn you two draped over the fan blade and went on the ride of her life," David said, chuckling, too.

"We tried to turn it off, but we ended up speeding it up." Lauren doubled over. "That poor cat. Bonnie felt so bad. She thought Buttons would never come near her again."

"Oh, that cat loved her more than anyone else in the house. It used to make her mother nuts. Abby thought Buttons should love her the most since she was the one who fed her all the time, but that cat would only cuddle with Bonnie. And you, if I remember correctly."

"She was a sweet cat," Lauren said wistfully. Mentioning Bonnie so much stopped the laughter, but Aaron could tell his sister had been lost in the memory long enough to recognize it felt good to talk about the way things used to be.

"You're not only Aaron's sister, but you're Bonnie's friend?" Sasha seemed to think that was a good thing until he started to put two and two together. He had to know that the Lauren who'd had a falling-out with Bonnie used to be a good friend. His smile faded and was replaced with a furrowed brow. "Please tell me you're not Bad Lauren."

"She's not bad," David said in her defense before Aaron could speak up.

"Lauren's lost her way a bit, but I know the two girls will figure things out."

Lauren's eyes were wet. "I should go. I... I need to go."

Aaron followed her out. "Hey, I don't think you're Bad Lauren, either. I hope you'll think about finding a way to make peace with me. And with Bonnie."

His sister wiped the tears on her cheeks. "I don't know, Aaron. I have to get back to work," she said, getting into her car.

It wasn't a no. He would consider that progress in the right direction. If Lauren and Bonnie could find a way to get along, maybe there was a possibility Bonnie would be open to exploring these feelings he thought perhaps both he and Bonnie were feeling for one another.

A guy could hope.

CHAPTER ELEVEN

BONNIE HOPED THIS wasn't a joke. Mary had texted her that she wanted to meet her for lunch. She wasn't going to let it hurt her feelings that Mary chose a restaurant fifteen miles out of Blue Springs—at least she wanted to get together.

"Welcome to Gianna's. How many for lunch today?" the dark-haired hostess asked.

Bonnie had seen Mary's car in the parking lot. "I think my friend might already be here." She scanned the eating area, spotting Mary sitting in the corner. "I see her."

She approached the table warily. There was no telling what might happen at this rendezvous. She was trying to be optimistic, but nothing much had been going her way lately, so there was no reason to believe this would be any different.

Mary offered her a slight smile when she caught sight of her. That was reassuring. Bonnie wanted so badly to regain the trust and support of at least one friend. She was so tired of feeling alone.

"Hi," she said, sitting down across from Mary. Her stomach ached from anxiety. Eating was the last thing she wanted to do.

"I'm glad you found it," Mary said, fiddling with the napkin on her lap. Perhaps she was just as nervous as Bonnie was. "I was worried since you said you'd never been here before."

Bonnie reached for the glass of water in front of her. "It wasn't hard to find."

Gianna's was a sweet little café in New Castle. The tables were covered in white tablecloths, and there was a candle and bud vase with fresh flowers on each one. None of the chairs were matching—instead they were an eclectic mix of different styles and colors. There were floor-to-ceiling windows on the west wall and exposed beams running across the ceiling.

Mary picked up her menu and then put it back down. "I know you're probably wondering why I asked you to meet me for lunch, and I feel like we should get that out of the way first."

Bonnie sighed with relief. "That would be

appreciated, because I don't think I can eat with the way my stomach is tied in knots."

Mary reached across the table and touched Bonnie's hand. "Mine, too. I've missed you. I've missed hanging out and getting our nails done together. I miss Margarita Thursdays at Tim's Taqueria."

Fighting back tears, Bonnie nodded. The lump in her throat prevented her from telling Mary how much she missed those same things. Lauren had taken not only herself out of Bonnie's life, but so many others who were important to her. Mary was one of those people. It wasn't fair.

"I feel like Lauren is close to changing her mind about you. I think she's beginning to realize that maybe she was wrong about what was going on or not going on between you and Mitch."

"Nothing was going on."

"I know," Mary assured her, leaning back in her seat.

"What happens if she decides to change her mind? Is she going to ask me to forgive her for what she's doing to me?" Bonnie needed to make it clear that Lauren was not the victim in this situation. Lauren was the one who needed to beg for Bonnie's forgiveness, not the other way around.

"I don't know that she'll be looking for you to forgive her as much as she'd let everyone know she's forgiven you."

"Forgiven me for what?" Bonnie's voice rose so much that some of the other patrons couldn't help but stare.

"Don't get upset. I know it's not ideal."

"'Don't get upset'? I didn't do anything. I was treated like a social pariah. She attempted to run me out of town. She got my dad fired. At the very least, I deserve an apology. A very public one, at that."

Mary picked up her menu again as if she needed to use it to protect herself from Bonnie's anger. Bonnie knew Mary hadn't come here to be yelled at. She was clearly here to negotiate the terms of this reunification. However, Bonnie wasn't ready to meet Lauren halfway. She wanted Lauren to do some crawling. It was only fair.

"You know Lauren. She's not going to fully admit being wrong. I also think there's a part of her that is so afraid that you will tell her you want nothing to do with her if she does try to make amends. I need to know that if

Lauren wants to be cordial, will you be open to it, or is there no coming back from this?"

It was a valid question and not one Bonnie wanted to answer without truly thinking about the potential consequences. There was a strong part of her that didn't want to talk to Lauren Cole ever again. There was another part that wanted to be invited over for a Netflix binge with wine and popcorn like they used to do all the time.

The waitress came over to take their orders, offering Bonnie some of that time to think about how she wanted to respond. If she let Lauren believe all she had to do was lift the curse, she'd be giving her the message that it was somehow okay to treat her friends that way. Not even just friends, but more so people in general.

Once the waitress went to put in their orders, Bonnie rested her forearms on the table. "Listen, I know it's hard for Lauren to eat some crow. She doesn't do it. Ever. But I guess that's why it's even more important for her to do it in this situation. Her strong opinions about me have nearly destroyed my career and my reputation. She actually got my father fired. It's not okay. She should be sorry about that."

"Here's what I know," Mary said, folding her hands together. "She should apologize, but I'm not sure she will. She wants to move on, but she won't even do that unless she knows you're going to move on as well."

Bonnie could feel her cheeks getting hot. "So what you're saying is that if I don't go along with her publicly forgiving me for something I didn't do, she's going to keep this going?"

Mary expression was sympathetic. "Pretty much."

"And you're okay with that? You're going to continue to shun me if that's what Lauren asks you to do?" Her temper was rising. Anger wasn't an emotion that Bonnie had had to manage very often until recently. She wasn't very good at it.

"Obviously I would keep trying to convince Lauren to stop. I know Cheryl thinks she should make up with you, too. We'll both keep trying."

Bonnie stood up and tossed her napkin on the table. She would not be staying to eat. Not with someone who wasn't willing to stand up for what was right. "That makes you a terrible friend. To me and to Lauren."

She found the waitress and canceled her lunch order, offering her a tip for her trouble. Bonnie got in her car, and a flood of emotion poured out of her. What kind of world was she living in where people would choose to follow someone so clearly in the wrong? Maybe what she needed to do was pack up her things and get out of Blue Springs for good. Leave the town and all the horrible people in it behind.

It felt like the right thing to do in this moment, but she knew she couldn't leave her father behind. He would never leave because everything in Blue Springs reminded him of her mother. He needed to be there, because that was where the memory of her still remained.

Bonnie couldn't run. In fact, the ultimate revenge against Lauren would be to stay in Blue Springs and act like none of this bothered her in the least. She wiped her face and checked her reflection in her rearview mirror. The people Bonnie wanted in her life would stand up for her. Sasha, her dad, her boss Gordon, and Aaron. He had stood by her through all of it. Even when his family turned on him. He knew what was right, and he was willing to fight for it.

From now on, that would be her focus. No more worrying about what Lauren wanted or how much she missed her old friends. She would appreciate those who had her back. She would be worthy of their loyalty.

"I FEEL LIKE IT would be easier to tear these walls down than to spend the rest of my life trying to take this godforsaken wallpaper off," Aaron said as he scraped another strip of wallpaper. It was tearing into small pieces instead of coming off in a big sheet. At this rate, he'd be stripping wallpaper the rest of this flip.

"It might seem easier, but it would be more expensive for you and more time-consuming for me," David said. He was busy working on the plumbing in the kitchen because the inspector was coming in a couple days to sign off on the electrical and plumbing. Sasha was in the master bedroom framing out the new en suite bathroom and closet.

Time was an issue. They had basically lost a week of work on the inside while the asbestos had been removed. Aaron had opted to contract out replacing the roof. He didn't even bother trying to get anyone local for fear that his father had threatened everyone in a fifty-mile radius not to work with him. He ended up hiring some guys from Sacramento and offering to pay for their lodging while they were up here.

Once they could get back inside, they had torn down the ceilings in the living room and framed it out. Next up was the master bath plumbing. Aaron had foolishly chosen to peel off wallpaper while he waited for the other two to finish their current tasks. He figured it was the next logical priority, since after plumbing and electrical, it was time to hang the new drywall and fix any flaws in the existing walls.

"Hello?" Bonnie called out from the foyer. Aaron's heart jumped. It seemed to do that more and more when she was around. "I come bearing gifts. I hope you guys didn't stop for lunch yet."

She walked into the living room carrying two pizza boxes from Aaron's favorite pizza place in Morris and a six-pack of beer. As much as he appreciated the gesture, David had mentioned she was having lunch with Mary today. It didn't make sense for her to be back here with food in hand.

"That was thoughtful of you, sweetheart," David said. "How was your lunch?"

"It wasn't great, but it doesn't matter. I want to have lunch with the people who really matter in my life."

Aaron again had mixed feelings. He was happy to be someone who mattered to her, but disappointed that things with Mary hadn't gone well. "You want to talk about it?"

"Not really," she said with a sad smile. She handed her dad the beer.

Aaron had been so hopeful after his visit with Lauren. It seemed like things were moving in the right direction when Mary contacted Bonnie. He couldn't imagine what had gone wrong.

He touched her elbow. "I'm here for you."

She reached up and placed a hand on his cheek. Her touch was electric. She made his heart beat faster. "I know you are, and that means everything."

It was as if the whole world dropped away and they were the only two people left. Sometimes he wished he could take her away to some private island far from all of this drama. Somewhere no one could hurt her and where he could have her all to himself. "You have the most beautiful eyes. Did you know that?"

The corners of her lips curled up. "You smell better than anyone else who has ever worked construction. Did you know that?"

"Can you two stop flirting long enough to hand over those pizzas?" Sasha said as he entered the room. "I'm starved and my growling stomach will be heard three states away if I don't get food."

Bonnie dropped her hand and set the pizzas on a card table in the middle of the room. "Eat up, my friend."

Aaron was glad Bonnie didn't protest that they weren't flirting, because he knew he was and hoped she was, too. Maybe when they finished this flip and sold the house for top dollar, he'd take her on that trip.

"I can't believe how much you guys have gotten done. I love this open layout. It's going to be so nice when you get all the cabinets in here, and that island."

"Speaking of which, I need to go pick out my fixtures, but I could use some help with the design. You up for going with me to do some shopping?" he asked her.

"Are you asking if I want to be hired as your designer?"

"I am absolutely asking you to be my designer. You have great taste and the most knowledge of what will sell in this area."

"Let me think about it." She picked up a huge slice of sausage pizza and took a bite as she mulled it over. She cracked open a can of beer and took a swig. He loved that she could just be one of the guys when she wanted to be.

The four of them ate and commiserated about how things were moving along. Sasha showed Bonnie some new pictures of his niece. She immediately oohed and aahed, offering to babysit if his sister needed a respite. Aaron finished off his drink and made eye contact with David, who hadn't said much during this impromptu lunch.

David held his gaze for longer than expected. Aaron looked away, feeling uncomfortable under his scrutiny. Did he realize how hard Aaron was falling for his daughter? Did he not approve?

When Aaron glanced back over at him,

David set his drink down. "Aaron, can you come help me with something outside for a second?"

His stomach dropped, but Aaron agreed as if there was nothing wrong. He followed David outside.

David placed his hands on his hips and stared down at the ground. "I'm concerned," he said solemnly.

"About the house?"

He lifted his head. "About my daughter."

Aaron reached up and rubbed the back of his neck. There was so much tension there. "I am, too."

"What do you think happened with Mary? I thought things were going to be resolved after their lunch."

"I don't know. I can try to get more out of her when we go shopping."

"I was hoping we had gotten through to Lauren when she was here a week ago."

"Me, too. I thought the lunch with Mary was proof we had."

David paced around. He tapped his work boot against the pile of landscaping pavers that had been delivered earlier in the day.

"She's strong. There's no one stronger than

my Bon Bon, but I don't like what's happening to her. Gordon asked her to take over administrative duties at the office for the time being because no one will work with her as their Realtor. She didn't get her real estate license to be an administrative assistant."

"Of course not," Aaron agreed.

"I also know you two got something going on." Before Aaron could assure him of his good intentions, David added, "I understand it's in the beginning stages. But I need you to know that being with you might not be what's best for her. I don't know how Lauren or your parents are going to feel about you and her getting closer. Not that I don't think you're a great guy."

Aaron could sense another *but* coming. "But you're concerned about how people might treat her if being with me sets Lauren off."

"Pretty much," David admitted. "Again, I think you are a great guy. I have nothing against you. In any other circumstance, you would have my full blessing."

It felt as though Aaron's heart had been punched until it was black and blue. It wasn't broken, just bruised. "I understand, David. I don't want to bring any unnecessary harm to Bonnie, either. I'd still like her to help me work on this house."

"Son, I'm not telling you what to do or not do, I am simply sharing my concerns with you. I certainly would never tell my daughter who to date or not date. I trust the two of you to do what's best. I just wanted to point out some things you might not have thought about because you're feeling so enamored with my daughter at the moment."

Aaron was even more taken aback. He wasn't used to a parent who didn't demand his opinions be the be-all and end-all. When Aaron's dad shared his feelings on something, it was because he wanted to make it clear that Aaron was to do it the way he wanted or else. It was refreshing to hear someone say they trusted Aaron to make the best decision for himself. That kind of faith truly inspired him to do better instead of driving him to rebel.

Mr. Windsor was good at this dad thing. Aaron's dad needed to take some lessons.

"She's an amazing woman. I really care about her, and I assure you I will not put her in harm's way."

David slapped his hand down on Aaron's shoulder. "I know. I believe you."

With that, he went back inside, leaving Aaron out there to put his thoughts together. He refused to believe that Lauren didn't miss having Bonnie in her life. There was no way she would be able to spend eternity mad about something that didn't even happen. Once Lauren and Bonnie were on good terms, there would be no reason he couldn't date Bonnie.

"You okay?" Bonnie came out with the empty pizza boxes and tossed them in the dumpster. "I hope you got enough pizza, because Sasha eats exactly as much as you would expect someone the size of the Statue of Liberty eats."

She made him smile, and that was only one small reason he enjoyed being around her so much. "I'm good. I am curious as to what happened at the lunch that made you unhappy. I don't like unhappy Bonnies. It's just not my thing."

"You hate all Bonnies who are unhappy?"

"No, no. Don't twist my words. I like Bonnies. I like all the Bonnies I know, at least.

I hate when something makes them sad. So, what made lunch so disappointing?"

"When Lauren and I were nine, we always went on the swings during recess. It was our favorite thing to do. We would run to the swings as soon as we were dismissed from lunch. We had to beat everyone else, because there were only three swings. There was one time that Timmy Johnson and Kyle Rodgers beat us and we had to share the one swing that was left. We took turns pushing each other so we could swing higher than the boys."

"I'm sure that was Lauren's idea. No one beats her at anything."

Bonnie shrugged. "She would call it being ambitious."

"I'm sure she would. Continue your story, even though I have no idea what this has to do with your lunch with Mary."

"I pushed Lauren first, because of course she had to go first, and she couldn't get as high as Kyle. He was really rubbing it in. She was livid, mostly at him but also at me for not pushing her hard enough so she could beat him. When it was my turn, as soon as I sat down she shoved me so hard, I fell off the swing. Kyle and Timmy laughed at me and made fun of Lauren."

Tim Johnson owned a Mexican restaurant in town. "I am never eating at Tim's Taqueria ever again."

Bonnie rolled her eyes but couldn't hold back a grin. "Anyway, Lauren was so mad at me. She told me I really hurt her feelings by not pushing her hard enough and then having the audacity to not hold on tight enough to stay on the swing when she was pushing me hard enough to go higher than the boys. She got all the girls in class to not talk to me until I apologized. *She* pushed *me* off the swing and made me apologize to her."

Aaron cringed at the thought. "I am sorry she did that to you, and I'm sorry that it doesn't surprise me that she did it, either."

"I haven't really thought about that day since it happened…until today. Mary basically told me that Lauren will most likely publicly forgive me for what happened, but she will not be apologizing for what she did to me. For a split second, I was almost good with that. End the feud. I'd get back in everyone's good graces, but then I realized that she was basically asking me to apologize for getting shoved off the swings. I'm not nine years old anymore and neither is she. I don't need her to be my friend. I don't think I want her to be my friend if she can't say she's sorry when she hurts me."

He couldn't argue with that. Bonnie did deserve better than that from her best friend. He also didn't want to believe that things weren't going to get better. He needed things to get better. "I hope my sister is better than that. Maybe Mary doesn't know what Lauren really wants to do."

"I don't know. But I do know that everyone is willing to stick by Lauren's side even though they think she's wrong because no one wants to cross her." She moved closer to Aaron. "I appreciate that you are not one of those people. I can't even explain to you what it means to me that you have sided with me on this. It's people like you that make me think I might be able to get through this without having to move far away to start over somewhere else."

He took her by the hand, and the contact made his heart beat double time. She was soft and warm physically and emotionally. "If you left, I might have to come with you."

"You would do that for me?" She looked up at him with those green eyes that made him weak in the knees. He was beginning to think he would do anything for her.

"I think I would."

Bonnie wrapped her arms around him and gave Aaron a hug that solidified for him that he would absolutely do that and anything else she asked of him. It also made him realize that he couldn't stop himself from falling for Bonnie even if David was concerned.

He pulled back enough to look her in the eye. He brushed his thumb across her cheek. Her green eyes were locked on his. His lips carefully pressed against hers. If she resisted even the slightest bit, he'd never kiss her again. She didn't resist, though. She actually deepened the kiss almost immediately. His whole body felt like gelatin, wobbly and like he wanted to bounce around. He would do anything for this woman. If she needed Lauren to apologize, he was going to see to it that Lauren did that and more.

CHAPTER TWELVE

BONNIE HAD ONCE read that one of the ultimate tests of a relationship was furniture shopping together. She was beginning to think they could add any kind of shopping to that list. She and Aaron weren't even a couple and fixture shopping was stressful. He had this annoying habit of falling in love with two choices for every single item on their list. He was a way better kisser than he was a shopper.

"I think the farmhouse sink is the way to go," she said, trying to guide him in the right direction after a thirty-minute discussion about cabinet styles. "They are really in right now."

"Agreed. But single or double basin? I like them both," he said, running a hand over the divider in the double basin on display. "Single is nice and simple, but is a double more functional?"

"I would go with the double. This one is perfect." Bonnie stood in front of the one that she liked the most.

"If we go double, do we pick the one that has two equal sides or the one that has one larger side? I like them both."

If he said *I like them both* one more time, Bonnie was going to scream. "I don't think it matters that much."

"What are people going to want?"

"I don't think there's a huge preference in either direction. You could go with the least expensive to save some money."

Aaron took off his baseball hat and scratched his head. "I'm going to have to think about it."

He was adding that to the list of other things he still had to think about, like which drawer pulls he was going to put on the cabinets and which showerhead he wanted for the master bath and which toilet was going in each of the bathrooms.

"We need faucets for the kitchen and bathrooms, but I feel like you might freak out when you see all the choices in that aisle."

"Why are there so many things? It's overwhelming," Aaron complained. "I feel like every decision is so critical. If I pick the wrong faucet, buyers won't buy the house. All I want is for someone to fall in love with it."

He was infuriating but also pretty adorable. Bonnie grabbed his hand. "Someone is going to completely fall in love with it, because it's going to be beautiful no matter which faucet you choose or if the cabinets are Shaker or traditional. Once we get it narrowed down to two we like, you aren't going to go wrong with either one. I promise you, there's nothing you're going to buy that's going to turn people away."

He gave her hand a squeeze. "I'm stressed."

"Do you trust me?" she asked.

He smiled down at her, showing off his perfectly white teeth. He kissed her, and it was soft and gentle. She felt her cheeks heat when he pulled back. "With my life," he answered.

"Whoa, that's way too much responsibility. I mean, I know the Heimlich, but if you were drowning, you'd be in trouble, because I am a terrible swimmer."

He threw his head back as he laughed. "My trust does not require you to save my life if I am in peril."

"Thank you. I would like you to trust me to pick all the fixtures after you help narrow it down to the two choices, though. Can you give me that responsibility? I promise I will not choose anything that will scare away potential buyers."

He took a deep breath in and let it out slowly. "I will trust you with the final decision."

Hallelujah. With that concession, the rest of the shopping trip went much smoother. At the end of the trip, everything was ordered, and Aaron's stress level was significantly lower.

He offered to take her to eat as they left the home improvement store. Even though she had wanted to strangle him in the store, they had survived, and she still wanted to spend time with him. That had to say something about their compatibility.

Aaron drove them to Tim's Taqueria. Bonnie used to go there with Lauren, Mary and Cheryl for Margarita Thursdays. She hadn't been there since before the wedding.

"I thought you said you were never eating here again," she teased.

Aaron's hand stilled on his keys in the ignition. "I did say that, didn't I?"

"I'm kidding. You do not need to punish Tim for something he did when he was nine. That would make me a huge hypocrite if I let you do that."

He turned his car off and took out the keys. "You are very correct. Let's go eat."

Always the gentleman, Aaron held the door of the restaurant open for her. The taqueria was brightly colored. Sunshine yellows and pinkish reds covered the walls. The booths were upholstered with colorful Mexican serapes, and decorative Talavera tiles covered the tables.

Since Bonnie was a regular, she knew most of the staff. Greg, the host, greeted them with a smile until he recognized her. She could feel the rejection coming before the words came out of his mouth.

"Bonnie," he said, like her name was a terminal disease. "Can you guys give me a minute?" He stepped away, and she knew he was going to get reinforcements to ask her to leave.

"We should go," she whispered to Aaron, trying to tug him back toward the door.

"What? Why?"

"They're going to tell me I'm not welcome. I don't want to make them say it, and I definitely don't want to hear it." When she lived in her little bubble, she could forget that much of the town thought she was a backstabbing wedding wrecker. She hadn't eaten out in Blue Springs since she'd been banished.

"Oh, I hope he went to get Tim. I will remind that guy that you don't hold a grudge for actual things he did to you, so it's pretty unfair of him to mistreat you for something you didn't do."

"I really don't want the confrontation." She tried again to pull him away.

"You can't run away from these people. You need to force them to be mean to your face. To explain why they are being horrible humans."

"They think I am a horrible human, so they don't feel bad," she tried to explain. The longer they stood there fighting about this, the greater the chance that she would have to live through another hurtful shunning. "Please, Aaron. I don't want to do this."

Greg and Tim exited the back kitchen area and were heading their way. Aaron didn't fight her any longer and left with her before the two men came to kick them out. She felt sick to her stomach, and the tears were threatening to fall. She punched the dashboard and immediately regretted it. Cradling her aching fist, she cursed her bad luck.

Aaron took her hand in his and gently kissed her throbbing knuckles before letting her go. Bonnie covered her face with her hands. It was so embarrassing that she couldn't even eat lunch somewhere without drama.

"Hey, come here," Aaron said. When she dropped her hands, he had his arms open. She shifted in her seat so she could fall into his embrace. He pressed his cheek against the top of her head. "I'm sorry. I can't stand that people make you feel this way. You do not deserve it."

She liked the way it felt to be in his arms. He made her feel safe and cared for. "Tim's margaritas aren't even that good. They don't even salt the rims of the glasses."

"Well, thank goodness we did not have to suffer through mediocre Mexican food and drinks. My famous tacos are way better than theirs, too."

Bonnie sat back and gave him the skunk eye. "You make famous tacos? You? The man who grew up in a house with a personal chef knows how to make tacos?"

"I'll remind you that I did go to college, and I did not get to bring Byron with me. I also live on my own and have to eat."

She loved that he didn't take himself too seriously. He didn't act as entitled as he was. "I can't wait to taste your tacos. I'll make you my famous margaritas, and we'll have the perfect meal."

Aaron started the car. "Frozen or on the rocks margaritas?"

"Frozen. It's summer. You have to have frozen margaritas in the summer."

Aaron snickered as he pulled out of the parking lot. "You and I would do perfectly fine on a private island. We don't need anyone else. I'm this close to kidnapping you and taking you away from all of this."

He made her skin tingle with his words. No one had ever made her wish to be kidnapped before until Aaron. Where he wanted to go, she would follow.

HONESTLY, AARON HAD never made tacos before. He had, however, eaten plenty of them.

He also knew how to google recipes and read, so thankfully it wasn't too difficult to make something edible.

"Those were quite possibly the best shrimp tacos I have ever eaten in my life," Bonnie said, leaning back in her chair and patting her stomach.

He raised a glass to her. "And I will need another margarita, because you were not lying about how good these are. I think it may have something to do with your heavy-handedness with the tequila, but I am not complaining."

"You better not be," Bonnie said, getting up and retrieving the blender and filling his glass and hers. They moved to the living room.

Aaron loved the quaintness of Bonnie's house. It was small but felt more like a home than his parents' mansion ever did. Bonnie's place was cozy. He wanted to sit on the couch and take a nap. She had fluffy-looking throw blankets in a basket in the corner of the living room, and her couch was covered in pillows. Framed black-and-white photos hung on the wall above the couch. She had a picture of her and her parents, and one of her standing outside a house with a For Sale sign out front with a big Sold sticker on top of it.

"Is this a shot of your first sale?" he asked, pointing at the photograph.

"It is. It was the best day of my life when it happened. I was so ridiculously proud, like I had accomplished something so momentous, helping someone find their dream home. That's lame, isn't it?"

"No," Aaron said. "Not at all. I understand that completely. Why do you think I changed careers? I don't think there's anything more satisfying than giving someone not just a house, but a home."

She sat next to him on the couch. "I love that."

"I love spending time with you," he admitted. He wanted to do more of that, and he didn't want his fear to keep him from letting her know. "What are you doing Friday night?"

"I don't know, what am I doing?" She took another sip of her drink and leaned in.

He didn't have a plan. There were lots of things they could do but only one that he wanted to do. He cupped her face with his hand and brushed her cheek with his thumb. "Anything you want, as long as I get to be there with you."

"Anything?" she asked a bit breathlessly. "Whatever you'd like."

She somehow got closer. Their noses were almost touching. "I'd really like to kiss you."

Heart racing and throat dry, he was falling hard. "That sounds like a great plan. Do we have to wait until Friday to do that?"

She didn't bother to answer with words. Tipping her head ever so slightly, she pressed her lips to his. The kiss was better than the tacos and the drinks. It was better than any kiss he'd ever had before. He stopped long enough to put their glasses on the coffee table. Taking her face in both hands, he went back to kissing her for as long as she would let him.

Bonnie pulled back with the biggest smile spread across her face. "I can't believe I've made out with Aaron Cole twice."

The way she said it made it sound like that was something she had been hoping would happen. "I can't believe I just made out with Bonnie Windsor. Twice."

"I'm fairly certain you and your friends never put my name on their dream girl lists when we were in high school."

"You and your friends put me on their dream girl lists?"

"Dream *boy*."

"And by *friends* I hope you mean everyone except for my sister, because that would be awkward."

Bonnie covered her mouth with her hand and giggled like she was back in high school. "Your sister never put you on her list. But she did put your friend Luke Ellington on there every time."

"Luke? Seriously? He would have dated Lauren in a heartbeat if he knew she was interested. How come she didn't say something? She never was shy about telling boys she wanted them to ask her out."

"I don't know why she didn't. Part of me thinks it was because he wasn't her usual type. She always seemed to think she needed to be with the most popular guy at school. She didn't give the guys who she actually had things in common with a chance."

That was so true. Mitch was a perfect example. Aaron had always wondered what Lauren saw in him. They didn't have any of the same interests. He usually annoyed her more than anything else. The only thing that made sense was that he ticked off all the boxes she imagined were more important.

"Who else had me on their list?"

Bonnie scrunched up her nose in the most adorable way. "I'm not telling. I don't need any competition."

"You think I would run off and date someone else who had a crush on me over ten years ago?"

"With my luck, yes."

Aaron couldn't let her think he had any interest in anyone but her. He pulled her close again, and this time he initiated the kiss. There wasn't a single person on this planet he wanted to be kissing other than Bonnie.

He would have kissed her all afternoon long if there hadn't been a knock at her door.

"Expecting someone?" he asked.

"No."

"Sasha says sometimes little girls come door to door selling cookies. Maybe we're about to get dessert. Let me answer it." He popped up off the couch and went to the door with Bonnie following behind.

"I doubt it's someone selling cookies. Like I said, I am not that lucky."

"Probably not the cops. There's no way they could accuse you of making too much noise."

"What?"

Aaron forgot he hadn't told her that story. He hadn't because he didn't want her to think that it was because of her.

He swung open the door—and it was worse than anything he could have imagined.

"Aaron? What are you doing here?" Mitch stood on Bonnie's front porch with an enormous bouquet of flowers in his hands.

Aaron did the only thing he could think of—he slammed the door right in his best friend's face.

CHAPTER THIRTEEN

JUST WHEN BONNIE thought things couldn't get worse, they managed. Her breathing became labored and she felt dizzy. Her heart was pounding in her chest. She leaned against the wall and put her hands on her knees.

"This is not happening," she said between breaths.

Aaron still had his hand on the doorknob and looked just as stunned as Bonnie felt. "I'll tell him he has to leave. I'll leave with him if I have to."

"Did you know he was coming home?" Being blindsided by Mitch was one thing, but if Aaron knew about this and hadn't warned her, she would be devastated.

"No. He never said anything about coming home the last time I talked to him. I figured he'd stay there the rest of the summer. That was the plan."

Mitch knocked on the door. There was no

getting out of this confrontation. Perhaps the sooner Bonnie told him she wanted nothing to do with him, the sooner he would find someone else to torture.

"I will get him out of here," Aaron promised before opening the door just wide enough that he could step outside. He promptly closed it behind him. Bonnie went to the door and looked out the peephole. Their distorted heads were all she could see. She pressed her ear to the door instead.

"What are you doing home?" she heard Aaron say. "Why didn't you tell me you were coming back?"

"I didn't know I had to inform you of my every move," Mitch said. "What are you doing at Bonnie's? You told me you didn't have her phone number, but here you are hanging out at her house in the middle of the day."

Bonnie had had no idea that Aaron had been talking to Mitch since he left. It made sense since they were friends, but it was still surprising given that Aaron was not happy with what Mitch had done before he left. It would have been nice to know that Mitch was trying to contact her. She would have sent him a clear message that she was not interested in anything he was offering.

"You need to get out of here. You being here could cause Bonnie a lot of harm. Come on, come to my place and let's talk about what's been going on since you left."

Bonnie waited for Mitch to protest, but he didn't. He followed Aaron off the porch. "Can I leave these for her? I feel bad that Lauren has been taking this out on her. I left and she took all the blame. I just want her to know I'm sorry."

That was nice of him. She could at least let him apologize to her face. She opened the door.

"Mitch," she called out.

He glanced at Aaron as if asking for permission before climbing back up the stairs of her porch. He held out the roses.

"I am so sorry for leaving you here to face all the wrath over my foolish decision. The last thing I wanted to do was hurt you and Lauren. I mean, I know hurting Lauren was inevitable, but I didn't mean to do it the way I did. I was emotional that day, and I am really sorry."

"I appreciate that. It has been incredibly hard."

"Well, hopefully things will get easier for you now that I'm back. Lauren can focus all of her revenge on me instead of you. I'm really sorry. I know I said that already, but I mean it."

"She heard you," Aaron said sternly. "You need to leave. If people see you here, it will only hurt her."

He wasn't wrong. Bonnie wanted to retreat back into her house. "Good luck, Mitch." She didn't know what else to say. He was going to need it if he was going to survive whatever wrath was headed his way as soon as Lauren found out he was home.

"Thanks, Bonnie." He left with Aaron, who looked more unhappy than anything else.

"Mitch is back, huh?" Bonnie hadn't noticed her neighbor Becca had been weeding the landscaping on the side of their house.

Great. It was only a matter of time before the town's gossip train had this news spread across the whole county.

"Unfortunately," Bonnie replied, feeling guilty for being mean while holding the gorgeous bouquet of roses he had brought her as a peace offering.

Becca raised her eyebrows as if skeptical that was truly Bonnie's feeling on the subject. "That should be interesting. I hope things work out for you guys."

Bonnie almost shouted that she'd been making out with Aaron Cole ten minutes ago. The only person she wanted things to work out with was him. This was going to be her new battle, but she didn't have the energy for it today. She would have to correct all the misconceptions out there about what kind of relationship she had with Mitch even though she had no relationship with him.

Aaron would figure out what to do about Mitch. At least he seemed genuinely sorry for what he had done and he hadn't come back professing his love for her. That was a huge relief. Still, she was disappointed that she didn't get to enjoy the fact that she and Aaron had taken things to the next level before this new issue popped up.

She took off for the Greenbriar house. The inspectors were supposed to come check the plumbing and electrical today so her dad and Sasha could start hanging drywall. Once they got all the walls up, things would start moving along much faster. She also hoped that Greenbriar would be Aaron's next stop after talking to Mitch. She texted him to let him know she was heading there just in case.

The loud pop of the nail gun greeted her as she walked in. "Hello," she called out.

"Back here!" Her dad's voice came from the master bedroom.

They were putting up the walls separating the bedroom from the bathroom. "Passed inspection?"

"I have never seen anyone work so hard to not pass someone in my life," Sasha said. "This guy was bound and determined to find something wrong so he could delay us, but he did not know who he was up against. Your dad is a master at what he does. There wasn't one thing he could find that wasn't up to code."

"We need to be careful," her dad said. "Next time they will simply not show up or try to show up when we aren't here. Someone might have to stay here all day to prevent them from putting it on us."

"It's bound to get worse before it gets

better. Mitch got home today," Bonnie announced.

Her dad was visibly disappointed. His shoulders dropped. "How do you know?"

"He showed up at my house with roses in hand."

He held up the nail gun like it was a weapon. "Me and that boy need to have a talk. He is not going to come back and put us in the middle of another war with the Coles."

"I'd be happy to meet this Mitch guy." Sasha punched his fist into his palm. "I'm sure I could be very persuasive about leaving our Bonnie alone."

The last thing she wanted was for either of them to get in the middle of this. "You two don't need to do anything to Mitch. He was actually very apologetic and didn't make things weird. No talk about being in love with me anymore. Aaron is with him now."

"Oh, Aaron's on the case," Sasha said with a chuckle. "He was probably all, 'Back away from my girl, loser. There's a new sheriff in Bonnie Town.'"

Bonnie could feel her cheeks flush. "There is no sheriff in Bonnie Town except for me.

I'm in charge of what happens to me, thank you very much."

"That's my girl," her dad said. "You don't need any man in your life other than your dear old dad."

She wouldn't go that far. She didn't mind having Aaron around Bonnie Town. He was welcome anytime, but he wasn't in control. She was.

"You two should get back to work. Can I do anything to help while I'm here?"

Her dad nodded. "Aaron would love you if you could get that wallpaper off the walls in the living room. He was really struggling with it the other day."

"I don't think she needs to do anything to make Aaron love her," Sasha said, picking up a sheet of drywall.

Bonnie shook her head, and her dad was not amused. At least Sasha was clear about where her heart was leaning. Maybe everyone else wouldn't be so hard to convince. She certainly wouldn't mind if Aaron was falling in love with her. The feeling would be mutual.

After twenty minutes of scraping wallpaper, Bonnie could see why Aaron hated this job. It was peelable wallpaper, which meant the top coat came off but the backing stayed stuck to the wall. She sprayed some more stripper on it to loosen it up. It smelled terrible, and her fingers were covered in it as she tried to get the backing off.

She could hear the alternating pop of the nail gun with the buzz of the saw from the master bedroom. The noise was distracting. There was a stereo plugged in and sitting on the card table. Music might help encourage her to persevere. She scrounged around for a rag to wipe her hands on. There was nothing out there. She went back to the bedroom to ask the guys where she could find one.

"Hey," she said, accidentally startling Sasha, who was holding the nail gun. It discharged, and her dad screamed. His finger was now attached to the drywall. Bonnie thought she was going to pass out. The room started to spin, and her stomach turned.

Off to the hospital they went.

HAD DAVID BEEN a minor, Aaron was sure that Blue Springs Hospital would have called the authorities on him for endangering his safety on a regular basis. He checked in at the front desk.

"Hi, again." He smiled at the receptionist. She was around his mother's age and had long nails with tiny American flags painted on them. "My friend is here again. Can I go back?"

"I'm thinking it might be more cost-effective to hire a doctor on-site at this point," she said, tapping those nails on her keyboard.

"I don't disagree. That or I need to wrap my foreman up in Bubble Wrap from now on."

"You sure Bubble Wrap would be enough?"

Aaron laughed, because no amount of Bubble Wrap would've stopped the speeding nail from puncturing David's hand. "I probably need to rethink that. Maybe I can cover him in some titanium. That's bulletproof, right?"

"I have no idea," she said. "But you can go back to Room 103 and check on him."

He thanked her and headed back. The doctor was in the room and had everything prepped to stitch David up. Bonnie was seated in the chair on the other side of the tiny room.

"I can't leave you alone one day without an accident?" he said, stepping past the curtain that was partially drawn in front of his door.

"I'm starting to think it's Bonnie," David

said. "Every time she's over there, something happens."

"No fair. I will admit that the sledgehammer accident was my fault, but the rest just happened while I was there. I played no part."

"You distracted a man holding a nail gun. That was a little bit your fault," David argued.

Aaron knew the last thing Bonnie needed was to be accused to being bad luck or the bringer of pain for her father. She had dealt with enough blows today.

"I think it's safe to say that the only person cursed on this job is you, David. You better go see Madame Katrina on Main Street and get your tea leaves read and have her perform some karma-fixing spell or do something to your chakra."

He managed to get a laugh out of Bonnie, who pushed him out of the room. "We'll get out of the good doctor's way," she said.

"Are you okay?" He knew it was a loaded question but asked it anyway.

"No and yes. But mostly no."

He pulled her close for a hug. To think an hour ago they were at her house kissing and forgetting about all the bad stuff that was literally right outside her front door. He wished he had better news to share, like Mitch had agreed to go back to Paris, but they weren't that fortunate.

"I'm sorry this day has been kind of a nightmare."

"Some parts were definitely better than others," she said, resting her cheek against his chest. He loved the way she fit in his arms. He rested his chin on the top of her head.

"Some parts were kind of amazing," he said. There was no "kind of" about it. Kissing her was beyond amazing.

"I don't suppose you convinced Mitch to go back to France. Permanently?"

"He's planning to talk to Lauren, which I warned him was a terrible plan. He thinks that he can fix everything by apologizing. As if my sister is going to simply accept his apology and move on."

Bonnie pulled back with a look of fear in her eyes that made him shudder. "You can't let him face her alone. I feel kind of bad for him. I think he sees the error of his ways and really is remorseful."

"Don't worry, there is no way in the world that Lauren is going to let Mitch get within a fifty-foot radius of her. She doesn't have any interest in anything he has to say."

Bonnie wasn't so sure. "If she thinks there's a possibility he's going to tell her he was wrong and beg for forgiveness, she might. Was he going to talk to her now?"

"He had dinner with his parents tonight, and then he was going to go over to Lauren's. I'll call Lauren and give her a heads-up that he's back." He knew he didn't really have to do that. Enough people in town had seen Mitch—there was no way the news hadn't gotten back to Lauren already. Aaron could only hope that no one mentioned he'd been on Bonnie's doorstep.

Pacing back and forth in the hall, Bonnie chewed on her thumbnail. "You have to go there."

"Maybe we should both go. You and me." Maybe they could even announce they were sort of a couple. Wouldn't that put all these rumors to rest? If she was dating Aaron, she couldn't be dating Mitch, too.

"I don't know. If she saw me and Mitch together—even though we aren't together—it could be a complete disaster." She stopped pacing and dropped her arms to her side. "I also can't keep putting you in the middle of this. You've strained your relationship with your sister enough for me already."

"If I didn't want to be in the middle of it, I wouldn't be. But I have your back. All the way."

Bonnie shook her head, her determination clear in her eyes. "It's time for me to stop avoiding her. I need to face her and finally have my say. It'll be better if Mitch is there, because then there won't be any confusion. Everyone will be on the same page about how I feel and who I want to be with."

She bit down on her bottom lip. Did that mean what he thought it meant? Did she feel things for him, and was she willing to tell Lauren about it? Aaron really wanted to be there for that.

"Any chance you're feeling things for someone I know?"

One side of her mouth curled up in a crooked smile. "I'll let you know after our date on Friday."

Their date. They had a date. Why did he pick Friday when it was only Tuesday? That seemed so far away.

"I look forward to it, Miss Windsor," he said with a little bow.

"As do I, Mr. Cole." She clasped her hands behind his neck and kissed him ever so chastely.

Aaron floated out of the hospital and back to the house. For all the drama today, one thing was certain. He was falling head over heels for Bonnie, and she might just feel the same way about him. The thought would get him through anything Mitch and Lauren would throw their way.

CHAPTER FOURTEEN

BONNIE FELT LIKE a stalker sitting in her car outside Lauren's house. She didn't want to go in until after Mitch got there. If Mitch didn't show up, she wasn't sure she was going to have this conversation with Lauren. All the bravery she'd showed Aaron at the hospital had disappeared as soon as she turned onto Lauren's street.

"It's just Lauren," she reminded herself in the rearview mirror. Lauren, who slept with a stuffed animal named Baby Hippo until she was fifteen. She acted way tougher than she really was. Bonnie knew that deep down there was an extremely fragile person in there. She was much more vulnerable than she let on.

A knock on the passenger side window nearly gave her a heart attack. Lauren pulled on the door handle and motioned for Bonnie to unlock the door. Bonnie let her in.

"Are you working up the nerve to come in and kill me, or are you waiting out here for the guy you hired to kill me to come out and tell you the job is complete?" she asked, sitting down in the passenger's seat. Her hair was up in a ponytail, and she had taken off all her makeup.

"I—I—I didn't come to kill you," Bonnie stammered. Why would she think that?

"Then why are you creeping outside my house?"

There was a simple answer to that, but she wasn't sure she wanted to say it out loud in case Mitch didn't show up. "I was working up the nerve to talk to you."

"About what?"

"Mitch is back in town."

"I know. I'm also not surprised you know that already. I'm assuming you two have seen each other since he returned from France?"

"He came over to apologize for making such a stupid spectacle at your wedding," Bonnie admitted. There was no doubt someone had told Lauren that they had seen him at her house.

Lauren fixed her gaze on something outside in front of the car. "You weren't excited to see him?"

"I like to believe that you are not half as self-absorbed as people like to think and you actually noticed that I was never overly friendly or nice to him."

"You are always nice to everyone, Bonnie." Lauren turned her head and smirked. "It's one of your more annoying traits."

Touché. "Are you implying I have more than one?"

Lauren shrugged and looked down at her nails. "I don't think you came here to hear all the reasons I think you're annoying."

It was strange to be sitting next to her best friend like she had a million times over the last twenty-plus years but not be friends. It sucked, actually. "Did Aaron call you?"

"Yes," she answered, giving nothing else.

"Did he tell you that Mitch was coming over here tonight to talk to you?"

"Yes."

"Did he tell you that I was coming over?"

"No. Did he know you were coming over as well?"

"Yes." Bonnie waited to see if using Lauren's short answers against her would get her attention.

She finally gave in and made eye contact. "Why did you want to come over with Mitch? To beg for my forgiveness and ask for my blessing? Because that is never going to happen. Let's be clear about that."

Bonnie pretended to slam her head against the steering wheel. Anything to stop this torture. "Do you even listen to anything I say? Do you hear yourself? It's ridiculous. There is no me and Mitch. There never was. There never will be. He was your boyfriend. Your fiancé. Your ex. No matter what title you give him, it's always preceded by the word *Lauren's.*"

Speaking of the devil, Mitch pulled into Lauren's driveway. The two women stayed in the car and watched silently as he got out and went to her front door.

"I don't want to talk to him," Lauren finally said. The hurt in her voice was palpable.

Bonnie didn't blame her. Nothing Mitch had to say was going to make Lauren feel any better about herself or the situation. He wasn't here to tell her he'd made a mistake.

He only wanted to remind her that he had left her for Bonnie.

Maybe if they knew how she felt about Aaron, all of this would be over. Of course, Bonnie wasn't sure how Lauren would feel about Bonnie's attraction to Aaron. She liked him. She knew he liked her. She really liked kissing him. He was funny and chivalrous and didn't take himself too seriously. He had a desire to make the world a better place, not only for himself, but for others. She loved that.

"He was going to tell you that you shouldn't blame me. At least, that's what he told Aaron he was going to say. He wasn't aware that I had taken the fall for his infatuation. Your wedding day was the first time he ever made me aware that he had any feelings for me. That is the God's honest truth."

Mitch stepped off the porch and peeked through the windows on the front of the house. He tried the doorbell one more time before giving up and going back to his car. Bonnie was glad she had parked on the street and not in the driveway. Mitch was oblivious to the two of them sitting right there.

"You were my best friend," Lauren said, reaching for the door handle. "I just don't know."

Lauren got out of the car and jogged across the street back to her house. Bonnie let her head fall back against the headrest. What was there to know? She hadn't done anything. Why couldn't Lauren admit that she was wrong? That she was sorry she hadn't believed her from the start? There was nothing left to say. If Lauren couldn't believe the truth, Bonnie was done trying to feed it to her. They had been best friends, but were no more.

Bonnie drove to her dad's, needing someone who loved her unconditionally to tell her it would all be okay. She found her dad sitting in his recliner chair in the living room when she got to his house. His feet were up and his TV was turned to the game-show channel, his favorite. She locked the front door behind her, and her heart rate was just about back to normal.

"What happened? Are you okay?"

Maybe she didn't look as calm as she thought she did. "Nothing. I'm fine."

"And I'm a ballroom dancer. What happened?"

"I talked to Lauren."

He put the footrest down and leaned forward. "How did that go?"

"About as well as you would expect."

"So, not well?" he guessed.

Bonnie wasn't sure what it was about her that made him guess she was frazzled. She fixed her ponytail and pressed the back of her hand to her cheeks to see if they were warm. "She isn't going to get over this. With Mitch back, it will probably only get worse. What do you think about you and me moving down to San Diego? Perfect weather. Plenty of real estate for me to sell. Lots of construction jobs for you to do."

"We are not going to be run out of this town, Bon Bon. Lauren is going to come around. Trust me."

She wanted him to trust her. She was beginning to worry it wasn't going to get better. At some point, Bonnie might have to leave Blue Springs.

"You have to help me." Mitch stood in Aaron's kitchen with his hands in his hair. "What's it going to take to get Lauren to forgive me?"

"Amnesia, a brain tumor that causes memory loss, divine intervention maybe," Aaron suggested. Those were really the only ways Lauren would ever forgive and forget.

Mitch dropped his hands to his sides. "That is not helpful. You are my best friend. You have to help me."

"I don't have to help you do anything. You're lucky I even invited you into my home. You crushed my sister by dumping her at the altar. You ruined my friend's reputation at the same time, and you come back without asking me once what I've been up to while you've been gone."

"So what have you been up to while I've been gone, Aaron?" he asked, taking a seat at the island.

"Well, thanks so much for asking, Mitchell. I have been super busy. I quit my job, bought a house to remodel and have been working nonstop to flip it so I can start doing that for a living. My dad's not speaking to me. My sister is mad at me for working with her ex– best friend's dad and doesn't know that I have also been working with her. And I learned I can make delicious tacos."

"Why in the world would you quit your job?

Your dad was basically giving you money. All you had to do was show up."

Aaron scrubbed his face with his hands. Sometimes he questioned how he'd ever become friends with Mitch in the first place. "You are the one who gets paid for doing nothing. I am the one who actually had to work long hours and was miserable."

"But you were making money."

"And now I make people happy by designing their dream home," he said with a flourish.

"So you hire people to fix up these houses and then sell them off for big bucks? I could do that."

"No, I actually do the work." He had the sore muscles and the cuts and scrapes to prove it. "I hired Bonnie's dad after my father fired him because you made everyone believe Bonnie knew you were in love with her."

Mitch didn't respond to the part where Aaron tried to hold him accountable. "You've got to be kidding. You do manual labor? That sounds horrible."

"I enjoy it. It's a million times better than sitting in a boardroom all day."

"Nope. I could sit in a boardroom all day

for the rest of my life as long as I had Wi-Fi and my computer and the administrative assistants kept bringing snacks and drinks in."

Aaron was certain that Mitch had never actually worked a day in his life. "You better pray your father's business never goes under."

"Speaking of food and drinks, you got any?" He got up and helped himself to what was in the refrigerator. "So where is this house you're flipping?"

"Over on Greenbriar. It's this ranch on a big lot. Lots of trees. It's nice."

"And Bonnie is helping you?"

Aaron didn't want to talk about Bonnie. Not with Mitch. "She helped design the interior."

Mitch nodded. "Okay, now that we've caught up on what you've been doing, how about you tell me how to win your sister's forgiveness."

Aaron had no ideas. If he had, he would have shared them with Bonnie, not Mitch. Mitch deserved whatever Lauren was going to do to him. He wondered if now was a good time to mention he was going on a date with Bonnie this Friday or not. He wondered how

Mitch would take that. He hadn't said anything about how he felt about Bonnie.

"I went to her house tonight, and she wouldn't even answer the door."

Aaron shrugged. "Lauren does what Lauren wants. She doesn't care what you want."

"I don't want her to hurt Bonnie anymore. Do you have any bread? I want to make a sandwich."

He pointed Mitch in the direction of the bread and then picked up his phone to send Bonnie a text. He wondered if she had seen him show up at Lauren's and if she'd tried to talk to Lauren as well.

"Who are you texting? You have the most serious look on your face." Mitch laughed as he took a bite of his sandwich.

If he told Mitch he was texting Bonnie, how would he respond? Aaron wasn't sure he wanted to know. If he told Mitch that they were kind of dating, everyone would know in a matter of hours. He wasn't sure how Bonnie felt about that information getting out just yet. It was better to let Mitch believe he was just a concerned older brother. "I was checking on Lauren."

His front door opened, and before he could

process what was happening, Lauren stormed in. "I need to talk to you," she said before stopping dead in her tracks.

Mitch froze midbite.

Without a word, she spun around and marched right back out the door. Aaron chased after her. "Lauren, hold up."

Red-faced, she turned back to him. "You are the worst brother in the entire world!" she shouted. "Every time I need you, there you are being buddy-buddy with my mortal enemies. You have made it perfectly clear that my feelings mean nothing to you."

"That's not true."

"Ha! When it comes to family loyalty, you have none. You are completely disloyal. You put everyone ahead of me. All I needed tonight was my big brother to talk to about how I'm feeling, and instead you're hanging out with Mitch. I guess I should be surprised it wasn't Bonnie, because all you do these days is align yourself with the people who hurt me."

Aaron felt like a complete heel. Even though Bonnie hadn't done anything, the same couldn't be said for Mitch. Aaron was currently being quite hospitable to the person who broke his sister's heart. "I'm sorry. He came over here to talk about how to make things better. I'm seriously trying to find a way to make peace. I can't do that if I leave him to his own devices."

"I'll never find peace as long as you keep allowing them to be part of your life. I can't do it anymore, Aaron."

"I totally understand why you feel that way about Mitch, but things are different with Bonnie. I know you and Bonnie are going to find a way to get past this misunderstanding."

Apparently that was the wrong choice of words. "Misunderstanding? I don't think anyone would call cheating with your best friend's fiancé a misunderstanding."

"She didn't cheat with him! Would you please stop saying that? You are the only one who thinks that's true. Go back in there and ask Mitch yourself. He'll tell you he didn't cheat."

Lauren had tears running down her face, making Aaron feel like an even bigger jerk. "Of course he's going to tell me he didn't cheat. He's a liar. That's what liars do. They lie."

"I'm not trying to hurt you by not agreeing with you. I am trying to get things back to normal. All I want is for everyone to get along. I'm not good with all this conflict. I don't know how to hate people. I know that's what you want me to do, but that's not who I am. I can promise you that I've made it known that I am not happy with how he treated you. I have been trying to get him to make better choices so he doesn't continue to hurt you. I know you think he's lying, but I don't. I don't think he's lying about Bonnie. I know he's not, because I also trust Bonnie. You used to trust Bonnie. Think about why you used to trust her."

"You've made your choice, Aaron. You didn't choose me. There's nothing more to say."

She was breaking his heart. "Lauren," he called after her as she walked away.

She didn't stop and he feared the pain in his chest wouldn't, either.

CHAPTER FIFTEEN

SOMETHING WAS OFF. Bonnie couldn't put her finger on it, but something had changed the night Mitch came back. For some reason, Aaron became more distant. The next day, he asked if they could postpone their date, claiming there was way too much to do on the house and he needed to work late and get there at the break of dawn on Saturday. When she stopped by the house to check on the progress, he had little to say to her and almost seemed to be avoiding her.

How could they go from kissing on the couch to not even speaking in less than twenty-four hours? She tried to brush it off. Could she be overthinking it? For sure. Days became weeks, and still this wedge existed between them. She wanted to ask him what had happened, but feared what his answer might be.

TODAY, SHE WAS working at the realty office, hating every minute she had to sit behind that desk. To her surprise, Mitch strode in. "Hey, I need to hire a Realtor," he said.

Bonnie didn't know what to say. "I'll let Gordon know you're here."

He stopped her from picking up the phone. "I don't want to hire Gordon. I want to hire you."

"Mitch, I don't think that's a good idea."

He held his hands up. "No, I get it. I don't want it to look bad. It's just that you're the only one who can help me find a new house. You are the one who can help me pick something that Lauren would absolutely hate."

It was one thing to need a new place to live—it was another to need a place Lauren would not want to live. "Why is that?"

He pulled one of the waiting room chairs closer to her desk. "Everywhere I look at home, I see Lauren. She's the one who made me buy that condo. She picked out all the furniture, every little knickknack, every photo, every book on my bookshelf. I need a fresh start. I need a new place that hasn't been touched by Lauren. I want a place Lauren wouldn't want to touch. Can you please help me?"

Mitch really had gotten out of that relationship in the nick of time. Lauren would have told him what to do the rest of his life had he not called the wedding off. There was a weird sensation in her chest. Was she actually feeling sorry for Mitch? She needed to suffocate that emotion immediately. She didn't want him to misconstrue her sympathy for anything else.

"I will happily guide Gordon to all the right properties. I, however, won't go with you to look at any of them."

"Come on, Bonnie. Aaron told me you've been missing getting out there and selling houses. He thought this was a great idea."

Bonnie imagined her chin hitting the floor. "Aaron told you to hire me?"

"More or less. We've been trying to think of ways to make things better for you. Please let me try to make things better for you."

There was no way it was better for her to be seen around town with Mitch. She could only imagine the gossip if they were house hunting. People would assume they were looking at houses to move into together.

It was unbelievable that Aaron would encourage Mitch to do that. He knew how she felt about being around him. He knew how Lauren would feel about the two of them being seen out in public together.

"I appreciate you wanting to get me out of the office, but I think it's better that we not give anyone the impression that there's something going on between us."

Gordon came out of his office. His glasses were resting on top of his head. He must have been in there reading something. That was the only time he took them off. "Everything all—" He put his glasses back on his face, and what he saw stopped him cold. "Mitchell Bennett, back from your trip abroad, I see."

"I am. It was good to get away. Clear my head. Decide my new path in life. My first big decision is finding a new place."

"I would be happy to help you find something. Bonnie isn't doing any of the hands-on stuff right now. She's taking a break behind the scenes."

"She helped Aaron Cole find a house, didn't she?"

"Well, yes, but—"

"Then she can help me, too. We're both in

so much hot water in this town, how much worse could it get?"

Bonnie had no desire to find out.

"We'll see what we can do," Gordon said, much to Bonnie's dismay. "Why don't you come on back to my office and let me know what kind of place you're looking for?"

Mitch got to his feet. "No need, Gordon. Bonnie knows exactly what I need," he said.

As soon as he was out the door, she turned to Gordon. "Why would you tell him we'll work something out? I am not going to look at any houses with him. That would be social suicide."

"I figured it was the quickest way to get him out of here."

He was probably right about that. She couldn't believe Aaron would set her up like that.

"Mind if I go check on the Greenbriar house? I haven't been over there in a week. I'm interested to see how things are coming along. We might need to start getting ready for an open house soon."

"Go ahead. Say hi to your dad for me."

Bonnie would happily say hi to her dad— right after she reamed Aaron out for conspiring behind her back with Mitch, of all people. It suddenly felt like he was backing off so Mitch could make his move. Why would he do that?

She was about to find out.

Sasha was outside in the driveway when she pulled up. He had gray paint sprinkled in his red hair.

"Hey there, stranger. Long time no see," he said as she got out of the car.

"Hello to you, my friend. How are things going in there? Are you guys already painting?"

"We are. It's looking pretty awesome. We're doing an amazing job, if I do say so myself. I kind of wish I had plans to stay in town when you guys put it up for sale. It's a really beautiful home."

She patted him on his thick arm. "Well, you know there's nothing I'd like more than for you to put down some roots here in Blue Springs."

"Good thing I know a great Realtor who could help me do that…"

"Anytime. Is my dad in there?"

"He is. Your father is probably the hardest-working man I have ever met in my entire life. I am in awe of him every day."

That was sweet. She thought he was pretty incredible as well. "I wish I had half of his stamina. Is Aaron here, too?"

"Boss man is inside as well. He told me putting on the finishing touches is his favorite part of this job."

Maybe Aaron was distracted by all the little details that had to be done. Maybe he wasn't really ignoring her on purpose.

The sound of classic-rock music greeted her when she opened the front door. When she walked inside, she was shocked at how different it looked. The kitchen cabinets were in, as well as the countertops and backsplash. The wood beams on the ceiling in the living room were up and absolutely stunning. The chandelier she'd chosen on their shopping trip was hanging in the dining room, and the pendant lights she'd fallen in love with were perfectly placed above the enormous island.

All the trim was done, and the paint was coming along. All that was left to do out in these common areas were the floors. When this place was staged for a showing, it was going to completely wow potential buyers.

"Bon Bon, what are you doing here?" Her dad came down the hall leading to the master bedroom.

"I was in the neighborhood. Thought I would check in on the progress. There's been *a lot* of progress since I was here last."

The pride on her dad's face was priceless. "It's coming together. I don't think Aaron sleeps. He's got an air mattress in the master that he says he's been using, but I think the man never stops."

"Funny, Sasha just told me you're the one with endless energy around this place."

He laughed and shook his head. "I'm just trying to keep up with Aaron. He's the one in charge now."

"Where is Aaron?"

"Painting the second bedroom, I think. That's where the music is coming from, so I assume that's where you'll find him. Everything okay?"

Her father had some kind of parental sixth sense. He knew her moods better than she did.

"Everything's fine. Just wanted to touch base with him about a couple things."

"If you say so," her dad said, not sounding the least bit convinced.

Bonnie followed the sound of music down the hall and into the first of the two guest bedrooms. Aaron was rolling more gray paint onto the walls. His light blue T-shirt had some paint on the sleeve. His jeans were like a memorial to all the work that had already been done. He had some cement on there from when her dad had taught him how to redo the concrete stoop. There was a tear on the leg where he'd gotten it snagged on a nail when they were putting in the bathtub. Black marker on his thigh from when he'd needed to jot down some measurements and didn't have anything to write on other than himself. Now he was adding some paint to the mix.

Unaware she'd been standing there watching him, he jumped when he saw her. "Are you trying to give me a heart attack?"

"Sorry. I was just admiring the view. I mean, all the work you've done. This place looks fantastic, Aaron."

He set his roller down in the paint tray and put his hands on his hips as he looked around. "It does, doesn't it?"

"It's going to fetch top dollar. I have no doubts."

He didn't seem to know what to do with his hands. He fidgeted a bit, almost like he was nervous. "Did you see the master bedroom yet?"

"I didn't get that far."

"You've got to check it out," he said, coming over to where she stood in the doorway. He stopped, and for a second she thought he might kiss her. "Come on, you have to see it."

Disappointment coursed through her veins. She was so foolish to think someone who hadn't spoken more than a few words to her in weeks would want to start kissing again.

The master bedroom was painted the same gray on three of the four walls. The new wall that had been put in to extend the room so they could put in a bigger en suite was painted a nautical blue.

"I know I was supposed to keep things neutral so people could come in and imagine their stuff in here, but I wanted to add just a pop of color for fun. I figure this wall is where the bed will sit, so it needed something. If people hate it, it's only paint. They can change it, right?"

"I think it's awesome. Blue and gray work together nicely. The gray keeps the blue from being too overpowering, and the blue gives this room a touch of masculinity. I like it."

"Yeah?" He seemed genuinely surprised.

"Yeah."

"I thought for sure you were going to hate it and tell me to paint over it."

She was surprised to hear that her opinion carried that much weight. "This is your house, Aaron. Not mine. If you want to paint all the walls purple, I'm not going to say anything except, 'Get ready for some lowball offers.'"

He laughed, and she wanted to listen to that all day on a continuous loop. His laughter was contagious. "Don't worry. No purple."

"Good to know. I can only imagine the kind of feedback we'd get." She took a deep breath. She'd come here to confront him. "Can I talk to you about something?"

AARON HAD A sinking feeling that Bonnie wasn't going to ask him about something related to the house. He'd been avoiding her, and it was making him miserable. He deserved to feel miserable, however, because he was a terrible brother. He figured the least he could do was put a little breathing room between him and Bonnie as well as him and Mitch.

He couldn't hate either one of them, but he owed it to Lauren not to be seen all over town with the two of them. Not hanging out with Mitch was easy. Not being around Bonnie was torture.

"You can talk to me about anything. You know that."

Bonnie seemed to think that wasn't exactly true. She hesitated a second before opening up. "Did I do something?"

"What do you mean?"

"Did I say something or do something to make you question your feelings for me? Because I thought we were on the same page, and now I'm not sure we're even reading the same book anymore."

Another smooth move on his part. By trying to ease Lauren's feelings of rejection, he'd managed to give them to Bonnie. "You didn't do anything. I'm sorry if I'm putting out a lot of mixed messages right now. I'm trying really hard to do the right thing, but it seems like no matter what I do, someone I care about gets hurt. First Lauren. Now you."

"I warned you that things would get messy if you placed yourself in my corner of the fight. I knew your sister wasn't going to handle it well."

"I know she's a pain. I know she's wrong about you. I know you deserve an apology and so much more. But I have let my sister down in ways I didn't realize, and I have to try to make it up to her. The only way I know how to do that is to let you and Mitch fend for yourselves for a little bit."

"Is that why you told Mitch he should hire me as his Realtor? Are you trying to help him spend time with me?"

Aaron's back stiffened. "What? Why would you think that?"

"Because Mitch came to the office today and said you encouraged him to seek me out and that you two have been trying to come up with ways to make things better for me."

Based on her tone, they both appeared to agree that spending time with Mitch was not better for her. "I have barely spoken to Mitch in weeks. I don't know why he would say that."

By stepping away, he hadn't meant to open

the door for Mitch. "I can talk to him. Remind him that it's in his best interest and yours if he leaves you alone."

"That would be extremely helpful. Thank you." Bonnie slid her hands into her front pockets. "Can I be honest about something else?"

He took a step in her direction, drawn to her in ways he couldn't explain. In ways he only saw in movies and read about in books. "I hope you're honest with me about everything."

"I understand you're trying to regain your sister's trust, but I really hope we're still going to go on that date. I think about it pretty much every day. It would be so disappointing if it wasn't ever going to happen."

Aaron shared her desire. He also thought about that date every morning and every night when he finally let himself rest. "I want to say yes so badly."

She shifted her weight from her heels to the balls of her feet. "I am scared to death there's a but at the end of that sentence."

"No but. I need some more time, that's all. I've got to make some things right with Lauren before I can let myself have you, but make no mistake, I want you."

Her cheeks flushed, and she looked down at her feet. "Okay, well, I can give you time. I don't want you to take too long, but I can accept you needing a little bit."

"Help!" David screamed from the living room.

Bonnie and Aaron exchanged "not again" looks and took off down the hall. Another trip to the ER would be absolutely humiliating. Another accident when Bonnie was here might make her start to question if a higher power was trying to tell them something.

Bonnie ran over to her dad, who was sitting on a folding chair in the kitchen. Sasha sat next to him, calm, cool and collected. "What's wrong? What happened?"

A smile spread across David's face. "Nothing. I just thought you two were alone back there a little too long. Sasha had me convinced I shouldn't intrude, so I decided to bring you to me instead. I'm impressed with how fast you guys made it out here."

"Me, too," Sasha said with a chuckle. They thought they were hilarious. Aaron watched as Bonnie's ears turned bright red.

"It was almost like they saw a mouse," David said.

"Are they scared of mice?" Sasha asked.

"Oh, you should see these two when they see a mouse. It's a toss-up who will climb on top of the other first to get away from the tiny little critter."

"Don't. Ever. Do. That. To. Me. Again," Bonnie said, slapping him on the arm with every word.

"Everything okay with you two?" Sasha asked Aaron, his gaze shifting between him and Bonnie.

"We're all good. We'll be even better when we get our revenge, won't we, Bonnie?"

"You two have no idea what you're in for. Revenge will be sweet."

Aaron tried being optimistic. Things would work out. Some playful vengeance would be served, and that date would happen. The worst had to be behind them.

CHAPTER SIXTEEN

"WHO IS THE prettiest baby in the entire world? Who is it? Who is it? It's Winter!" There was nothing sweeter than the sound of baby's laughter. Bonnie was one hundred percent, utterly and absolutely in love with Sasha's niece.

"Stop stealing all the giggles. Hand her over here," Sasha said, reaching for the little girl in Bonnie's arms.

There was also nothing cuter than the manliest of men holding a baby. Throw in some baby talk and Bonnie was reduced to mush.

"Who's going to ride in Uncle Sasha's side-car when she's bigger? Who is? Winter is!" He gave her belly a poke with his finger, and the baby laughed like he had told her the funniest joke she'd ever heard.

"Never in a million years would I have believed my brother would be good with babies." Sasha's sister, Athena, handed Bonnie a glass of water and sat down like it was the first time she'd done so in days.

"He's a natural," Bonnie said, watching him bounce little Winter on his knee. "Isn't it sort of annoying that Sasha is good at everything he does? I feel like if we went bowling, he'd knock down the pins in my lane and his at the same time. That's how good he'd be."

"Yeah, try growing up with that. Guess who was valedictorian of his class and who got a perfect score on his SAT?"

Bonnie's eyes went wide. Wonders never ceased when it came to Sasha. "You were valedictorian of your high school? Is your picture on a wall somewhere?"

"I was, and it is. I can't help it that I was graced with so many abilities. Look at me. I'm huge. Can you imagine how big my brain must be?"

"Ginormous," Calvin, Sasha's brother-in-law, said as he came out of the bedroom. He was dressed in a suit and tie.

Sasha wolf whistled. "Wow, look at your daddy. He's all dressed up to take Mommy on a date. Maybe in nine months you'll have a little brother or sister."

"Don't even say it. One baby at a time,

please," Athena said, forcing herself to get up off the couch. "Thank you again for helping him babysit tonight, Bonnie. We appreciate it so much."

"The pleasure is all mine. I've been begging Sasha for weeks for some baby time. Have fun, you two."

"But not too much fun, Calvin. Athena doesn't want another baby just yet."

"If you weren't holding my beautiful baby daughter, I would throw something at you right now," Athena said with a playful scowl. She had the same beautiful red hair and fair skin as her brother. They were very much alike except for the fact that she was literally half his size.

Sasha chuckled. "Go, get out of here."

"Thanks again, Bonnie," Calvin said, holding the door open for his wife.

"I like them. Almost more than you," Bonnie said when they'd left.

"All I take away from that is you like me the most." He held Winter up over his head. "Did you hear that, Winter? Bonnie likes me the most. Yes, she does. Yes, she does!"

"Careful," Bonnie warned a second too late. Winter spit up right on her uncle's face.

Once again, she was impressed with Sasha's skills. He kept his cool, handed the baby to Bonnie and went to the bathroom to clean up. "That was disgusting," he said when he returned.

"Never bounce a baby after she's eaten and then shake her over your head. It's like tossing some Mentos into a can of soda. You would be a fool to think nothing is going to happen."

"And I am no fool. I was valedictorian, after all."

"I was happy to just graduate high school." School was hard for Bonnie. She'd struggled with reading when she was little, and she had to work hard for every grade she got. She knew college wasn't for her and, after a few dead-end jobs as a young adult, she'd talked to Gordon about what he did for a living and was convinced to get her real estate license. She'd never regretted it.

"You and Aaron went to school together?"

"We did. He was a couple years older than us."

"Us?"

Funny how even now after everything that had happened, Bonnie still thought of them as inseparable when she spoke about them in the past. "Me and Lauren, his sister."

"Bad Lauren. How does someone like you become best friends with someone like her?"

Someone who didn't know them well might think it was an issue of opposites attracting, which in some respects was true. Bonnie and Lauren were different in many ways, but it was the things in common that had made them as close as they were.

"You love Aaron, right?" she asked him.

Sasha nodded. "He's the best."

"There are parts of Lauren that are very similar to her brother. I love those things about her as well."

"You love Aaron, too, right?"

The question struck Bonnie as more serious than when she asked it of him. "I like Aaron a lot."

An evil grin spread across Sasha's face. "*Like* him. Uh-huh."

"Are you thirteen years old or something? Sometimes I think Winter is more mature than you are."

"Oh, Bonnie, Bonnie, Bonnie, Bonnie. Thou dost protest too much. Just say it. Out loud. Don't be afraid."

"Say what?" she asked, even though she knew exactly what he wanted her to say. Did she love Aaron? Sure, the same way she loved Sasha. Was she in love with Aaron? Thinking it made her heart skip a beat and her palms sweat.

"Say it! Say it! Say it!" he chanted, much to Winter's delight and Bonnie's horror.

"Would you please stop? You are so embarrassing. Your poor sister. I can just imagine the torture she had to endure growing up with you."

"He loves you. I can tell. He's been in love with you pretty much since I started working for him."

Bonnie's throat went dry. She tried to laugh it off like he was kidding. "Oh, really?"

"Really. I know these things." He tapped his finger against his temple. "Big, big brain, remember?"

"We like each other. We're thinking about going on a date, but it's complicated."

"Because of Bad Lauren."

"Stop calling her that," Bonnie said, feeling strangely protective of Lauren all of a sudden.

He sat forward, leaning across the space that separated them. "If she's not bad, then why is she keeping you from being with her brother? If I was in love with someone, Athena would be happy for me. She would wish me well. Not try to tear us apart."

"What if Athena thought the woman you were in love with tried to steal Calvin away?"

"But she didn't try to steal Calvin away. It never happened, and if I told Athena what really happened and explained to her that I trusted this woman I loved, she would get back on board with wishing me the best."

Bonnie picked up a toy for Winter to play with to stop her from fussing. She wasn't a fan of this conversation any more than Bonnie was. "In a perfect world, in your perfect world, maybe that's true. Lauren isn't Athena. That doesn't make her bad, though. It just makes her Lauren."

Sasha spread his arms out wide. "Then what are you so afraid of?"

"What do you mean?"

"If she's not a bad person. If she's a good person going through some bad stuff, then why are you and Aaron so afraid of jumping all in and being happy? What's the worst that can happen?"

When he put it like that, Bonnie didn't have

a quick retort. She had to stop and think about it. "I don't know."

"Can I give you some advice?" Sasha asked, as if he wasn't going to give it anyway.

"Go ahead. I know what you're going to say."

"Be happy, Bonnie. It's okay. Sometimes other people are happy while you're sad, and sometimes you're happy while other people are sad. That's the way the world works. We aren't all happy at the same time. But don't skip your turn at being happy because someone else is having their turn at being sad. I'm going to tell Aaron that, too."

His words struck a chord. That's what they had been doing. They had been waiting for Lauren to be happy so they didn't feel guilty about being happy. If Lauren wasn't a terrible person, she wouldn't want her brother to give up happiness. Lauren wasn't a terrible person.

"You are ridiculously wise."

Sasha sat back in the recliner and put his hands behind his head. "I know. Big brain, great wisdom."

"It's still so annoying," Bonnie teased. "Isn't it, Winter? Is Uncle Sasha annoying? Giggle if he's annoying." The baby squealed in delight. "Even the baby agrees, so it must be true."

"Yeah, yeah. You'll thank me later."

AARON'S PHONE RANG in his pocket as he finished putting the second coat of paint on the walls of bedroom number three. Wiping paint from his hand onto his already destroyed jeans, he pulled the phone out. It was his mom trying to video call him. He clicked to accept, and her face popped up on the screen.

"Aaron! Darling, how are you?"

"Hi, Mom. To what do I owe the pleasure of seeing your lovely face today instead of the usual phone call?"

"I haven't seen you in so long I was beginning to forget what you look like. Then at mah-jongg the other day, Sandra Polites was telling me about how she does this video chat with her grandchildren in New York once a week and I realized I could do that as well. Never mind the fact that both of my children live in the same town as I do but never come visit me."

Her guilt trips were legendary. "I've been super busy with this house, Mom. We're in the final stretch. Do you want a virtual tour?"

"Of course I do!"

Aaron showed her around and pointed out all the little upgrades and special details he had added over the last few weeks. She was particularly fond of the kitchen. It was very similar to what she had in their house in Arizona.

"You have done an incredible job. You should be so proud of yourself, sweetheart."

For the first time in a really long time, Aaron did feel pride. That was something he'd truly lacked when he worked for his dad. There'd been nothing for him to feel good about. But after taking a run-down, dirty, mice-infested pit and making it into this gorgeous home, he felt extraordinary.

"I can't wait to stage it and have you come see it in person when we have the open house in a couple weeks."

"I cannot wait, either. Which reminds me, I hope that you haven't forgotten something that's happening one week from today."

Aaron scrunched up his face and tried to remember. He couldn't think of anything he had committed to recently. "Are we doing a family dinner?"

"The library gala! Aaron, please tell me

you have not forgotten. Do you need to do any last-minute alterations to your tuxedo? When was the last time you wore it?"

Aaron hadn't been in a tux since Lauren's wedding. "I'm sure it's fine, Mom. Do you really need me to go, though? Are you sure Dad is okay with me going?" It may have felt like forever to his mom since the last time the two of them had spoken, but Aaron knew for a fact that it had been forever since he talked to his dad. They had not seen one another or spoken since the day he had been summoned to his father's office and told he couldn't work with Bonnie or her father. Or else.

"Your father is expecting you, and so is Hilde."

"Who's Hilde?"

"Ingrid Rutherford's daughter. Your date to the gala! Aaron, sweetheart, please don't do this to me." She placed her hand over her heart as if he was giving her palpitations.

He had completely forgotten about having to take a date. There was only one woman Aaron wanted to go on a date with, and her name was not Hilde. Bonnie would not be interested in the Cole library gala, however.

It was probably the last place she would want to be.

"I'll be there and on my best behavior. I promise."

"Thank you. Have you spoken to your sister lately? She's been avoiding my calls, and it has me a bit worried."

"I have not. Has she been showing up for work and such?"

"Apparently. But I'm still concerned. With Mitch back in town, she can't be in a very good place. Maybe you could check on her and make sure she's okay."

His mother clearly wasn't aware that Lauren hated his guts right now. "I'll see what I can do."

"Thank you. Well, I'll let you get back to work. I will talk to you after you visit your sister. Bye, honey."

"Bye." Aaron hung up and pushed the phone back in his pocket. He couldn't tell if this was an elaborate ploy to get him and his sister in the same room together before the gala or if his mom was truly worried about Lauren's well-being. Either was possible. He would do as she asked and check on his baby sister, because that was what a good brother would do and he was trying to be a good brother.

He sent her a text about checking in and got no reply.

"Flooring is here," Sasha said, popping his head in the master bedroom where Aaron's tour and video chat had come to an end. "Want to get started on the kitchen and living room?"

"Yeah, let's see how much we can get done before it gets dark."

The three men worked until dusk and finished the entire main living area. The wood Bonnie had picked out was perfect. Aaron was more than pleased with the way it tied everything together.

"I am going home and soaking in the tub until the water turns cold. That is the only way this old body is going to function tomorrow," David said, stretching his arms over his head and clasping his hands together. He leaned to the right and then to the left.

"I'm going to go downtown and get some food and a couple drinks. You want to join me, Aaron?" Sasha asked.

"Well, since David didn't offer to make

room for me in the tub, I guess I can grab something to eat with you."

"You're pretty, Aaron, but not pretty enough to share my bathtub, buddy," David joked.

Sasha and Aaron stayed a little bit longer to tidy things up before heading over to the Trusty Steed, a new gastropub in the center of town. They ordered a bunch of appetizers and each picked a different burger as their entree. No one would be going home hungry. Aaron sent another text to his sister, letting her know he was at dinner but would check on her when he was done. He got an automated reply that she was driving and couldn't respond to his message.

When the waitress brought their drinks, Aaron raised his glass. "To almost being finished with my first flip, thanks to you and David."

"Cheers to that, except we can't forget Bonnie. If it wasn't for her, I wouldn't have gotten added to the crew, you would still be trying to choose a cabinet style and both of us would be worse for wear."

"Absolutely. To Bonnie as well." Nothing

would be right without Bonnie. They clinked glasses and drank.

"Speaking of Bonnie, I was thinking I might ask her out on a date."

Aaron set his drink down and stared blankly at Sasha's giant head. First of all, Sasha was too old for Bonnie. Second of all, if anyone had picked up on the fact that there was something going on between Bonnie and Aaron, it was Sasha. Why on earth would he try to get in the middle of that?

Sasha's fist came down hard on the table, rattling everything on it as he laughed hysterically. "I'm messing with you, kid! Oh my goodness, you should have seen your face. You would have thought I told you I was going to rob a bank tonight."

Aaron's shoulders relaxed, and he picked his drink back up. "That was not cool."

Sasha couldn't stop laughing. "You are seriously so transparent. How did you ever get away with anything when you were a kid? Your face gives away your emotions every time."

"Oh, really?"

"Really. I know that you have been in love

with that woman since the day I met you. It was all right there." Sasha pointed at Aaron's face.

In love from the beginning? No way. He was still trying to figure out his feelings. There was no chance he'd been in love months ago.

"You're a funny guy."

"Don't worry. She loves you, too. She's just afraid you'll regret making your sister mad. I say if your sister cares about you half as much as you care about her, she'll get over it."

"Did you talk to Bonnie about me?" How else would he know any of this stuff? Had she really told him that she was in love?

The waitress with the worst possible timing on the planet showed up at that moment with baskets full of appetizers. As soon as she set them down, food went into Sasha's mouth, making it difficult for him to answer questions.

Aaron couldn't eat until he knew exactly what Bonnie had said. Sasha grabbed a napkin out of the dispenser on their table and wiped his mouth. "These wings are delicious. Aren't you going to eat any?"

"Aren't you going to answer my question?"

"Did Bonnie talk to me about you? Kind of."

That was an insufficient answer. That was the kind of answer that only led to more questions and put knots in Aaron's stomach instead of buffalo wings. "What does that mean?"

Sasha had moved on to the fried mushrooms. His eyes closed as he chewed. "Those are also really good," he said once he was done savoring a mouthful. "You've got to try some."

"What does it mean that you kind of talked to her about me?"

"It means we talked. I probably talked more than she did, but you came up."

"And she told you that she's in love with me?"

"You truly don't see it? Every time the two of you are in the same room together? You don't see it, hear it, feel it?" Sasha seemed genuinely perplexed.

Aaron needed to think about it. Did he? He knew what he felt. Did he know what she felt?

"Hey, Aaron!" Mitch came up to the table and gave Aaron a slap on the back. "I feel like I haven't seen you in ages. Where have you been hiding? At that house you're working on?"

"Pretty much. We're almost finished. The open house should be in a couple weeks. Truth be told, I sometimes wonder if I should sell it or move in myself," Aaron said, noticing Sasha was glaring at him, most likely for not introducing him to their unexpected guest. "Mitch, this is Sasha, a friend of mine. Sasha, this is Mitch."

"Mitch? The Mitch?" Sasha questioned Aaron, who nodded. "Mitch, why don't you join us? We have plenty of apps to share."

That was the last thing Aaron wanted, but there was no way to rescind the offer now.

"That would be great. I was just going to get a couple beers before I headed home, but I could eat." He snagged an empty chair from another table and sat between Aaron and Sasha. His phone buzzed, and he read it and set it down on the table. "My mom is driving me nuts about this library gala. She thinks we need to make an appearance as a family. I think we need to stay home."

"I agree with you. Stay home." The last thing they needed was for Mitch and Lauren to be in the same room for any period of time.

"If I could stay home, I would, but my mother bribed me into taking Hilde Rutherford."

"Never heard of her," Mitch said. "Is she hot?"

Lauren had really dodged a bullet with this one. "I have no idea. I don't know that I've ever met her."

Mitch helped himself to a chicken wing. "Blind dates are the worst."

Sasha's brows were pinched together. "You're going on a date?"

"Not a real date," Aaron said. "I don't even know the woman. I'm doing my mother a favor."

Mitch wiped his fingers on his napkin. "It's about time you got back in the dating scene. I can't remember anyone you've dated since Lara, and that was last year."

"How long have you guys been friends?" Sasha asked Mitch.

Mitch popped some cheese curds in his mouth. "Since high school," he answered after devouring them.

"Oh, then you know Bonnie. Bonnie Windsor?"

Aaron didn't like where this was headed. Sasha knew who Mitch was, and bringing up

Bonnie was a bad idea. Unfortunately, he was helpless to stop this conversation from going off the rails. It was a runaway train with no brakes and a mangled track up ahead.

"I know Bonnie Windsor very well. She's great."

"She is," Sasha said. "Aaron thinks so, too. I'm trying to explain to him that when two people connect the way he does with Bonnie, he's foolish to let that slip through his fingers."

"Aaron and Bonnie?" Mitch's forehead creased, and his lips dipped into a frown. Aaron squirmed. This conversation train wasn't just going to go off the rails—it was going to plummet into the deep cavern of doom.

"Don't listen to him," Aaron said, trying to minimize the damage. "He has no idea what he's talking about. Try one of these fried mushrooms, they're delicious."

Sasha shook his head. "Deny, deny, deny. You can't deny it forever, Aaron. That woman is your soul mate."

Boom! The train crashed into a fiery grave.

"Bonnie and Aaron? That's…hilarious. I don't see it," Mitch said.

Aaron tried to smooth things over. "Like I said, he doesn't know what he's talking about."

They finished off two of the appetizers before the waitress came back over to check on them and offered to take Mitch's order.

"Oh my gosh," Mitch said, looking at his phone. "I totally forgot I'm supposed to be on a conference call with China in like fifteen minutes. I have got to go. I'm so sorry." He pulled out a money clip and threw a twenty-dollar bill on the table. "Let me get the appetizers. It was nice to meet you, Sasha. Aaron, I'll see you around, buddy."

"Too bad he couldn't stay," Sasha said after Mitch was out of sight. He also snagged the last chicken wing.

"That was the guy who left my sister at the altar because he thought he was in love with Bonnie."

Sasha popped a fried mushroom into his mouth. "I know."

"Then why did you say all that?"

Sasha laughed. "All what?"

"The stuff about me and Bonnie."

"Because I'm right. You two should be together. I wanted everyone to be clear about who deserves Bonnie's heart, and it's not Mitch."

Aaron shook his head. He wished he could be as sure as Sasha was. He also had no idea how he would fix all of these issues. Sasha picked up the bill, refusing to let Aaron throw in any money.

After dinner, Aaron tried texting his sister again and got the same automated response that she was driving. He called her, but it went straight to voice mail. He left a message, asking her to call. He knew she was still upset with him, but the least she could do was respond with an "I hate you" or "Leave me alone."

Maybe the first person Aaron would tell about him and Bonnie was Lauren. If she knew they were in love like Sasha believed they were, she would finally get past this.

He was in love with Bonnie. The thought made laughter bubble out of him. He loved Bonnie. According to Sasha, she loved him back. What a wonderful world it would be if he could hear those words from her lips.

He turned onto Greenbriar, heading back to the house to do a little more work before he turned in for the night. He'd been sleeping there off and on for a couple weeks. It made it easier to get things done. They had fallen a bit behind because of a couple of the setbacks, but they weren't too far over.

Aaron's heart stopped when he turned into the driveway. It felt like he was starring in his own horror movie. Everything he'd spent the last two hours putting in his stomach threatened to come back up. Had he fallen asleep on the drive home and not realized? Because he had to be in the middle of a horrible nightmare.

In pink spray paint, the words *I Hate You* were written across the garage door. The windows that looked into the dining room were broken. It was possible that was where the missing landscaping bricks had gone. The front door was kicked in, and Aaron could only imagine the horrors that would be waiting for him inside.

He dialed 911 and cried while he waited for the police to come.

CHAPTER SEVENTEEN

IN BONNIE'S MIND, there was only one person who would have done this. There was only one person who was mad enough, hateful enough and out-of-touch-with-reality enough to do this.

"It had to be Lauren," she said to the police officer who was interviewing her. Who else would have chosen pink paint? It was like she wasn't even trying to hide that it was her.

Not only had the outside been defaced. All of the kitchen cabinets had gotten spray painted, and the beautiful quartz countertops were ruined. The chandelier in the dining room was hanging by one wire. The fireplace had the words *Blame Bonnie* written across the brick. Classic Lauren.

"It wasn't Lauren," Aaron said. His eyes were red and swollen. "She wouldn't do this to me. She wouldn't."

"Why not? You said yourself that she's mad at you. We know she's mad at me."

"I know it's hard to think the worst about a family member, but is there anything that might lead you to believe that what Miss Windsor is saying might be true?" the officer asked Aaron.

Tears fell down his face, and Bonnie's heart broke in two. How could Lauren do this to him? It took him a good minute to speak. His voice cracked as he explained the situation.

"She felt like I deserted her. That I was disloyal to her and chose Bonnie and Mitch over her after everything that happened at the wedding. I talked to my mom today, and she said she hadn't been able to get ahold of her lately and that she was worried. She was afraid that Lauren might be struggling with Mitch back in town. That would have easily pushed her over the edge."

"When was the last time you talked to your sister?"

"I texted her a few times tonight, and I called her right before I came back here. She didn't answer the texts or the call."

Because she was a coward. Because she was coldhearted. Bonnie watched as her dad stood in the middle of the living room with his hand over his mouth and tears welling in his eyes. It was unbelievable all the hard work that could be undone in a matter of minutes.

"Is there anyone else who would do something like this? Anyone who has it out for you?"

"She has a whole posse of followers. They could have all been here with her. I bet she had help from Theresa Gilmore, Kathy Cole, Wendy Hillbrand, and Jeanne Watson. Even Mary James and Cheryl Cooper could have tagged along." It made Bonnie sick to her stomach, but everyone she used to call friend could easily have had a hand in this. Everyone knew that if Lauren said something had to be done, they all would have done it, because no one questioned Lauren. No one stood up to her. No one told her she couldn't have something, do something, say something. Lauren did whatever she wanted, and this time, she'd gone too far.

The officer took all the names down and promised he would follow up with every one of them.

"Bad, bad Lauren," Sasha said from where he sat on the floor. He hadn't even gone into the bedrooms to see what had been done in there, because he had collapsed on the ground when he walked in.

"She wouldn't do this," Aaron repeated.

Bonnie walked over to where he stood and wrapped her arms around him. This was one tough pill to swallow, but the proof was written all over the house.

"I have to go talk to her. I need her to tell me to my face that she did this."

"I think you should let the police handle it. I don't think it's a good idea to confront her when everything is still so raw."

Aaron let her hug him, but he stood like a statue, motionless and rigid. She couldn't think of any words of comfort to offer him. While he was devastated and despondent, she was full of rage. If she were to confront Lauren right now, Lauren wasn't the only one who would be spending the night in jail.

"We should go," her dad finally said. "We need to get out of here and come back in the morning and make a punch list."

"Ha!" Sasha's laughter lacked any and all humor. "That's going to be one long punch list."

"There's nothing we can do about this tonight. It's best we rest up and start fresh in the morning." He offered Sasha a hand up.

Bonnie let go of Aaron and held out her hand. "Come on, let's go."

"She wouldn't do this to me," Aaron said again.

Denial was not easy to overcome. It was going to take a lot for the truth to sink in. Even when Lauren admitted to it, Aaron would probably still grapple with the reality of it.

"Do you want me to drive you home?" she asked, taking his hand instead of waiting for him to take hers. She tried to pull him toward the front door, but he wouldn't budge. "I can stay with you if you want."

Sasha placed a strong hand on her shoulder. "I got this. You go home with your dad. It's probably not safe for you to go to your house alone. I'll take good care of him, I promise."

Bonnie lifted up on her toes and gave Aaron a kiss on the cheek. "We can fix the house."

She knew that wasn't the real issue, though. They could fix the house. Repaint, repair, redo. But Aaron's heart would forever be broken. This kind of hurt caused by a betrayal from someone he loved would never fully heal. He knew that.

Bonnie went with her dad and cried the whole way to his house. She wiped her face and clenched her fists. She was so angry she spit her words. "How could she do this? How could she hurt him like that?"

"Maybe it wasn't her. Maybe Aaron's right. She wouldn't do something like that. Not the Lauren I know. Not the Lauren you know."

Bonnie shook her head. The Lauren she knew was long gone. That Lauren had disappeared the second Mitch began his speech about not wanting to get married. The Lauren that was left behind from that event was worse than Bad Lauren, as Sasha liked to call her. She was Evil Lauren. The wickedest of the wicked.

"Don't defend her. Don't ever defend her to me again. I won't hear it."

Her dad gave her leg a pat. "Let's get some sleep. We've got a long day ahead of us."

Bonnie didn't sleep a minute all night. She texted back and forth with Sasha, who had managed to get Aaron to leave the house eventually. They were both staying at Aaron's.

Sasha didn't think Aaron was sleeping, but he was at least lying down.

In the morning, she and her dad stopped to get some coffee and then made the depressing drive to the house. Aaron and Sasha were already there, and so was Mitch.

"What are you doing here?"

"Word spread pretty fast about what happened last night. I was calling Aaron all night, but he never picked up. This is bad. Who would have done this?"

"Are you serious? Who do you think did it?" She waved her hand in the direction of the garage door. "Lauren didn't even try to hide that it was her."

Mitch's expression was solemn. "I'm so sorry. I feel like this is all my fault. If I had handled things differently—if I had told Lauren I didn't want to get married before the wedding, none of this would have happened."

She shook her head. "This is not your fault. It's not yours or mine or anyone's fault except for Lauren. I am done feeling bad for her. She is a grown woman who has to take responsibility for what she's done."

"Come here. I know I'm not your favorite person, but you look like you are in desperate need of a hug." He opened his arms wide. Bonnie didn't even think about it—she just fell into his arms, because he was right. She needed someone to hold her, and she appreciated the fact that he didn't jump to Lauren's defense.

"Is there anything I can do to help?" Mitch asked. "I'm not very handy, but I can try."

"That's really kind of you." The true test of someone's character was how they responded in a crisis. Maybe she had misjudged Mitch's character. "Why don't you come on in? I'm sure we can find something for you to do."

THERE WAS NO WAY Lauren had done this. Lauren would *not* do this to him. Not when she knew how hard he had worked. Not when she knew that he was trying to be a better brother. She was hurt and she was angry, but she wouldn't ruin everything Aaron had worked for. He couldn't accept that.

"We've got some extra hands on deck today," Bonnie said, entering the room with Mitch trailing behind her.

"Hey, man. I'm so sorry this happened. Put me to work. Tell me what you need to get done and I will do it. Or at least I'll try."

"Thanks, Mitch. I appreciate you coming out."

David looked the way Aaron felt. Tired, beaten down, completely crushed. This house was like their baby. Their first baby, and someone had come and broken it. They all thought it was Lauren, but it wasn't Lauren. Aaron's heart told him it couldn't be her.

His phone rang, and for a second he expected it to be Lauren. She would tell him that she had gotten in her car and driven to Arizona or maybe San Francisco for a long weekend. It wasn't, though. It was his dad.

"Hey, Dad. Can I call you back? I'm kind of in the middle of something."

"No, you can't call me back. I'm at the police station trying to get your sister released from custody, because for some reason you told the cops that she vandalized your house. What is wrong with you? Why would you do that?"

"Dad, I told the cops I didn't think it was her. I pray it's not her, but…" All the evidence pointed to it being her.

"You need to get over here right now and tell them that you made a mistake and your sister had nothing to do with this." He hung up in typical Walter Cole fashion. He didn't need to wait for a reply, because when he summoned you, you came.

"I have to go. I'll be back, though."

"Wait." Bonnie stopped him. "Where are you going? Do you want me to come with you?"

It would be a very bad idea for Bonnie to come with him, given the fact that she believed beyond a shadow of a doubt that Lauren had done this. "I'm good. You stay here and help your dad. I'll be back before you can miss me."

"I doubt that," she nearly whispered.

Aaron drove straight to the Blue Springs Police Department. His mom was sitting in the tiny waiting area when he got there. His dad was pacing around.

"He's here!" his mom exclaimed.

"Here's my son," his dad said to the sergeant behind the counter. "He's the one who made the accusation. He's here to take it back. Where's that detective?"

Of course, he assumed that Aaron would simply let Lauren off the hook. As if it was that easy. This was part of the reason everyone else thought she was guilty. Their parents never made her own up to her mistakes. She was never held accountable for anything she ever did.

"Can I talk to the detective in charge of my case?" Aaron asked.

Detective Rogers thought it was a great idea for Aaron to talk to Lauren himself. She wasn't being very cooperative with the questioning and their dad had brought a lawyer, which significantly slowed things down.

When Aaron came into the room, Lauren sat up straight. "Aaron, thank God you're here. Can you believe that they think I did this?"

"I strongly suggest you not talk about anything that the police have asked you about," her lawyer said.

Lauren ignored him. "They're asking me to account for my entire evening and said they're going to be checking all the local hardware stores to find someone who will identify me as someone who bought spray paint. This is nuts. Can you please inform these detectives that I would never vandalize your stuff?"

"Can you ask your lawyer to leave?" Aaron knew the only way he was going to get the truth out of her was if it was only him and her. No police. No lawyers. Not even their mom and dad.

"Leave," Lauren told the man.

"I strongly advise you not to—"

"Leave," she repeated a little louder.

The man closed his briefcase and grabbed his jacket off the back of his chair before exiting the room.

"Now can you tell them this is ridiculous?"

Aaron sat across from his sister and tried to picture her destroying his house. He knew Bonnie could see it, but he couldn't visualize it no matter how hard he tried. "I know you've been mad at me," he said.

"Aaron, there's being mad at you and there's going berserk. I've been mad at you."

"All I need you to do is look me in the eye and answer one question. Did you destroy my house?"

Lauren didn't blink, she didn't shift her gaze, she didn't hesitate. "No. And I feel like the worst sister in the world, because if you even thought for a second that I would do that to you, then I've really ruined our relationship by being so hateful."

"I didn't think you did it. I knew you wouldn't do that to me."

Tears filled Lauren's eyes and rolled down her cheeks. "You did? You believed in me? Because I wouldn't blame you if you didn't. I haven't given you a lot of reasons to trust me not to do mean and terrible things. I asked Daddy to fire Mr. Windsor. That's pretty horrible. I have been nothing but hateful for months."

"Where were you last night? I tried texting and calling. I kept getting messages that you were driving."

"I just drove around. I didn't have a destination in mind. I just couldn't sit in my house anymore. I know it's a terrible alibi."

"You don't need an alibi." At least Aaron didn't need her to have one. If she said she was driving around, she was driving around. "I have one more question, though. Is it possible that you may have said something to someone else and accidentally inspired them to vandalize my house?"

"I hope not. I don't think so." She wrung her hands. "It's possible, I guess. I've been encouraging people to lash out at Bonnie. I've been complaining about you. Maybe one of my friends thought that by attacking you, they'd make me happy."

That was a distinct possibility. A lot of people worshipped the ground Lauren walked on. If they thought hurting Aaron or being mean to Bonnie would make Lauren happy, they might just have decided to do something illegal instead of simply shameful.

"We need to tell the police everyone you've been talking to over the last couple weeks so they can interview them. Anyone you complained to about me, about Bonnie, about Mitch."

Lauren nodded. "I'll tell them whatever they need to know." She reached across the table and touched his hand. "You look like you haven't slept. I am so sorry if someone did this because they thought I would want them to. I know how hard you worked on that house. I hope you can fix it back up."

"We can fix it. It's going to mess up my timeline and cost me more money, but we'll fix it. I was worried that you were so angry with me that our relationship would be irreparable. That's why I couldn't sleep last night. I'm sorry I've been such a lousy brother the last few months. I should have held Mitch more accountable for what he did to you. For that, I'm sorry."

"Apology accepted."

He gave her hand a squeeze. "I won't apologize for standing up for Bonnie, though. I'm in love with her, Lauren. I'm in love with her, and I think she's in love with me. We're really good for each other, and just like I knew you didn't wreck my house, I know she didn't wreck your wedding. She doesn't want to be with Mitch. She wants to be with me."

Lauren didn't respond right away. She sat with that news for a minute, but she didn't let go of his hand. That had to be a good sign.

"You're in love with Bonnie?"

Aaron nodded. His nerves were upsetting his stomach.

"You think she's in love with you?"

He nodded again.

"You know, I've heard this before." She tapped a finger to her chin. "Where have I heard this before? Oh, right! During my wedding vows."

"I know Mitch said the same thing. The difference between me and Mitch is that Bonnie is aware of how I feel. She wants to date me—we've actually talked about it."

Lauren rested her cheek in her hand. She stared right into his eyes. "Answer me one question. If I told you that I forbid you to be with Bonnie, that I would never speak to you again if she was the one you wanted to be with, who would you choose, me or Bonnie?"

Aaron's heart sank. She was supposed to see the light. She was supposed to want him to be happy, not make him choose between two of the most important people in his life. He shouldn't have to. He also knew that if Lauren actually gave him that ultimatum, Bonnie would refuse to be with him. She would never allow him to destroy his relationship with his sister to have one with her.

"I would say, Lauren, I love you. You are my sister, and I care about you and I want the best for you. I also expect the people I love to love me back. And if you really loved me, you'd never ask me to forsake my happiness for yours."

He waited anxiously for her reply, because he hadn't really answered her question. He'd instead asked her to reconsider asking it. "That was one heck of an answer. You somehow managed to choose Bonnie without not choosing me. You must really love her."

"I do. And I know deep down in that broken heart of yours, you do, too."

"Let's not go that far. Can we please get out of here? I don't know who you have to convince, but I need to go home."

Lauren cooperated with the police. She gave them all the names of everyone who she had complained to about Bonnie, Mitch and Aaron. She did her best to account for her time. Aaron even suggested they get her cell phone record, because he had texted her most likely right before the vandalism and immediately after. If she was way out in Morris like she thought she was during that time, the cell phone towers would confirm it.

They released her, much to their parents' relief. With that settled, Aaron was in a much better mental state to take care of things back at the house. His sister had confirmed what he knew to be true. She hadn't done that to him. She would never have done that to him.

Everyone was in the kitchen, gathered around the island when he returned. David had the list of repairs, and it was long.

"Good news," Aaron announced.

Bonnie spun around. "She confessed."

He couldn't blame her for thinking the

worst of Lauren. Lauren had admitted she had done some terribly hateful things to Bonnie over the last few months.

"No, the good news is she didn't do it."

Everyone stared back at him wide-eyed and slack-jawed. "How do they know?" Sasha asked.

"They don't know for sure yet, but I do, because she told me she didn't."

Bonnie put both hands on her head. "Are you kidding? Are you seriously joking right now? Aaron, please tell me you did not let her talk her way out of this. Please tell me you are going to hold her responsible for one time in her entire life."

He pulled her close. "Hey, I know it's hard to believe right now, but the evidence is going to show she didn't do it. Please trust me. I know my sister better than anyone."

Bonnie stepped away from him and covered her mouth with her hand. She shook her head. "She's playing you. You're being played by the master of manipulation. She did this when she was mad. She doesn't want to deal with the consequences, so she's lying and she's going to play on your emotions and your good heart and your complete denial so she can get away with it."

"I spent a long time talking to her. We aired out a lot of our differences. She's in a much better mental space than she's been in in months. We're not going to blame her anymore."

Bonnie exploded. "I'm going to blame her forever! If you want to live in your denial, you go right ahead, but I won't live there with you. I am going to live in reality."

"Bon Bon," her dad said, trying to refocus her, but she would have none of it.

"No! No one defend her. I won't listen to it anymore. No." She was shaking with anger. Aaron was at a loss for how to help her calm down. "I can't be here if everyone here is going to pretend that Lauren didn't do this."

She stormed past Aaron, bumping his shoulder on her way out. Everyone else was frozen in their spot until Mitch moved.

"I'm going to go after her. I don't think she should be alone right now."

CHAPTER EIGHTEEN

"OF ALL THE MANIPULATIVE, horrible, monstrous things she has done this summer, this really takes the cake." Bonnie had spent the last half hour raging about Lauren to Mitch. They had gone back to his condo. He seemed to be the only one who understood. Maybe it was because he had lived under Lauren's control. He knew exactly how conniving she could be.

"You're right. I don't understand how the rest of them don't see it. It's like one of those things where what people are looking for is sitting right in front of them but they don't see it. They won't look right in front of their faces."

"Exactly! What else could she have done to make it more obvious? What's Lauren's favorite color?"

"Pink," Mitch replied, not missing a beat.

"Who does she blame for everything that has gone wrong in her life?"

"You."

"Me. 'Blame Bonnie.' That's what she wrote on the fireplace!" She opened her eyes wide and flailed her arms around. "How much more obvious can she be?"

"It doesn't get more obvious, if you ask me."

She continued to pace in front of his giant eighty-inch wall-mounted television set. The television Lauren had picked out, no doubt. "And where was Lauren last night?"

"No one knows."

"No one knows. She was in her car. Where could she have been going? I just can't think of anywhere she might drive to. Maybe she went…to the house! I mean, how do they not see it?"

Mitch shook his head. "I don't know. You are so right about everything. I think Aaron is too blinded by family loyalty to see it, or maybe he knows the truth, but like you said, they never hold Lauren responsible for her actions. She gets away with everything. Maybe he's simply letting her off the hook, contributing to the cover-up."

"If that's true, I'm going to be so mad. I can't accept that. I can't go along with it. I can't enable it. If that's what he's doing, then whatever we thought was going on between us is over before it even started."

She sat on his black leather couch. The one Lauren had made him buy, because that was the controlling person she was. Bonnie was going to make sure she helped Mitch find a new home, new stuff, new everything so he didn't have to live in a Lauren-created world anymore.

"I'm so tired." Emotionally and physically, Bonnie was exhausted. She couldn't think straight anymore. Maybe that was why everyone was able to believe Lauren. They were too tired to fight her lies.

"Why don't you go lie down?" Mitch suggested. "I have a guest room. You can close your eyes for a little bit, give yourself a chance to relax."

That sounded pretty spectacular at the moment. "Thank you. I can't tell you how much I appreciate you being here for me. And listening to my nonsense at this point."

Mitch wouldn't hear it. "You are not speaking nonsense. You're the only one I've heard be real all day." He showed her to the room, which had its own bathroom. She washed her face and lay down on the bed. She could sell this condo for good money. She would sell it for him and she would find him a new place to live. Maybe she would talk him into moving out of Blue Springs. Maybe it was time she moved out of Blue Springs. Her eyes grew heavy, and her thoughts slowed and quieted down.

Bonnie didn't know how long she slept; she only knew she was awakened by raised voices in the living room. It took her a minute to realize what was going on.

"What do you think is going to happen?"

"Keep your voice down. She's sleeping."

"Bonnie wants nothing to do with you, and it doesn't matter what you do or what you say, that's not going to change."

"Do you think you get to speak for her because you love her? She isn't yours to control. She gets to make her own choice and have her own opinions. You Coles are all the same—you love to tell people what to do. Love to be the boss, and you pretend it's love so that makes it okay. Well, I got away from your sister just in time, and I'll help Bonnie see you for what you are before it's too late as well."

Bonnie sat up. Her heart pounded in her chest. Had Aaron said he was in love with her? Why did Mitch think that? She shook her head. That was beside the point right now. She didn't want anyone to fight over her. She rolled out of bed and went to stop them from arguing. Aaron's face was red, and Mitch was standing much too close. Aaron pushed Mitch, and he stumbled backward and tripped over the footstool in front of the chair in the corner. He landed hard and almost hit his head on the glass coffee table.

"Stop it!" she shouted at Aaron, going over to Mitch to help him up. "Are you okay?"

"Come on, Bonnie," Aaron said. "I'm here to take you home."

"I don't need you to take me anywhere. I will go home when I'm ready to go home."

"I know you're upset. We need to talk about this. Me and you, without anyone else muddying the water." He glared at Mitch.

"I'm okay, Bonnie." Mitch winced as he tried to get up. "If you need to go, you should go. Don't worry about me."

He was clearly in more pain than he wanted to let on. She helped him to his feet.

"Please, Bonnie. Come with me. Your dad is waiting in the car."

So much for not involving anyone else who might muddy the waters. Her dad had been soft on Lauren from the get-go. He was part of the problem, not the solution.

"There's nothing to talk about. You believe your sister. I don't. I won't."

"What if the evidence proves she's innocent?"

"The cell phone tower her phone pinged off when you texted her? Easy, she could have had Theresa or Kathy driving her phone around, away from the house, so no one would know she was there."

"Do you hear yourself right now? Do you really believe that Lauren would be that diabolical?" Aaron asked. "Do you think she planned an elaborate scheme to vandalize my house and cover it up with multiple accomplices?"

"Yes," Mitch answered for her.

Aaron tugged at the front of his hair in frustration. "Literally no one is talking to you."

"I agree with him," Bonnie said in Mitch's defense. "I think it's more than possible."

"Oh my gosh." Aaron smacked his forehead with the heel of his hand. "You have turned into Lauren. You sound exactly like her. You're doing to her what she did to you. That is so hypocritical."

He might as well have stuck a dagger in her heart. That was what it felt like. She certainly hadn't gotten enough sleep to be able to take that hit with grace.

"Get out!" She pointed him toward the door. "Get out and tell my dad that you two can defend Lauren until you're blue in the face, but I am going to tell everyone and anyone that she was behind this."

Aaron's laugh was somewhat maniacal. "You just did it again. You're making the same arguments and threatening the same smear campaign. Listen to yourself."

"She told you to leave," Mitch said, getting in between them.

"I'm going to give you a couple days to come to your senses. You are better than this, Bonnie. You don't want to be hateful for the sake of being hateful like Lauren was."

"Is," she corrected him. "Your sister continues to be hateful. You're either too blind to see it or are choosing to ignore it."

He shook his head and left with nothing else to say. There wasn't anything else he could say. The damage had been done. Bonnie sat on the couch and held her head in her hands as the tears threatened to fall. Mitch sat beside her and gently rubbed her back.

"I'm sorry that got so ugly," he said softly and in such a contrast to the tone he had been using a moment ago.

"I thought he loved me."

"Aaron isn't a bad guy. You know that. I mean, he does some questionable things sometimes, but he's not bad."

She lifted her head. "What do you mean, questionable things?"

"I shouldn't say. That's gossiping, and I don't want to make you any more upset than you already are."

Now he had to tell her. "Spill it," she demanded.

"Last night, I met Aaron and Sasha out at that new gastropub downtown. Have you heard about it? Their appetizers are really good."

"I've been banned from all the local restaurants because of Lauren, so I wouldn't know."

"I'm sorry. I should be quiet. I'm not making things any better."

"Tell me." Her irritability level was at an all-time high. She didn't mean to snap, but that was the way it came out.

"We were hanging out, and Aaron started telling us about this date he has next week."

Their date. Had he planned to take her out as early as next week? Not getting their first date was another reason to be angry with Lauren. The list grew longer and longer with each passing minute.

"I guess he's going to the library gala with Hilde Rutherford. I didn't think anything of it at the time, but now that I know he's been trying to get something started with you, it seems a little sketchy."

Hilde Rutherford? Bonnie didn't know who that was. She'd heard of the Rutherford family, but Hilde wasn't familiar. Aaron had never mentioned her before. Of course, he'd been distant lately. Maybe that was the reason. Maybe he was spending time with Hilde.

"I'm sure it's nothing. It's not like the gala is very fun. Boring music, boring food, even more boring speakers. I mean, come on, have you ever had fun at that thing?"

Bonnie had never been to the library gala. She couldn't afford a ticket, and there was no way the Coles would have welcomed her this year. It was no wonder that Aaron had had to find a more suitable date. And if she wasn't good enough to take to the gala, how would she ever be good enough for something more? Aaron would never choose her over his family. Today made that evident.

"I've never been to one."

Mitch back straightened. "What? How have you been best friends with Lauren this many years and haven't gone to the Cole library gala?"

She shrugged. Who cared about a stupid gala? She hoped Aaron had a great time with Hilde and that the Coles welcomed her into their cult with open arms.

"You got a nice dress at home?" he asked, pulling her out of her head. Thoughts were getting dark in there—she needed to go home and get a real nap.

"I have plenty of nice dresses, why?"

"We're going," Mitch said with a quirked brow.

She was too tired to follow this conversation. "We're going where?"

"To the gala."

She barked out a laugh. "Do you have a death wish? Mr. Cole would flip his lid if you and I walked into the gala together."

Rubbing his hands together, he smirked like the Cheshire cat. "He absolutely would. And imagine how enraged Lauren would be."

She would be completely beside herself. There was no telling how Aaron would react. But he'd have Hilde to keep him distracted. "What time will you pick me up?"

IT HAD BEEN almost a week since Aaron had spoken to Bonnie. She didn't answer his calls or texts. Her dad had shared the news that Lauren's cell phone records cleared her from being a suspect. The only person whose cell phone pinged near the house was Mary, but she seemed the least likely of Lauren's friends to have vandalized the house unprompted. She didn't have a solid alibi, though, so the police were taking a closer look at her.

Bonnie couldn't care less that the evidence didn't line up and point a finger at Lauren. She was bound and determined to prove that it was Lauren, regardless of what the facts truly were. It was worse than trying to convince Lauren that Bonnie didn't cheat with Mitch. The two of them were more alike than either of them would admit.

"It frustrates me that whoever did this didn't stick to spray painting the walls. Why did they have to get it on the floors and the counters?" Sasha asked as he finished sanding down the painted floorboards.

"Because if they only sprayed the walls, it wouldn't be a pain in our butts to fix. I'm fairly sure their purpose was to make us miserable."

"Mission accomplished," David said from the kitchen. He'd decided they should sand down the cabinet doors that weren't broken and repaint them.

The alarm on Aaron's phone went off. He had to go home and clean up. He was due to pick Hilde up in two hours for the gala. His plan was to make an appearance, shake a few hands, chat up a couple major donors and get out of there. If Hilde wanted to stay longer, she could leave with her parents.

"I have to go," he said, putting his tools away. Looking at all the work that still had to be done was depressing. They had been so close to being done, and now it felt like they were basically starting over. Such a waste of time and money. Thank goodness for insurance.

"Will we see you tomorrow?" David asked, wiping his hands on one of his work rags. "I was going to pick up the new toilets in the morning."

"Tomorrow is Sunday. I think we need to take the day off and relax a little bit before we have to work our butts off the rest of the week," Aaron replied.

"Whatever you say, boss," Sasha said.

"Say a prayer for me, gentlemen. Between dealing with my mother and all the sucking up I have to do, I may not make it out alive."

"It's shame you have to be subjected to a party with caviar and champagne," Sasha said. "While surrounded by the town's rich and famous."

"Don't forget having to collect all those checks to help fund the library so people like you and me can read all the books we want for free," David added. "The sacrifice is real."

Aaron slapped his knee a couple times. "You two are a real comedy act. Hilarious. Let me know when the show is hitting the road. I'll be sure to buy a ticket in every city."

Sasha couldn't stop laughing. "I've got the perfect joke for the opener. A biker, a carpenter and a tortured rich guy walk into a gala…"

David shook his head but still chuckled at the big man's ridiculousness.

"Careful now, or the punch line of that joke will be, '…and the biker got fired,'" Aaron warned him.

Sasha's expression immediately turned serious. "That's not funny, boss man."

"You would know all about things that aren't funny." Aaron pretended to drop a microphone. "Boom."

"That's because everything about you is funny. Your face, your hair, your unusually long fingers."

Aaron glanced down at his hands. He didn't have unusually long fingers. Did he? "You're not worth the comeback. Have a good night," he said as he walked out the door.

He would survive a few hours of hobnobbing, he kept telling himself as he struggled to tie his bow tie and slid his feet into shiny dress shoes that rubbed his heels and left blisters every time he wore them.

He checked his phone. No new messages. No missed calls. What was Bonnie doing?

Was she really going to let Mitch fill her head full of conspiracy theories? At this point, she probably believed his father had hired someone who'd purposely made it look like Lauren did it, knowing she'd be vindicated and the case would go unsolved.

He stopped in his tracks. What if his father had done it? Or paid someone to do it? That wasn't such a far-fetched idea. His father had been beside himself when the police were holding Lauren for questioning. He wouldn't have expected her not to have an airtight alibi. He could have been freaking out that he set her up to take the fall.

He also wanted nothing more than for Aaron to give up house flipping and come back to the family business. His mom had been warning him all week that his dad wanted a couple minutes of his time at the gala tonight. Maybe he planned to make a big deal out of the vandalism and use it to lure Aaron back on board.

The more he thought about it, the more he was sure his dad had paid someone to destroy his house. He was the most likely suspect, hiding in plain sight. Getting him to admit it wasn't going to be easy, but Aaron would make him confess. He'd use his pride against him, forcing him to take credit because the plan was brilliant.

HILDE RUTHERFORD WAS not a talker. In fact, they had been together for more than an hour and the woman had said approximately seven words—if he counted "mmm-hmm" as two words. Aaron had schmoozed with all the important donors but had yet to see his father. It wasn't like him to not be front and center on this night. Maybe he was busy paying off his hired hand and getting the vandal out of town.

"Mr. Cole," someone from behind him said just as Aaron spotted Walter Cole enter the gala.

"Can you hang on one second? I need to speak to my father about something. I'll be right back."

"It's kind of an emergency," the young man in waitstaff attire said, following him as he crossed the room to get to his dad.

"Can you handle it on your own for five more minutes while I talk to my father? Please."

His dad held a drink in one hand and laughed at what was most likely a terrible joke.

"I'm not sure Mr. Bennett and Miss Windsor will wait that long. I sense they're ready to make a scene."

space in a minute. They don't have the cash, trust me."

Mitch's big plan was to demand a refund for the tickets he'd paid for when they were refused entrance. Then, while the others re-fund was in thought, he would threaten to sue the library for installing a paid ghost.

CHAPTER NINETEEN

THERE HAD BEEN multiple points in time leading up to this one when Bonnie thought this might be a bad idea. Now that they were in the library and she could hear all the voices coming from the party, she was sure of it.

Dressed in the blush-pink bridesmaid's gown she'd worn on that fateful wedding day, Bonnie wished she could be transported back in time to that morning. She would have confronted Mitch and told him to break up with Lauren, not because he thought he was in love with her, but because he was sure he wasn't in love with Lauren. There were no time machines in the library, however.

"Maybe we should leave," she whispered to Mitch as they waited at the check-in area. "Their reactions may be less satisfying than we think."

"It's fine. We'll be making our grand entrance in a minute. They don't have the cash, trust me."

Mitch's big plan was to demand a refund for the tickets he'd paid for when they were refused entry. If they didn't give him the refund in cash tonight, he would threaten to sue the library for not allowing a paid guest entry, guessing they would rather let him in than take the risk of losing all the money they were trying to make tonight in court.

"You have two minutes remaining," Mitch announced to the young man assigned to guard them.

"We're doing everything we can to resolve this issue, sir."

The Cole library was one of the most beautiful buildings in Blue Springs. Inspired by the Guggenheim in New York, it had a spiraling tower and rotunda. Each of the four floors housed different genres of books as well as classrooms and computer labs. They often had charity events on the main level under the magnificent domed ceiling.

The other young man who had been tasked with finding out what to do with them returned with Aaron in tow. He looked less than pleased to see them there. Instead of that making Bonnie feel empowered, she was quickly overwhelmed with shame.

Aaron spoke only to Bonnie. He didn't even spare Mitch a sideways glance. "This is what you want to do? This is the statement you want to make in front of everyone here?"

Bonnie swallowed hard. Her throat was suddenly too tight to let the words pass. She wanted to shake her head no, but she nodded yes against her better judgment. The disappointment in his eyes was almost too much to bear. He wasn't angry—he was sad.

"I'm surprised they pulled you away. I thought for sure they were going to bring the big guns. Your dad and sister are here, right?" Mitch asked. When Aaron didn't respond with more than a glare, he continued, "How is the date with Hilde going so far? Are you two hitting it off?"

Mitch had reminded her why she was there. If Aaron could go on dates, so could she. Straightening her shoulders, she found her voice. "Are we free to join the party?"

"I hope this makes you feel better, but I'm betting it won't." He stepped aside and waved them past.

Mitch offered her his arm, and they strode

past Aaron. Bonnie's stomach rolled, and her heart was beating so fast she was afraid she was going to have a full-blown panic attack. They walked out into the festivities. Wait-staff with trays of champagne flutes glided by. Mitch snagged two and handed her one.

The whispers and stares began immediately. Bonnie felt more like a zoo animal on display than a guest at a fancy party. All the years she'd dreamed of coming to the gala, she had not imagined herself as a spectacle. Every reasonable part of her brain was screaming for her to leave. She didn't need to do this. Aaron had seen her. That was enough. He knew that she knew he had brought someone else as his date. Angering Lauren didn't seem worth the negative attention she was receiving from everyone else there.

"You are not here. You are not here with Mitch. You are not here with Mitch wearing that dress." Lauren's cousin Kathy gaped at them. "You have no shame. I don't even know you."

Jeanne Watson and her tightly curled blond hair was also there. "You need to leave right now," she said.

Mary came swooping in and grabbed Bonnie by the arm, ushering her down one of the halls to the library offices. "Why are you doing this? Are you some kind of glutton for punishment?"

"Did you help Lauren destroy Aaron's house?"

"Bonnie..."

"Yes or no? All I need is a one-word answer."

Mary pushed her long brown hair over her shoulder. "No. Why would I do that?"

"I don't know," Bonnie admitted. She'd felt so paranoid all week, sure that everyone had conspired to ruin every good thing in her life.

"When you accused me of being a bad friend, I deserved it, because I have been. By not standing up *for* you and by not standing up *to* her, I let you both down. But now you're accusing me of vandalism? When do you think I had the time to turn into a criminal?"

Bonnie shrugged.

"What about you? Why are you here trying to convince the whole town they were right about you? Why would you spend all summer professing your innocence and then do this?"

Bonnie hung her head. She didn't have a

good answer to that, either. She was angry. She'd wanted to hurt Lauren like she had hurt Bonnie since the wedding. Mitch had simply been a willing accomplice.

"You should leave now. Lauren will hear things, but if she doesn't see you, maybe it won't bother her as much."

"Too late," Lauren said from down the hall. She slowly made her way to where the two women were huddled together. "Nice dress."

"You win, Lauren," Bonnie said. "I thought I could be as mean and hateful as you've been, but I don't have the stomach for it."

"Well, for someone who doesn't believe they're cut out for the revenge game, I think showing up in your bridesmaid dress on the arm of my ex-fiancé is next-level hatefulness. Kudos to you for really knocking it out of the park."

Her tone was so dry and flat, it was hard to tell how angry she was. Bonnie didn't care. She'd thought sticking it to her would make things better, but it hadn't. "I was trying hard to think like you, and that's what I came up with. Unlike you, however, I can't spend the whole night here making you and everyone else uncomfortable, so I'm leaving."

Lauren blocked her from going. "Do you love him?"

Bonnie was so tired of this rivalry that neither one of them was going to win, because Lauren couldn't win and Bonnie didn't want to win the prize. Bonnie didn't love Mitch. She never would.

"Because he loves you," Lauren said before Bonnie could respond. "And I don't mean he thinks he's in love with you because you smiled at him one time like Mitch. I'm talking about he cares about you and wants what's best for you and would give up everything for you kind of love."

Bonnie's brows drew together. "Wait, you weren't asking me about Mitch?"

Lauren pressed the palm of her hand to her forehead and closed her eyes. "Mary, please help her out. I can't."

"Aaron," Mary whispered.

His name made her heart skip a beat. The way she felt about Aaron wasn't like anything she'd ever felt with anyone else. It killed her that she had been a disappointment to him tonight.

"Do you love my brother?" Lauren asked again.

"What makes you think he loves me when he asked someone else to be his date tonight?"

Lauren barked out a laugh. "You think he asked Hilde to be his date? My mother is trying to get Hilde's father to invest in some run-down museum she wants to renovate. She made Aaron bring Hilde to get in her parents' good graces."

Always the dutiful son. "Okay, so he's not dating someone else, but I'm not sure he's in love with me. In fact, I think he might be more disappointed in me tonight than I am."

"Do you love my brother?" Lauren asked one more time. "Answer the question. Don't come up with reasons why he couldn't possibly love you, because I have already talked to him about this and he's extremely clear about how he feels."

Bonnie's heart shuddered. Being loved was a gift.

"Yes," she answered. "I love your brother."

She'd done it. She'd said it. Admitting her feelings out loud felt good, even if she hadn't said the words to Aaron himself.

Lauren actually smiled. Could she be pleased about this? "I wish someone would have made sure Mitch and I were on the same page about the whole love thing before we walked down the aisle. That's why we didn't make it." Lauren gave a little shrug and rolled her eyes. "That, and he's a doofus."

Bonnie covered her mouth, feeling guilty for laughing. "Now what?" she asked.

"Now I let my brother be happy even though I'm maybe not." Lauren pressed her lips together and dropped her eyes, like she was trying to maintain control of her emotions. She looked back up. "I'm also going to let my best friend be happy, because she deserves it after the way I treated her."

Where had this Lauren been for the last few months? Why had she stayed away for so long? "I'm sorry you're not happy. I know you think you were supposed to marry Mitch, but fate has bigger and better plans for you."

Lauren laughed. "Two minutes ago you were telling me how evil I was, and now you feel bad for me? You are the opposite of mean and hateful. It's just not in you, Bon. You are too nice."

Sometimes nice didn't feel like a compliment. "I don't want to be a pushover, though."

"You have stood up for yourself more times than you should have needed to this summer. You're no pushover. And don't feel bad for me. I won't always feel this way. There's someone out there who will love me the way Aaron loves you."

Aaron loved her. He loved her in spite of her flaws. *Hopefully*.

Lauren touched Bonnie's arm. "I also should take a minute to say I'm sorry. I'm sorry for everything I said and did that hurt you. And I'm sorry for asking other people to hurt you as well. Most of all, I'm sorry for not trusting you even though you'd never given me a reason not to."

Okay, this wasn't real. Could she have hit her head at some point? Maybe Lauren had walked up to her and knocked her out instead of talking to her. *Sorry* wasn't in Lauren's vocabulary unless she was referring to how someone else was about to feel. Bonnie discreetly pinched herself.

"Can you repeat that?"

"Ha ha. You heard me. I. Am. Sorry. I grew up thinking I didn't need to apologize for being me, but let's be honest, that attitude is what got me left at the altar."

She wasn't wrong.

"If we're apologizing, I better go," Mary

said. "Lauren, I'm sorry for not telling you that you were being a terrible person and for not being honest with you about how I felt. Friends don't let friends be jerks."

"Apology accepted. I'm sorry I asked you to shun someone you care about. I shouldn't dictate how anybody lives their lives." Lauren and Mary hugged it out.

When they were finished, Mary turned to Bonnie. "I'm sorry for being more worried about my social standing than being a good person to another good person. You deserved better than that."

"I'm sorry for thinking both of you would ruin Aaron's house. I'm also sorry for putting on this dress tonight and for showing up with Mitch. That was a low blow. It didn't make me feel good, and all I want to do is tell Aaron the same thing."

"I can't believe you're still here." The gang was all here. Kathy's sneer and Jeanne's scowl came to fight. "Do you want us to get security to throw her out, Lauren?" Kathy asked.

Lauren took Bonnie by the hand and gave her a reassuring smile. "No." She looked over at the two of them. "I would like you both to apologize for being mean to Bonnie to impress me. Anyone who is impressed by meanness and cruelty shouldn't be someone you *want* to impress."

"What?" Jeanne's scowl turned into a confused grimace.

"You want us to apologize to her?" Kathy clarified.

"You should want to apologize. You have been really mean."

Bonnie didn't want them to say anything. If they had to be commanded to apologize, it wasn't much of an apology. "Let's just agree the slate is clean between us all. How about that? Let's start over."

"That's more than we deserve," Lauren said. "Have you two seen Aaron around? We need to find him."

"He was waiting to talk to your dad last I saw him," Kathy said.

"Perfect. I need to talk to him as well. I don't suppose your dad would want his job back, Bonnie?"

"I think he likes working for your brother, but he wouldn't have to work so hard if some of his friends felt like their jobs weren't at risk by helping him out."

"I will make sure that happens. Your dad

was way nicer to me than he should have been this summer."

Bonnie gave her a side hug. "He loves you like one of his own."

"Let's get my dad on the same page."

"DAD, I NEED five minutes," Aaron said for the third time. Once he confronted his dad, he was leaving. The sooner the better. His heart couldn't handle watching Bonnie and Mitch whisper to one another or seeing her laugh at something he said. He didn't want to be here when Lauren's hyenas attacked.

"There's something I wanted to talk to you about as well. Come out here." His dad took him through some doors and into a room with books in sealed boxes. Rare Books was written on the label on the shelf.

"What did you want to talk about?" Aaron asked, figuring after his dad made his comeback-and-work-for-me speech, Aaron would question if it was possible that he'd hired someone to vandalize the house.

"Your house."

"My house? What about my house?" Aaron couldn't believe he was going to admit it without Aaron having to trick it out of him.

"I know who vandalized it."

Of course he did. Why was he being honest about it? Aaron suddenly had a sinking feeling that he was going to use it as a warning. Come work for him or he would destroy every house he tried to flip.

"Dad, I'm never going to come back to Cole Industries. Nothing you do can stop me from fixing up houses. You could wreck them and I would simply rebuild. That's my life's work now."

The lines on his father's forehead creased deeper. "Why would I wreck your houses?"

"You said you know who vandalized the one on Greenbriar."

"I do. I've had a PI following Mitch around since he landed in Paris. I wanted to make sure he didn't do anything else that would get back to your sister and cause her any more pain. When he came back to Blue Springs, I wanted to make sure he stayed away from Lauren and see if Bonnie had anything to do with him."

Aaron couldn't breathe. Mitch. Bonnie wouldn't believe it. Not without more proof.

"She didn't, by the way." His dad pulled an envelope out of his inside jacket pocket and handed it to Aaron. "The investigator didn't realize you owned the house when he took these pictures. We only meet once a week to go over what he sees, so I didn't find out until yesterday. I wanted to give you a chance to decide how you want to handle this. If you want to turn it over to the police, you can. If you want to use it to perhaps make a deal, you could do that, too."

Aaron opened the envelope and unfolded the small stack of photos. Photo after photo of Mitch buying the spray paint, throwing landscaping bricks through the front windows, kicking down the door, destroying all of Aaron's hard work.

It all made sense now. He had heard Sasha say Bonnie and Aaron were meant to be and got jealous. He'd wrecked the house, making it look very Lauren-esque. Then, he'd showed up at the house first thing in the morning to "help" clean up and offer Bonnie a shoulder to cry on and stoke her anger at Lauren, knowing that could drive a wedge between Bonnie and Aaron.

It was actually a well-thought-out plan. Aaron needed to be sure never to underestimate Mitch's ability to be cutthroat again.

He put the pictures back in the envelope. "Thank you for giving me these. I need to think about how I want to handle this."

"I trust you'll make the right decision." He started to leave, but Aaron stopped him.

"Dad, I have to apologize. I wanted to talk to you tonight because I thought maybe you had something to do with the vandalism. I'd convinced myself that you didn't want me to be successful."

His father tipped his chin down to his chest. "Why wouldn't I want you to be successful?"

"Because you want me to work for you instead."

"I do want that, but I also want you to be the best at whatever you do. Once you hired David, I knew you'd be fine. And according to your mother, you are very good at what you're doing. She's been so inspired by you, she wants to do some renovations around town."

The ton of bricks Aaron had been carrying around since quitting his job lifted off his shoulders. To hear his dad accept his decision gave him a peace he'd thought was impossible.

"I'm not going to have to compete with Mom, am I?"

"Your mom isn't going to do residential stuff. Don't worry."

"Oh my goodness, you two are hard to find." Lauren came barreling in, dragging Bonnie by the hand. "We need to talk to you guys."

Aaron wasn't sure what was happening, and it wasn't clear if Bonnie was here willingly or under duress. He was stressed for her either way.

"Dad, Bonnie is my best friend. I was wrong to attack her because Mitch was a jerk with bad timing. We need to change the narrative in this town. I don't want Bonnie to ever feel unwelcome again."

"Okay." Their dad threw his hands up. "Whatever you want, princess."

"Don't say that," she said, looking a bit flustered. "I want you to tell me no sometimes. If you and Mom always do what I say, I don't know if I'm making the right decision or not. You let me make a lot of bad decisions this summer."

"I want you to be happy."

"Being hateful didn't make me happy, Daddy."

"Should I be recording this so we have proof that you said it when Dad tells you you can't have something or do something?" Aaron asked.

"No, but you're all my witnesses."

"Okay, I'll tell you no sometimes. Anything else?"

"We're done with you. You can go back to the party," she said, shooing the older man out of the room.

Bonnie pressed her lips together to hold back her laughter. It made Aaron happy to see her smiling. Although he was curious how they'd gotten to this point.

"Aaron, if you break Bonnie's heart, I'll forgive you, but I'll be super mad. Don't break her heart. Tell her what you told me." She turned to Bonnie. "And you should also tell him what you told me. I'm going to get some more champagne and pay someone on the waitstaff to drop a tray of champagne flutes on Mitch."

She left them alone. Aaron's head was spinning. "Did you crash the gala with Mitch wearing your bridesmaid dress and make up with my sister?"

"Trust me, I don't really understand what is happening, either."

They both chuckled softly. Lauren was being Lauren. Good Lauren, thankfully. Unless your name was Mitch Bennett.

"You have to try to explain," he pleaded. He had gone from brokenhearted to hopeful in one hour.

"Your sister apologized. She said she wants us to be happy even if she's going through a hard time. Then she asked me if I loved you."

Aaron was caught off balance by the *L* word. He wasn't sure he should ask the next question, but given the evidence he was holding in his hand, he felt confident that if she hadn't answered the way he hoped, he might be able to change her mind.

"What did you say?"

Bonnie fidgeted with the clutch in her hands. Her teeth worried her bottom lip. Those green eyes lifted to his, and she didn't have to say a word. He knew.

"I said yes."

"I love you," they said at the same time.

"How did you know what I was going to say?"

He didn't know how to explain it with words, so he took her hand and placed it on his chest. "Do you feel that?" She nodded. His heart was beating like a jackhammer. "That's how I knew. I could feel it." He leaned down and pressed his lips to hers. There was no doubt she felt his love. He felt hers from the hair on top of his head to his toes.

"I owe you an apology," she said.

He placed a finger on her lips. "No apologies. We have been stuck in the middle of someone else's drama for too long. I am certain that once we break free of that, we're never going to need to say we're sorry again."

"I never want to hurt you. I hope you know that I went off the deep end because it killed me to see you so sad. I wish I knew who did that to your house. I agree with you that it wasn't Lauren or Mary."

"It wasn't them. I thought maybe my dad had paid someone, but it wasn't my dad, either. And it wasn't some random guy. I know exactly who it was."

"You do? How do you—" Before she could

finish her sentence, Aaron handed her the envelope.

"My dad saved the day by being his over-protective self."

Bonnie's brows pinched together as she slid the photos out of the envelope. "You have got to be kidding me." She flipped through page after page. "I am so stupid. I believed he was actually worried about you, worried about me. I thought he showed up that morning genuinely willing to help his friend. He's...ugh!"

"My dad said I can do what I want with these pictures. He said I could turn them over to the police or I can use them how I see fit."

"What does that mean?"

"If he's convicted, he's going to pay a fine, he's going to owe me money, but there's no real consequence other than a financial one, which won't bother him at all."

"That's not fair."

"Or I could show him the pictures and let him know I know what he did and offer him a deal."

Bonnie, sweet Bonnie, had no idea what that meant. He loved that she had a hard time even thinking in a conniving way. "What kind of deal?"

"I could run him out of town. He leaves. We never have to see him again. I feel like that would be good for Lauren, it would be good for me and I hope you think it would be good for you." He wouldn't do it if she didn't agree. She knew what it felt like to have people try to push her out.

"It would be good for me," she agreed.

"Then that's what we'll do. Goodbye, Mitch."

"Goodbye, Mitch." She kissed him again. He could feel her smiling under his lips. He could kiss a smiling Bonnie all day long.

"Before he leaves, though, I need to do one thing," she said, taking him by the hand and leading him back out to the party.

She took a champagne glass off one of the passing trays and strode right up to Mitch, who was leaning against the bar and doing what he did best. His face lit up when he saw her coming his way. Aaron could relate to that feeling. Seeing Bonnie brightened a day. She had a light inside her that warmed his soul.

Once Bonnie was close enough, she lifted her glass and dumped the champagne on Mitch's head. He leaped back and shouted something about her being crazy. Nobody called Aaron's girlfriend names. He rescued her even though it didn't seem like she needed it.

"You are not a nice person! Not nice!"

Aaron laughed as he pulled her away. "I love your use of very powerful insults."

"There were other things I wanted to say, but I didn't want people to think I was that kind of a woman."

"Good idea." They happened to walk right by Hilde and her parents. He quickly introduced them all. "Hilde, would it be okay if I took my friend home? Do you think you could get a ride home with your parents?"

"Mmm-hmm," she answered.

Nine words total between them. There was no way she was going to miss him.

"Let's get you home. You need to change out of that dress. And maybe we should burn it."

"Hey, this is the dress I was wearing the first time you came to my rescue. It was also the dress I was wearing when your sister apologized to me for the first time. This is a dress I never want to forget."

Aaron took her by the hand. "You, in that

dress, are pretty unforgettable, but I'm in love with the woman, not the dress."

She didn't even bat an eye. "We burn it, then."

CHAPTER TWENTY

"Two new toilets ready to be installed," her dad announced.

"I feel like we should throw the broken ones in Mitch's living room. He breaks it, he buys it," Bonnie said.

"I think we should get to tie him to a tree and spray paint him," Sasha suggested. "Do you think we can fit that in the agreement?"

"I feel like that could get us arrested," Aaron said, cocking an eyebrow.

"Fine, I'll spray paint his car on my own," Sasha said, shaking one of the paint cans.

Bonnie looked over the project list. There was so much to do. She needed to reschedule the open house, which was a huge bummer. Houses always sold better right before school started. If they had to push the open house until sometime in September, they were going to miss that window. The three of them could only do so much. Even if they worked around the clock, they needed at least a month.

A knock on the door got everyone's attention.

"Are you expecting something?" Bonnie asked Aaron, who shook his head. She went to answer it, since the men were all busy.

"Please be little girls selling cookies, please be little girls selling cookies," Sasha muttered.

Bonnie pulled the door open and was blown away. Lauren, dressed in overalls and brand-new work boots, was on the front stoop, holding a bucket full of paint brushes and rollers. She looked ready to work, but that wasn't what took Bonnie's breath away. Lauren wasn't alone. Behind her were probably about thirty people. Mary, Theresa, Cheryl and Kathy were all there. A bunch of guys who used to work with her dad at Cole Industries had come with their tools and their skills. There was a plumbing van, some landscapers, dozens of able-bodied men and women.

"What did you do?"

"I put my power to influence others to

good use. These guys are all here to help get things done, and it's all free."

There might not have been any little girls selling cookies, but the kindness of these people was priceless.

"Come on in, everybody!" Lauren marched them all inside.

When Aaron saw what Lauren had done, he had tears in his eyes. This time, Bonnie was happy about the fact that his sister had made him cry. Aaron couldn't thank everyone enough for their willingness to help him get this place on the market.

Her dad got the overwhelming job of managing an entire crew and then some. No more wearing multiple hats. He got to be the real project manager now.

By the end of the day, they'd finished what would have taken the three of them all month. Their helpers scraped the paint off the countertops, salvaging them so they didn't have to order new. All the drywall was repaired, the whole house was painted, the landscaping was fixed, ceiling fans were replaced, floors were stained and the toilets were installed.

"I can't believe what happened today," Aaron said, lying down in the middle of the living room. Most everyone had gone for the day except for the original four, Lauren and Mary. "I feel like we can start moving the staging furniture in. I mean, we went from not even close to being done to done in twelve hours."

"That was amazing. The people of this town really stepped up," Sasha said before he took a long swig from his water bottle.

Bonnie's dad sat at the card table, reviewing the project list.

"How's it looking, Dad?"

"We can definitely start filling this place up. Did you call and set up the appliance delivery?" he asked Aaron.

"I did," Aaron replied. "They come Tuesday."

Bonnie couldn't care less about when the appliances were coming. They had been working all day, and she was looking forward to some alone time with her new boyfriend. Everyone needed to get out.

"My work is done here," Lauren said, wiping her hands on her overalls. She had done more work today than she had probably ever done in her life. "I will happily come back when your stagers show up."

Aaron wrapped his little sister in a bear hug. "Thank you so much for everything you did to make this happen."

"You are so welcome."

Seeing them getting along and working together warmed Bonnie's heart. It was nice to see them not only interact as family but as friends.

Sasha open his arms to Lauren. "Good Lauren, we are so grateful for you. I am glad David was right and told us not to give up on you."

"Big Sasha, I am grateful for you and your superlong arms, because without you, I wouldn't have been able to get that piece of pizza."

Bonnie chuckled. They had ordered pizzas for all the workers at lunchtime, and Sasha had come to Lauren's rescue when she wanted the last piece of pepperoni. Lauren wasn't the only one who was fond of Sasha—Mary had found him quite interesting. Every time Bonnie walked past her, she was next to Sasha and laughing about something.

She opted not to go with Lauren, instead asking Sasha if he wanted to grab some dinner with her. He was more than willing to oblige her. They cleaned up and headed out. The only one left was her dad.

"Can I take anything to the car for you, Dad?" she asked, hoping to help move him along.

"Nope, I'm good," he said not picking up on the hint. He got up from the table and was inspecting the kitchen cabinets.

Bonnie lost her patience with him. "You do know that the kitchen cabinets will be here tomorrow, right?"

"Why do I feel like you're trying to get rid of me?"

"Probably because she is," Aaron said.

The old man nodded. "Okay, I'll get out of your hair." He gave Bonnie a kiss on the cheek. "I'm glad you two have worked things out. For the record, I wasn't too keen on you being a couple when we first started this thing."

"And now?" Bonnie couldn't see what he would object to anymore.

"Now, I want you both to be happy, and I think you'll be happiest together."

She couldn't agree more. As soon as her dad left, Bonnie fell into Aaron's arms.

"Alone at last," she said.

He pressed his cheek against the top of her head. "It's funny you say that, because I was just thinking about how nice it is that we don't ever have to be alone again because we have each other."

His words melted her heart. "I love that."

"I love you."

She pulled back and looked up at him. "I love you, too."

He bent down and kissed her in a way that made her feel that tingle all the way in her toes. She felt so safe in his arms. For the first time in a long time, she didn't worry about what the next day would bring. She wasn't afraid of what someone was going to think about her. There was such a feeling of contentment deep in her soul that assured her everything was going to be all right.

"I don't know about you, but I am starving," Aaron said as they swayed back and forth in a tiny circle even though there was no music.

"I could eat."

"Please tell me you have some marshmallows at your house, because I am craving some PBM sandwiches."

"I do not," Bonnie said. "But I am no longer banished from the town market. I can go in there and buy whatever I want. No one will stop me. Is it wrong that part of me wants to go into every place that refused me service and be like, 'Whose money aren't you getting now? Mine!' The other part of me wants an apple danish from The Bean right now."

"I think we should give people a second chance. Everyone except Tim over at Tim's Taqueria. I don't want his tacos, and his margaritas aren't that good. The day we went there was his second chance, so too bad, Tim."

Bonnie giggled into his chest and waved her hand. "See ya, Tim."

Outside the skies were getting dark. The shadows began to grow longer in the house, and the world seemed just a bit quieter. Aaron took her hand and spun her around and pulled her close.

"You know, had Lauren and Mitch got married, we would have been dance partners that night at the reception," Aaron said.

"That's true. We missed out on our first dance because of those two."

"I hope we dance a lot. I could see us dancing right here twenty years from now. We'll have four kids."

"Four? I am an only child. I wouldn't know what to do with four children."

"Fine, three."

"Two."

"I read somewhere that the average couple has two and a half. Let's split the difference," he joked.

"You think we should have a half of a kid?"

"Maybe we share him with another family. We get him Mondays, Wednesdays, Fridays and every other Saturday."

"I think that could work."

"You think so?" Bonnie nodded her head. "Yeah?" She shook it. "No?"

"No, I don't think that will work," she said through the giggles. If the rest of her life was this lighthearted and silly, she'd be a happy girl.

"Me, either. Let's stick with two or three. We round up or round down depending on how we feel after we have two. Two can be draining, especially when the second child is like Lauren."

Bonnie stopped. "Promise me our children will only be like Good Lauren."

Tipping his head a little, Aaron replied, "I'm not sure we get to decide their personalities. I feel like that's determined before we get our hands on them. But if we get a firecracker like Lauren, we will teach her to be kind and patient, like her mama."

"Sounds like a plan."

"I don't think I can sell this house," Aaron said. "We just decided how many kids we're going to have here, and I've imagined dancing with you when I'm old and you're gray."

She smacked him lightly on the arm. "I am not going to go gray. I'm blonde—I'll stay blonde."

"Fine, I'm going to get old and gray and you will stay young and forever blonde, but I want to do it here. We put so much work into it, and you picked out all your favorite things."

Bonnie shook her head. "This house is very nice and it has a lot of things I like in it, but this is not our home. Trust me, when we find our house, we'll both know it."

"Are you sure? I mean, your dad had three near-death experiences in this house. That gives it character, right?"

"Rule number one when flipping a house—don't get too attached," she reminded him. "Don't break the rules on the first flip."

He resumed their dancing. "You're right. Good thing I've got you here to keep me on the right house-flipping path."

"Always."

THE OPEN HOUSE was set to begin at noon, but Aaron was there a little early. He'd walked around the outside of the house four times. The landscaping looked good.

"Everything looks amazing," Bonnie assured him when he came inside and couldn't stop pacing. "Don't worry."

That was easy for her to say. She had been there all morning setting up vases of fresh flowers, organizing her materials, dusting everything for the third time. Her nerves had already been worked out.

"This is my big day. This is my house-flipping final exam. Whatever grade I get here will determine my final grade in the class."

Bonnie slipped her arms around the back of his neck. "If I was handing out grades, I would give you an A."

Panic shot through him. "Not an A-plus? What's wrong with it? Is something not right? I can have your dad over here in a couple minutes to fix whatever made you say A instead of A-plus."

Bonnie put both hands on his cheeks. "Aaron. Relax. I didn't realize your grading scale allowed for pluses and minuses. This place is an A-plus. Someone is going to buy it and give you enough money to do it all over again with a new house. There's a good one that just went up on Timberland. We should check it out this week."

How could she be ready to move on to another house when they still owned this one? Aaron was a one-house-at-a-time man. He needed to see this one through to the end before he could focus on the next one.

"What time are you meeting my dad?" Bonnie asked, moving the brochures back to where she had them after he moved them an inch to the right. "You know you can't be here when the open house starts."

He'd been told that repeatedly. Everyone was so worried he was going to oversell the place. He had to trust that Bonnie knew what she was doing, so Sasha and David were coming to get him and they were going to shoot pool until the open house was over.

"They should be here any minute."

"Wow! Look at this place!" Sasha's voice boomed through the house. "It looks so different with stuff in it."

"Please get him out of here before he wears a path into the wood floors with his pacing. Go, have fun, and when you come back, I'll tell you all about the nice people who want to make an offer."

Aaron scanned the open living area one more time for any noticeable flaws. There were none. This place was perfect. He left with Sasha to meet up with David, who was sitting in the car.

"You did good, kid. For your first flip, you handled all the setbacks with grace," David said once they got to the pool hall and ordered their round of drinks. "I hope you feel like you learned something."

"I learned don't go poking wasps' nests behind old pantry doors, never give Bonnie a sledgehammer and don't trust this guy—" he pointed at Sasha "—to be paying attention when using a nail gun."

Sasha tried to defend himself. "It was one time. And it was Bonnie's fault for distracting me."

"Well, hopefully you learn from some of my successes as well as my slipups," David said.

"You were a great teacher." Aaron held up his glass. "I can't wait to see what we learn on the next house."

"When we can hire a bigger crew," Sasha said, raising his.

"And can use local contractors," David added, holding up his ice water.

"And don't have anyone breaking in to wreck it right at the end." Aaron clinked his glass against theirs. "Seriously, I could not have asked for two better people to get me through this first flip. I really appreciate all your hard work. Drinks and pool are on me today."

Sasha and David readily agreed to that. They spent the next couple hours laughing and giving each other a hard time. Before he knew it, the open house was over and Aaron could go back and find out how things went.

David gave him a little pep talk as they walked inside. "Now, just remember, an open house hopefully brings in some potential buyers, but it also attracts nosy neighbors and people who want to see what you did to update the place. You're going to get people looking at this place for the next couple weeks. Open houses give Bonnie feedback. Don't be upset if people don't go write up offers today."

Keep expectations low was the overall message Aaron was getting from that little speech. Bonnie was cleaning up in the kitchen when they arrived.

"How did it go? Please tell me it went well even if you have to lie to me."

She wore an easy smile. "It went great. Lots of people. Lots of questions. Lots of interest. I had a few Realtors walk through so they could speak about it to potential buyers down the road. They thought we had it priced right. They loved a lot of the things you did here. It was a good day."

"Anyone talk about making an offer?" he asked, forgetting all about lowering those expectations.

"I did have one couple say they might go home and talk about it."

"Really?" Sasha said. "But did you have anyone actually write up an offer like this one?"

Aaron's brow furrowed. "What are you talking about?"

A BRIDESMAID TO REMEMBER

Sasha pulled a folded piece of paper out of his back pocket. "Bonnie and I wrote this up last night. I think you'll find the offer is quite fair."

Aaron snatched it out of Sasha's hands. Sure enough, his redheaded friend wanted to buy the house for five thousand dollars over the asking price.

"You want to buy this house?"

"I love this house. I love this town. My family is here. My friends. I think it's time I settle down, and I can't think of a better house to do that in than this one."

Aaron was speechless. He wrapped his arms around Sasha the best he could and hugged that giant of a man hard. "Why did you torture me all day when you knew I had a sale all along?" he asked the three of them.

"We wanted you to have the full experience," Bonnie said. "You won't be selling every house to the guys who helped you build it moving forward."

He knew that would be the case, but he was happy that the first one would be somewhere he would be welcome to visit in the future.

"I guess we can go look at that house on Timberland."

"Which house on Timberland?" David asked.

"Bonnie wants me to look at a house over there for my next flip."

"Not *the* house on Timberland?" David asked Bonnie, who shrugged coyly.

David shook his head and laughed.

"What?"

"Nothing," Bonnie replied, giving her dad a warning look.

"It's clearly not nothing. What's up with the house on Timberland?"

"It's her dream house."

"It's not my dream house. It was my dream house when I was little. Who knows how I'll feel about it as a grown woman?"

Aaron placed his hands on her hips. "You want me to flip your dream home?"

"So much for flipping houses your crew won't want to buy," Sasha noted.

"If I flip your dream home and you buy it, I'm going to have to live in it with you. Forever."

He leaned down and kissed her so she'd know without a doubt he meant it. She was the only one he wanted to spend forever with. When she pulled back, the smile on her face made his heart skip a beat. There was no question she felt the same way.

Bonnie put her arms around his neck and tickled the hair on his nape. "I'm counting on it."

* * * * *

Be sure to look for Amy Vastine's next Harlequin Heartwarming book in May 2020!

Get 4 FREE REWARDS!

We'll send you 2 FREE Books plus 2 FREE Mystery Gifts.

Love Inspired® Suspense books feature Christian characters facing challenges to their faith... and lives.

FREE Value Over **$20**

YES! Please send me 2 FREE Love Inspired® Suspense novels and my 2 FREE mystery gifts (gifts are worth about $10 retail). After receiving them, if I don't wish to receive any more books, I can return the shipping statement marked "cancel." If I don't cancel, I will receive 6 brand-new novels every month and be billed just $5.24 each for the regular-print edition or $5.99 each for the larger-print edition in the U.S., or $5.74 each for the regular-print edition or $6.24 each for the larger-print edition in Canada. That's a savings of at least 13% off the cover price. It's quite a bargain! Shipping and handling is just 50¢ per book in the U.S. and $1.25 per book in Canada.* I understand that accepting the 2 free books and gifts places me under no obligation to buy anything. I can always return a shipment and cancel at any time. The free books and gifts are mine to keep no matter what I decide.

Choose one: ☐ **Love Inspired® Suspense**
Regular-Print
(153/353 IDN GNWN)

☐ **Love Inspired® Suspense**
Larger-Print
(107/307 IDN GNWN)

Name (please print)

Address   Apt. #

City   State/Province   Zip/Postal Code

Mail to the Reader Service:
IN U.S.A.: P.O. Box 1341, Buffalo, NY 14240-8531
IN CANADA: P.O. Box 603, Fort Erie, Ontario L2A 5X3

Want to try 2 free books from another series! Call 1-800-873-8635 or visit www.ReaderService.com.

THE FORTUNES OF TEXAS COLLECTION!

18 FREE BOOKS in all!

Treat yourself to the rich legacy of the Fortune and Mendoza clans in this remarkable 50-book collection. This collection is packed with cowboys, tycoons and Texas-sized romances!

YES! Please send me **The Fortunes of Texas Collection** in Larger Print. This collection begins with 3 FREE books and 2 FREE gifts in the first shipment. Along with my 3 free books, I'll also get the next 4 books from The Fortunes of Texas Collection, in LARGER PRINT, which I may either return and owe nothing, or keep for the low price of $5.24 U.S./$5.89 CDN each plus $2.99 for shipping and handling per shipment*. If I decide to continue, about once a month for 8 months I will get 6 or 7 more books but will only need to pay for 4. That means 2 or 3 books in every shipment will be FREE! If I decide to keep the entire collection, I'll have paid for only 32 books because 18 books are FREE! I understand that accepting the 3 free books and gifts places me under no obligation to buy anything. I can always return a shipment and cancel at any time. My free books and gifts are mine to keep no matter what I decide.

☐ 269 HCN 4622   ☐ 469 HCN 4622

Name (please print)

Address   Apt. #

City   State/Province   Zip/Postal Code

Mail to the Reader Service:
IN U.S.A.: P.O Box 1341, Buffalo, N.Y. 14240-8531
IN CANADA: P.O. Box 603, Fort Erie, Ontario L2A 5X3

*Terms and prices subject to change without notice. Prices do not include sales taxes, which will be charged (if applicable) based on your state or country of residence. Canadian residents will be charged applicable taxes. Offer not valid in Quebec. All orders subject to approval. Credit or debit balances in a customer's account(s) may be offset by any other outstanding balance owed by or to the customer. Please allow three to four weeks for delivery. Offer available while quantities last. © 2018 Harlequin Enterprises Limited. ® and ™ are trademarks owned and used by the trademark owner and/or its licensee.

Your Privacy—The Reader Service is committed to protecting your privacy. Our Privacy Policy is available online at www.ReaderService.com or upon request from the Reader Service. We make a portion of our mailing list available to reputable third parties that offer products we believe may interest you. If you prefer that we not exchange your name with third parties, or if you wish to clarify or modify your communication preferences, please visit us at www.ReaderService.com/consumerchoice or write to us at Reader Service Preference Service, P.O. Box 9049, Buffalo, NY 14269-9049. Include your name and address.

50BFT19R

ReaderService.com has a new look!

We have refreshed our website and
we want to share our new look with you.
Head over to ReaderService.com
and check it out!

On ReaderService.com, you can:

- Try 2 free books from any series
- Access risk-free special offers
- View your account history & manage payments
- Browse the latest Bonus Bucks catalog

Don't miss out!

If you want to stay up-to-date on the latest at the Reader Service and enjoy more Harlequin content, make sure you've signed up for our monthly News & Notes email newsletter. Sign up online at ReaderService.com.

INTRODUCING OUR
FABULOUS NEW COVER LOOK!
COMING FEBRUARY 2020

Find your favorite series in-store, online or subscribe to the Reader Service!